HILL FARM

Hill Farm

MIRANDA FRANCE

Chatto & Windus

LONDON

Published by Chatto & Windus 2011

2 4 6 8 10 9 7 5 3 1

Copyright © Miranda France 2011

Miranda France has asserted her right under the Copyright, Designs
and Patents Act 1988 to be identified as the author of this work

First published in Great Britain in 2011 by
Chatto & Windus
Random House, 20 Vauxhall Bridge Road,
London SW1V 2SA
www.rbooks.co.uk

Addresses for companies within The Random House Group Limited
can be found at:
www.randomhouse.co.uk/offices.htm

The Random House Group Limited Reg. No. 954009

A CIP catalogue record for this book
is available from the British Library

ISBN 9780701185800

The Random House Group Limited supports The Forest Stewardship
Council (FSC), the leading international forest certification organisation.
All our titles that are printed on Greenpeace approved FSC
certified paper carry the FSC logo. Our paper procurement
policy can be found at: www.rbooks.co.uk/environment

Mixed Sources
Product group from well-managed
forests and other controlled sources
www.fsc.org Cert no. TT-COC-2139
© 1996 Forest Stewardship Council
FSC

Typeset by Palimpsest Book Production Ltd, Falkirk, Stirlingshire

Printed and bound in Great Britain by
Clays Ltd, St Ives plc

To Carl, and to Caroline

Hill Farm

In nature's infinite book of secrecy
A little I can read.

William Shakespeare,
Antony and Cleopatra

ONE

The air had grown cooler now and Mikey rubbed his hands together, to make them more agile with the match. Usually he was good at starting fires, but the conditions for this one had been all wrong. Although it felt dry to the touch, the straw must still have been damp from the rain that had fallen two nights back. It was the first week of September and the sun was weakening. Ten times or more Mikey had struck a match, made a cave of his hands for the flame and transferred it to the pile he had assembled from straw and cut-up pieces of cloth. The cloth burned quickly enough, sending indigo flames and sparks shooting down the shafts of straw, but then they met the damp resistance further in and the fire would not take.

He sat back on his heels, rubbing his hands on jeans that were stiff with dirt. He had been up since dawn and barely taken a break even for tea or a sandwich. An aimless hatred filled him up: he could taste its bitter edge at the back of his throat. When a pair of partridges emerged from the long grass close to him, then skittered together across the field, Mikey found no interest or pleasure in the sight. Instead, he examined his kneecap, which showed red against the torn fabric of his jeans. A latticework of old scars and newer scratches was criss-crossed by the white strands of cotton stretched against his skin.

He said to himself that he would give this 'one more go' and the words must have worked like some secret convocation, because just then a trick of the wind scooped up the flame. Seconds later fire was tearing across the field, devouring the upper layers of chaff and threatening the hedgerow that separated the farm from the rest of the village. On the other side of that hedge were the playing field and the cricket pavilion, which was never used for cricket any more and seemed to have no purpose other than as a place for teenagers to snog and scrawl obscenities on the walls.

Seeing the way the flames moved so fast filled Mikey with exhilaration. There was nothing to beat the sheer power of setting a fire. What would the boys at the pub say to that? Mikey, who everyone thought was thick. Mikey, who had never graduated to being 'Mike'. Davie was Dave now, and Tony was Tone, but the childish variant of his name had stuck with him. He suspected it affected the way people saw him. His mum was always saying he was grumpy. His last girlfriend, Karen, had said he was 'moany' and she had humiliated him in other ways, behind the cricket pavilion.

Up at the farmhouse, they could not feel that smarting heat, but the spectacle of advancing flames was enough to halt all usual domestic activity. The Hayes' house sat right in the middle of their land, halfway up the hill on one side of a valley. It was a seventeenth-century building, small-windowed and dark in its downstairs rooms where the thick, diamond-shaped panes seemed to keep out more light than they let in. Open the windows, though, and you could put the dark to your back as the view swept across a valley of fields and copses. This was the kind of England people thought about when they had lived for a long time abroad and yearned for greenery and rolling hills, for generous leafiness. The Hayes' land extended down to a river which formed the natural boundary with their neighbour's farm. Their fields were sown with wheat, barley, oats and oilseed rape. Some, too steep for a tractor, were left to grass and prettily dotted with sheep and cattle. On the other side of the river were more billowing hills; a line of silver poplars filed up one side of a slope, while telegraph poles strode to the horizon on another. On a day of sun and clouds the play of light across the valley brought the scene marvellously to life. The poplar leaves sparkled like tinsel as they turned in the wind. The sun also appeared to dance about, picking out for a brighter treatment metal objects – agricultural parts or abandoned cars – that were scattered in the valley, or the windows of other houses on other hills. As these patterns of light and shade travelled across the ground, you could imagine that the countryside itself knew about sombre moods and the relief of feeling them lifted.

Now that expanse of sky was dominated by smoke. Mattie and her mother watched from the dining-room window as the racing flames barrelled across the field, leaving behind a steaming, blackened underlay. There was an ominous viscosity to the smoke ballooning above them. Beyond it the sooty figure of her father looked distant, as though stranded beyond rescue.

The police had just been on the telephone and now, without moving away from the table, Isabel Hayes stood looking out of the window. The moment called for speed, for action. Beside her, Mattie hopped anxiously from one foot to the other. Anxiety ought to have quickened Isabel's movements, too, yet it seemed to have had the opposite effect. Very slowly she had replaced the receiver, then rubbed a corner of her mouth, and now she said, apparently to no one, 'I think it's already too late.' She seemed to take comfort in conceding this defeat, and she drew her cardigan protectively across her chest as if to say, 'At least we two are safe.'

'We have to do something!' Mattie cried. 'I mean the police said . . . for God's sake!'

'Please don't swear, Mattie.'

Behind them, a grandfather clock marked the hour in a reproving tone. Mattie's little brother had once mispronounced this as the 'dying room' and, among the children, the name stuck. They ran and crashed around the rest of the house, as children will, but in this room they maintained a respectful hush, without quite understanding why. It may have been because of the portraits of dead ancestors, of dead aunts and uncles many times removed, bearing down on them from the walls. Hayes' father had been the last of four children, much younger than his siblings and the only one of them to marry and produce offspring. Along with the farm, Hayes had inherited a strange assortment of old furniture and paintings. Some of the portraits had been made two centuries ago, by itinerant merchants who would arrive at the homes of the landed gentry with a canvas that was already three-quarters painted, then append a likeness of the flattered squire or his wife onto a ready-made body. The match was never perfect, and the ancestors displayed in this room suffered from cricked necks, crossed eyes and problems of proportion. They may have been pleasant men and women, but in these paintings they could not help but look askance, and the children felt their opprobrium travel across the centuries. The furniture bequeathed to Hayes was just as imposing – like yet more difficult relations, tallboys, bureaus and commodes were jammed in wherever they might fit.

The clock ticked on, and on raced the fire. Together they watched as the wind tugged the flames, drawing them ever closer to the cricket pavilion. 'I'm going to go,' said Mattie. It was better not to give her mother any option about this. If asked, she would have to say 'no'.

'I don't think you should, darling,' Isabel said, without making any move to stop her daughter, but Mattie ran out of the front door and grabbed her bike, which was always left at the garden gate, flung on the grass.

She had been given a new bike for her tenth birthday and was always eager for missions demanding its use. Isabel tried to oblige, sending her down to the post office with letters, or even to the vegetable patch for a lettuce. When no missions were forthcoming, Mattie had to invent them for herself. In her imagination, she recast the farm as a magical kingdom; a unicorn inhabited the fertiliser shed, and there was an oracle in a far-off land, about a mile from the house. Skirting the edge of one field was a glade where, under a green canopy of leaves, the earth bulged and swelled over the dugouts of an extensive badger sett. A stream meandered through it, and the children floated questions along it, on boats made from sticks. Even Tom, who was six, could pose some rudimentary questions: 'wil ther bee mor choklit?' Mattie's older sister, Jennifer, was the one who interpreted the oracle; sitting on a gnarled log they called the 'throne', she read its answers in the play of light on the leaves. 'There shall be chocolate, but not until Sunday.'

Now Mattie went fast down the hill, standing up on the pedals, mindful of gruesome stories her mother had told her, and fearing for her teeth. At the bottom of the hill the continuation of the road was a dirt track, hard to negotiate with the bike, so she dumped it at the field's edge and ran towards her father, along the edge of the path. All around her the land was steaming, small heaps of blackened chaff looking like the relics of a razed miniature city. By the time she reached Hayes she was out of breath, but that was partly a matter of design: when you are a child, melodrama is so much harder to resist. On the way down the hill on her bike Mattie had planned not only what she would say, but how she would convey the message. She wanted to shape her face in a sufficiently serious way, but feared accidentally smiling. Hayes was already looking expectant as she approached, his sooty hands hanging by his side. Mattie had planned to run all the way to him before delivering her message, but then, finding she could not wait, started shouting while she was still running.

'Daddy, the police called! They said that smoke is blowing across the road at the bottom of the village and you have to put out the fire.' And then the difficult phrase she had practised on the way down: 'The smoke's *obscuring visibility*.'

'Oh, heck – the blasted thing's nearly done now!' Hayes glared at her, then away at the racing flames, then collected some windswept strands of hair and smoothed them back over his head. Now Mikey came towards them from the other corner of the field exhibiting his own tic, which was to scratch at a place on the crown of his head with all the fingers of one hand, in a way that reminded Mattie and her brother and sister of a very funny comedian they had seen in a black-and-white film. Mikey, the farm labourer, was tall and gawky and somehow slack-looking. His soft, padded cheeks were often dappled red, as though smarting from a blow, and they merged into his neck without the interruption of a jawline. This feature gave his face a babyish look, especially as his mouth tended to gape open, revealing crooked teeth that had not known the intervention of an orthodontist. Mikey had a way of swallowing hard that made it look as if he was about to advance some interesting point – but he never was. In fact he spoke very little, and his thoughts, such as they were, were not considered illuminating by anyone who knew him. Even his mother was dismissive of Mikey, and his father had dismissed both of them a long time ago. That afternoon Mikey had on the same jeans he had worn every day of the harvest, and now they had acquired such a sheen of oil and dust over the thighs as to become vaguely reflective. His face was streaked with smuts and sweat.

Harvest, so often made to look golden in paintings, was on Hill Farm a season of unremitting dirt. Fine particles of dust rose in clouds from the combine harvester, as the wheat was disgorged into the waiting trailer, then again when it was dumped in piles by the augers. If you wore a filter over your mouth and nose it was quickly blackened, but they were uncomfortable, so mostly everyone did without, although Isabel insisted on them for the children. Then at the end of the harvest came this orgy of dust and grime, when the stubble was burned. Hayes and Mikey, with matching plumes of soot emerging from their nostrils, looked as if they might be the fire-breathing creatures that had caused this devastation.

Behind Mikey, the fire continued to gallop towards the cricket pavilion. Now came the wail of a siren.

'Hell, that's all we need! Some busybody's called out the fire brigade.'

As if to illustrate the wind's capricious design, a sudden gust caught some of the strands of hair that were combed over Hayes' pate and raised them comically aloft for a few seconds before depositing them on the other side of his head.

'You'd think people would know better,' said Mikey. He gave a scornful little laugh and shook his head, as if he could not believe people's lack of sophistication. He did this to please Hayes, whom he regarded as a kind of father.

Now Hayes' watery blue eyes, strikingly set in his besmirched face, narrowed dangerously. He looked up towards the brow of the hill. Beyond it, out of sight, was a cottage that was on his land, but did not belong to him. Some years ago Hayes had sold the cottage to raise capital, and now it was rented out on a long lease. The present incumbents were Mr and Mrs Payne. All Mattie knew about Mr Payne was that he was a 'pseudo-intellectual'; she understood this to be something mysterious and dreadful. He had moved to the country with his wife after many years living in London, 'for a change of pace'. The couple could often be seen walking around the farm, holding hands, 'enjoying the countryside' in a frenzy of sniffing and sighing. Mr Payne wore an expression of profound, of blissful happiness, as if he might burst into song or even into tears (Mattie's mother had told her that you could cry from joy as well as pain). The hand that was not holding Mrs Payne's swung in a vigorous demonstration of his contentment. It had not occurred to Mattie beforehand that the countryside might be enjoyed; ploughed, cultivated and harvested, yes, but 'enjoyed' – that was something new. Mr Payne was an oddity to the Hayes children while, to their father, he was a source of deep mistrust.

His dislike dated from their first meeting, when he and Isabel had gone to introduce themselves to the new tenants and found the Paynes making gazpacho ('gaz-what?' Hayes had asked). Mr Payne had explained that this was a Spanish soup, 'a very refreshing appetiser when served chilled', but the scene did not sit well with Mattie's father. What sort of a man spent the afternoon cooking? Besides, soups should be hot.

Undeterred, Mr Payne had pursued a policy of neighbourliness. One evening the previous week he had suddenly appeared at the kitchen window, making Isabel Hayes jump when she caught sight of him. He had tapped on the glass. Perhaps he had seen country people tapping on each other's kitchen windows on television. Isabel went to let him in at the back door.

'What a delicious smell!' said Mr Payne, inhaling deeply as he came into the kitchen. 'What are you making?'

'A steak-and-kidney pie,' said Isabel doubtfully. She was not as confident about her cooking as Mrs Payne was. 'Would you like to join us for supper?'

'Oh heavens, no!' His smooth city hands had sprung up to hold the suggestion at bay. 'But thank you, all the same. Actually I only eat white meat. Anything that swims, flies or clucks.'

There was a pause then; the children were unused to the fine distinctions city people used to define their eating habits, and Tom, the six-year-old, could not resist clucking a little himself. Mr Payne laughed nervously and put out a hand, skinny as a chicken's talon, to ruffle the boy's hair. Tom dodged it, though, and ran to join his sisters at the table.

For a few seconds Mr Payne's mouth moved, as though he was trying to feel the shape of something he had only just now discovered inside it. Everyone waited. Then he spoke: 'I hope this won't seem like a nuisance. It's just that, well, one of the reasons we chose the cottage – that is, chose to move here, to this particular cottage, I mean – was the "AONB" status. The AONB status is important to us – I can't stress that enough.'

Voicing this acronym seemed to give Mr Payne confidence. He took a step towards the range and leaned against it companionably. 'We really would hate to see that status threatened in any way.'

'Of course,' said Isabel, whose instinct was usually to agree, especially with things she did not understand. 'But I'm afraid I don't think I know what a . . .'

'An AONB is an "Area of Oustanding Natural Beauty",' said Hayes, who had arrived silently in the doorway. 'It's an area designated for preservation by the Department of the Environment. We are in one now, thanks to some bureacratic regulation or other. That's why we weren't allowed to build the conservatory, remember?'

Hayes' sudden appearance had made Mr Payne flush. Isabel stood in the middle of the kitchen holding a ceramic pie-dish. It was a piece of crockery inherited from her mother and cooking with it always provoked in her a certain emotional turbulence, which this scene in the kitchen threatened to aggravate.

'Oh, I see,' Isabel said. 'Of course I remember.' She

found a space on the counter and put down the dish, and with it the troublesome associations.

'Well, yes, we are in one!' said Mr Payne, who now attempted to turn the flush of his embarrassment into a glow of pride. 'And very nice it is too – glorious, in fact.'

'But forgive me, your concern is . . . ?'

Here Mr Payne appeared to falter. His eyes darted around the kitchen, until they were detained by a sign pinned on the fridge door, reading VERRUCCA (the aide-memoire had been placed there by Jennifer, who otherwise forgot to apply her ointment). This sign seemed to disconcert Mr Payne, for he said nothing for a few seconds, concentrating instead on a tea-towel he had found on the oven beside him, neatly folding it and patting it with his smooth hands.

'I just feel that some of the practices on this farm, intensive practices such as the use of nitrates, stubble-burning – that kind of thing . . . I wonder if they are, well, consistent with AONB development policy.'

'Which is?'

'Well, you know, sustainable farming,' said Mr Payne, as though this were some obvious formula.

'Excuse me,' said Isabel, moving to retrieve a pan of boiling courgettes from the hob beside Mr Payne. Usually she let vegetables boil for ten minutes, but now she feared that the courgettes might have been on for as long as half an hour. Mr Payne's presence by the range, at this time of day, struck her as especially inconsiderate.

'Stubble-burning is one of the oldest forms of controlling disease in the world, as any countryman knows.' Hayes spoke in a low, measured way that suggested an internal battle to contain his annoyance. The inference was that Mr Payne was not a countryman, was not, perhaps, much of a man at all. 'I would argue that it is very much a part of what you call "sustainable farming".'

'Ah,' said Mr Payne, 'but does it not strip the soil of organisms?'

'One thinks,' continued Hayes, 'of Kipling, of the autumn fields filled with "cloud and fire".' He seemed to swell with these patriotic thoughts, to fill the door-frame. 'How, otherwise, would you propose to control the slugs?'

'I'll answer your slugs with hedgehogs,' said Mr Payne, with another nervous smile, and the tip of his tongue appeared between his teeth, to show that he wanted to be good-humoured about this. 'If left alone, they would eat the slugs for you. But there's lots of evidence to show that field-burning is killing them off.' He had stepped away from the range and spread his hands out in front of him, as if laying out all this evidence for the benefit of his audience in the kitchen. The children, sitting at the table in a solemn row, weighed it up. Tom started clucking again, and was hushed by his sisters.

'Oh, for heaven's sake! You're not living in the real world.' The retort was ruder than one might usually expect of Hayes, except that it was harvest time, when it was understood that all tempers ran higher. There was, besides, something about Mr Payne that invited derision. Small and neat, he was like a poseable figure one might pick up and bend into different positions. All his points of articulation looked shiny, as though oiled, and when he was indignant or embarrassed, blood raced first to his nose, before fanning out across his cheeks. Indeed the very tip of his nose was permanently red, as though acting as a pilot light for future embarrassments. But it was Mr Payne's hair that made him look particularly ridiculous: thick, wiry ringlets stuck straight out from his scalp, shaping his head like a pyramid or some artful piece of topiary.

'I don't think we are getting anywhere,' said Mr Payne. He must have known that he was beaten: his hedgehogs were no match for Kipling. If Hayes had been more alert, though, he might have detected a resolve in the way Mr Payne laid the folded tea-towel down on top of the range and gave it a pat.

'No, and I have had a hard day, and now I would like to sit down and eat my supper, as I'm sure you would too.' Hayes stepped into the room in a motion that invited Mr Payne to step out of it.

'Quite. I'm sorry to have disturbed you,' said Mr Payne, who had smiled and nodded at Isabel before taking his cue to leave.

So Mattie's father had good cause to look warily towards the brow of the hill, where Mr Payne lived, and where a fire engine now appeared on the farm's top road, causing sheep in a field that ran alongside it to raise their heads and bolt away in woolly consensus.

Isabel also saw the red engine streak past as she stood at the dining-room window, from which she had watched so many farming events unfold. It was easier for her to watch life than to step into it: she had a dread of awkward social situations. It crossed her mind to walk down the hill and join the men, offering some charming extenuation that would help everyone to laugh off the accident. Was this not the role of a farmer's wife – to provide working men with the balm of good food and feminine under-standing? Fires had got out of hand before on Hill Farm, and she knew that Hayes found it irksome to keep apol-ogising. She could picture him now, growing red and clap-ping a dirty hand to his dirty face. As compensation he would probably want to offer the firemen a beer, when they had finished dousing the hedgerow. With this thought in mind, she went to check if there was any beer in the fridge. She puzzled, for a moment, over the word VERRUCA, and its distribution of 'c's and 'r's. If her children could not spell, she thought, perhaps they would be doomed in life. Then she disappeared into the gloomy territory of the back corridor, where a crate of beer bottles was kept – and wished that she could remain there, hidden for a few hours, beyond the reach of her family.

Her peace did not last long. The firemen, who were old hands at dealing with stubble fires, made quick work of extinguishing this one and were soon on their way, having declined the offer of a beer. By the time the party returned to the house, Hayes alone was fuming.

Mattie's first thought was to find her siblings, who had been playing in the orchard all afternoon, and regale them with the story of her own part in the day's drama. In her imagination, her role as messenger had grown to heroic proportions. 'I could probably have died,' she confided to Tom and Jennifer, before the three of them disappeared in an excited gaggle.

Meanwhile Hayes and Mikey leaned against the range in the kitchen, drinking their beer straight from the bottle.

'If there is one thing I deplore – I mean *deplore* – it's not being able to finish the job in hand,' said Hayes. 'That's another ruddy day wasted.'

Mikey shifted from one foot to the other. His Adam's apple bobbed up and down, as though he was about to make some important observation. Instead he took a swig of beer and said nothing.

Hayes, begrimed and sooty, looked like a thunderous god poised to smite a group of miscreants. 'There are times when I wonder – when I have to ask myself – if there is actually any point in carrying on,' he said. He spoke with a quietness that alarmed his wife at first, but his voice rose as anger pushed through it. 'Why in God's name would anyone go into farming these days? Can anyone tell me why a man would choose this way of life?' The question was directed at his wife and at Mikey. The three children, who had come back to the kitchen hoping to witness a row, stood in the doorway looking like young farm animals, with their mouths open. Mikey shrugged and fiddled awkwardly with his hands, and Isabel, feeling that she ought to think of something to say, remained silent. Hayes shot smouldering glances around the room. 'Well, I'll tell you something. You certainly don't go into farming for the money! You don't do it for the glory or the job satisfaction. Ha! The only good reason for it is masochism. That must be it. I think I must be in love with pain.'

Isabel could think of no response to this display of petulance other than to nod sympathetically, while thinking of her bed-sheets, which had been fresh on that morning. If only she had left them another day. It intrigued her now to see a little curl of smoke rising from her husband's head.

She had not known that it was possible for smoke to cling to a person. Was Hayes literally smouldering with rage? For, there it was, unmistakably, a thin plume of smoke that flowed upwards, towards the ceiling.

'What's that smell?' said Hayes, sniffing and frowning. With a start, Isabel realised then that the smoke was coming not from her husband, but from the oven behind him.

'Oh God! I forgot about the pie!'

'Blast! That's all we need.'

Mikey scratched the top of his head with all of the fingers of one hand. 'I think I'd better be getting off home, Mr Hayes. Thank you for the beer, Mrs Hayes. I'll see myself out.'

When the labourer had gone, the family gathered around their kitchen table, as they did every night, with expressions of resolve.

Isabel set the pie down before them, then took her place to the right of Hayes, who always sat at the head of the table. On Sundays they said grace before lunch, but these weekday meals were godless in every sense.

'We can always have cheese, if it's too awful,' Isabel said, without looking up. She tried to avoid eye-contact at meal times, knowing herself to be a disappointment in the kitchen. Instead, she looked down on the charred contents of her plate and consoled herself that this evening's offering represented a triumph of sorts. The day's stubble-burning may have been a failure. Supper, on the other hand, had burned very well indeed.

TWO

'Are you really in love with Mr Payne?' Tom asked their father, the morning after the stubble-burning. Hayes made no answer, except to reprise the previous day's thunderous expression. As usual, Tom was misunderstood: he was not trying to be facetious. As the youngest member of the family he was often regarded as an irritant, his ideas and preoccupations rarely given attention. Receiving no reply from his father, Tom took the same quandary to the girls who, having established for their brother the difference between 'pain' and 'payne', wondered what such a love could be like. They had a second cousin who could administer shockingly painful Chinese burns, but neither of them could imagine falling in love with him. Once Mattie had fallen on a concrete step near the sheep dip and cut open her knee – that must have hurt a good deal, though all she could remember now was the shock of seeing so much blood, a slice of red flesh and beneath it something whitish that must have been her kneecap. 'That means,' Jennifer had said gravely, 'that you are one of the only people in the world to have seen their own skeleton.' At the hospital stitches had been put in by an Indian doctor, the first Asian Mattie had ever seen – apart from on television – so her overriding impression of the day came to be one of wonderment and new sensations, rather than the pain of her injury.

Their father often experienced pain: his hands covered with welts and scars were a testament to that. Even the top of his head was sometimes wounded, under its sparse cover of hair, because he was tall and kept hitting it on the low lintels in their farmhouse. In centuries past, shorter, nimbler men would have glided under these beams without even noticing them, but Hayes was neither short nor nimble and, for all that he seemed hearty, his daughters worried that their father concealed some deadly frailty. Jennifer had read that stress was a 'silent killer', and their father seemed perpetually worried. The weather was a source of dread for all farmers – either there was no rain for weeks, and then the government had the nerve to charge you for diverting water from the river, or there were heavy downpours and the crops rotted in the field. The day that the fire brigade had come should have been safe for burning stubble. No one could have predicted that the wind would change direction, blowing the flames towards the sports field.

What other silent enemies endangered Hayes? He was a mystery to his children. Their mother was quantifiable, neatly contained in cardigans, tweed skirts and tights, while their father, unfathomably large and rugged, seemed to have been hewn out of woolly jumpers. As he went about his work on the farm, his abdomen swelling under the green furrows of his old patched sweater, he looked very much in keeping with the paunchy green hills. The voluminous jumpers hid some secret machinery that made industrious work of the meals their mother assembled in the farmhouse kitchen. He could summon surprising noises from deep recesses: prolonged rumblings that made you think of far-off detonations or Indians thundering across a plain on horses. Not all his battles with wind were confined to the fields.

Their father's sneezes came like controlled explosions, accompanied by a claxon shout; his coughing fits shook the house. Even rooms away, they could hear his rumblings and throat-clearings as clearly as the sharp bleating of the premature lambs that were sometimes brought in to be revived by the range. Large movements were no puzzle to Hayes. He could easily heft a bale of straw and throw it onto the back of a trailer, but to negotiate a tea set – when elderly relations came to visit – or even turn the page of a book was something he found frustrating. The tips of his fingers had been roughened by their work outside. Mattie cherished their slight abrasion on her cheek when he kissed her goodnight.

In some ways Hayes seemed too big for the house. He found it easy to trip over a rug or to misjudge an uneven threshold. The low lintels caused him particular misery.

'BLAST!' he would shout when his head whacked against the wooden beam. Sometimes, in the style of an old-school preacher prophesying doom, he would strike the offending beam with his open palm and shout, until the whole building seemed to quake and tremble: 'Damn this godforsaken house!'

Then again, anyone might feel foolish in a home like theirs. Over the centuries the house had been afflicted by bouts of subsidence and alterations, until finally its foundations had made an awkward truce with the surrounding soil. The building was secure, but inside it nothing was even, and Hayes complained that there was not a single ninety-degree angle anywhere. Everything was lopsided, every line was at odds with the next. Downstairs the low ceilings, criss-crossed with timbers, bulged and sagged under the years' accumulated to-and-fro. There were some areas in which Hayes must remain between the beams, truncating himself, if he wished to stand entirely straight. Upstairs the floors sloped to the degree that castors had to be removed from the furniture or it would roll away. Pictures could not be hung in a line that corresponded with both floor and ceiling, because there was no room in which such an agreement prevailed. Just to walk from one side to the other of the upper floor gave one an insight into life on the high seas. Pitched about like sailors, the Hayes family could not move around their home without causing boards to creak, furniture to judder against the walls, and windows to shake in their frames. The children, coming downstairs to steal food at night, taught each other how to jump over the noisiest steps.

Isabel despaired of the furniture, these hulking pieces of inherited Victoriana that lurched away from the walls and needed to be checked, often, for woodworm. Hayes would spot the telltale heaps of sawdust and, cursing, go to retrieve his spray. The children knew, if they came into a room to find his feet sticking out from underneath the sideboard or dressers, that their father was once more engaged in one of his hopeless campaigns to eradicate the enemy.

Now there was a new problem, because Hayes suspected that the house had fallen prey to death-watch beetles. He had heard the tapping – the beetle's characteristic mating call – as he sat up late at night. Death-watch beetles had a superior kind of appetite: not content to gnaw on a table leg or the soft base of an old chest, they preferred to feed on the supporting timbers of the house itself.

'We are being eaten away,' said Hayes looking up through the beams that concealed their hungry enemy, as he and Isabel lay in bed at night. 'Woodworm, moths and death-watch beetles are eating the house. Rabbits, pigeons and aphids are eating the crops.'

Isabel wanted to say something comforting, but found her throat paralysed. The thought of such a frenzied sating of appetites alarmed her, especially when set against the quiet starvation of her own marital bed.

At thirty-six, Isabel was not the first woman to wonder what had become of her life. The middle years are bound to be a time of reckoning, of totting up what has gone and what is left to come. At night, men and women around the world lie awake in bed making silent surveys of their achievements and failures and wondering what the future may hold. Isabel was no different, except that her nocturnal accounts were particularly punishing. As she lay in the dark, listening to the rumblings of her husband and the tapping of the death-watch beetles, she felt that she had achieved very little in life and that the future promised even less. She adored her children, but regarded their existence as a miracle in which she had played only a small part. It seemed to her that mothering was, in essence, a mystery: children either turn out well or not, and one cannot do much to influence the matter either way. At night, when the thread of life can seem so tenuous, she was prey to dreadful fears about their safety. It seemed there was an infinite number of ways in which one could suffer and be hurt. Her heart, she felt, was doomed to be broken. She wished there was some method for safeguarding hearts.

These fears began to stalk her by day, too, and she could not tackle them with any logic, because this quality seemed unavailable to her. In its place reigned a kind of mellifluous sorrow that carried her through the day, sustaining her at the same time as it did her harm. She knew that it would be better to do without this secret sadness, but she dared not begin the process of giving it up. Isabel would have liked to talk to Hayes about her worries, but she did not know how; he seemed always to be walking away from her, dwelling mostly in doorways, or just beyond them. It was true that they spent the evenings together, in front of the television, but then all his most eloquent communications were abdominal. While Hayes slept, sympathetic noises issued from under his jumper: soft entreaties, sighs and maundering elegies. Isabel alone stayed awake to watch television dramas in which the male leads listened with great attention when women spoke to them, stroking their hair and touching their cheeks. She wondered if such men really existed or were no more than a scriptwriter's conceit, invented to facilitate dialogue.

Sometimes, as she went about her daily work, she paused at the dining-room window and spotted Hayes in the distance, bouncing on his tractor. The seagulls following behind also bobbed up and down, as though they were being drawn along on invisible threads. He looked cheerfully occupied as he came to the end of a furrow, then swung the vehicle round to make a return trip. Isabel was not sure, though, that she shared her husband's love of the land; she feared that the farm had robbed her of more than it had yielded. There was little time for family life, and none for holidays. Her youthful energy had been dissipated in a routine of cooking, housework and child-care. She had grown sarcastic in the kitchen.

'One day meals will no longer be necessary and everyone will eat pills instead,' she told her children, as they sat, waiting for supper as though waiting for a comeuppance. 'And when that day arrives I will raise a hearty cheer.'

Over the years Isabel's grievances had come to occupy the larger part of her thoughts, until she became obsessed with them and could think of almost nothing else. It was partly in the hope of dispelling them that she had become pregnant again, with her fourth child. An unborn child may be charged with all kinds of weighty expectations and Isabel was relying on this one not only to complete her family, but to restore her faith in marriage and in life. With this prospect in view, she was for a time much happier, antici-pating pleasant days to come with her brood of children. Then, halfway through the pregnancy, she lost her baby, and the loss hit her very hard. Six months had passed since the miscarriage, but thinking about it still caused her a keen pain. She had always wanted a large family, being herself the only child of a couple who had expected to remain childless, a gift in later life that they were determined to cherish (they called her 'treasure', among other pet names). Wanting to give her the best of everything, Isabel's parents had loved her to a fault. Successive Christmases saw her spoiled with pet rabbits, her own puppy, a record-player, oil paints, a subscription to *Life* magazine. They were, in her father's words, a 'happy threesome', by which he seemed to imply that no one else was necessary. At bedtime her mother's hands enfolded hers and they prayed fiercely that all would be well with their little family group. Isabel never lost that fierce habit of willing things to go well, while fearing that they would not. She was successful at school and aspired to have the sort of career she had read about in *Life*. She pictured herself as a diplomat or a lawyer, perhaps living abroad – but Isabel's parents counselled against university. Privately, her father believed that it was wrong to educate a woman who was destined to be a mother and a housewife; one should not raise expectations that were bound to be disappointed. Isabel's mother, meanwhile, had heard about a friend's son who became a drug-addict at university and died. Every time she thought of her daughter leaving home, the world came alive with dangers, and even a redoubling of prayers was not enough to fend off the fear that something awful might happen to her only child, her treasure. So it was with love and kindness, with sad half-smiles, that Isabel's parents militated against their daughter's ambitions and kept her at home. 'A secretarial qualification is always useful,' offered her mother.

And if there had been resentment, fate gave it no time to flourish, for very soon afterwards Hayes was on the scene. Isabel met him at a barn dance for young farmers. 'He is twenty-nine,' she wrote in her diary that night. 'I hope that I'm not playing with fire.' Hayes presented an avenue of escape; for one thing, he owned a car. He was ten years older than Isabel, too, a fact that endowed him with an unearned charisma.

The truth was that Hayes was far from fiery, but was everything a young farmer should be: ruddy, reassuring and capable. Recognising these virtues, Isabel's parents reluctantly surrendered custody of their treasure on Saturday evenings. He came to pick her up in a Morris Minor to take her to a film and afterwards for coffee. Their romance progressed haltingly among awkward exchanges, blushes and a good deal of nervous laughter, until a point came when they blushed less, but laughed almost constantly. It was easy to mistake such merriment for love.

On one of those evenings, as they were driving home along a coast road, Hayes said, 'It's such a beautiful night, let's go swimming.' Before Isabel knew what to say he was pulling into a lay-by and leading her to the beach, which had been busy earlier in the day and was now the lone domain of razor-fish and hermit crabs. In the dusky half-light they stripped down to their underclothes. He took her hand and they walked into the sea, laughing even as they gasped with cold. Isabel had never swum in the dark before – how could she have done, with such anxious parents? The freezing-cold water felt delicious against her skin. This new sensation would have been revelation enough, but that night there was also an extraordinary phenomenon at work. As she moved in the water, Isabel's body was embraced by tiny lights. A thousand luminous jewels encircled her arms and legs. It was as though this dark, cold world was charged with a secret electricity about which only she and Hayes knew. At that moment she was filled with a pure exhilaration that convinced her she must be in love with Hayes.

He was a few feet away. 'What is this?' she shouted, laughing, struggling to produce the words because she was so cold. 'What's happening?'

'It's phosphorescence.' He was laughing too. 'They're little sea creatures that absorb light on hot days and give it off when you disturb them at night.'

His authority thrilled her. It was as if he had ordained this entertainment for her. As Hayes swam towards her, trailing thousands of lights, Isabel's heart pounded, and she gasped to think that he was going to kiss her, and that he might press his body against hers. Faced with this possibility – both wonderful and dreadful – for a moment she could not decide if it had been a very foolish or a very clever idea to take off her clothes and leap into the sea with a man of twenty-nine. Of *twenty-nine*. She wondered if she was about to lose her virginity, and how awkward this procedure might be, given the razor-clams and other seashells scattered on the beach. She hoped that she could make herself sufficiently alluring.

But Hayes proved to be disappointingly gentlemanly that night. He neither kissed her in the sea nor when they had returned shivering to the car, even though she had peeped winningly at him through tendrils of wet hair. Instead he passed her a blanket to dry herself, apologising that he had no towel and averting his eyes from her transparent underwear. Then he opened the driver's side door and changed behind it, using his own jumper to dry himself, and turning his back so that there would be no danger of seeing Isabel naked.

She returned home that evening as chaste as she had left it a few hours earlier, but, as far as her parents were concerned, Isabel's status had changed. Although they said nothing that day, the evidence of her wet hair and clothes shocked them: it was clear that Hayes could no longer be regarded merely as a boyfriend. The following Saturday when he came to visit, Isabel's father took them both into the study and asked Hayes formally what his intentions were.

'I would like to marry Isabel,' Hayes said, blushing tremendously. He had declared himself and, before Isabel had a chance to say anything, her father's shout of congratulations sealed the matter. So it was that she found herself engaged. They were married soon after her twentieth birthday, their lives linked for ever on the evidence of an evening swim.

THREE

She did not know it, but Isabel's life was about to change, and the change began one Sunday morning, when a visitor came, unannounced, to the farmhouse.

It was a sunny morning, early in October, and the Hayes children were going with their father to church, which did not seem entirely fair to them, given that their mother stayed at home. For years Isabel had been a faithful member of the congregation, taking her place without complaint on the rota for polishing brasses and arranging flowers but, after losing the baby, she had announced that she was going to 'have a break from church'. Such luxury of choice was not open to the children, who made their annoyance felt as, every Sunday morning, they set off for Holy Communion, following their father through the small orchard at the back of the house. With exaggerated ill-humour they stamped a path beneath the apple trees. The four geese that were kept there fell into line behind them and trudged with equal resignation, prattling like old ladies, towards the fence at the top of the orchard.

There was a stile at the gate. Hayes hoisted himself over it with large, horny hands – those thumbs that struggled with pages – then the children took their turns to jump over. At this point Tom always liked to look over his shoulder back down the hill, to see his home getting smaller as they travelled away from it. They left the geese at the stile, but in the next field the cows flanked their church-bound party. These were the Charolais, whose white coats lent them a pious look to match the family's Sunday intentions. The cattle did not belong to Hayes, but to Henry Bourne, who had a smallholding on the other side of the river and was 'a gentleman farmer', according to Hayes. For a long time Mattie had supposed this designation to be admiring, and she pictured Henry, dressed in tweeds and galoshes, out and about on his land performing acts of chivalry to ladies who were trying to cross muddy patches. Later she found out that her father felt no admiration for 'gentlemen farmers' at all, regarding them to be every bit as despicable as 'pseudo-intellectuals'.

When he talked about their neighbour to his wife Hayes painted Bourne as a slick fellow who had bought land as an investment, and to avoid tax. He still worked most days in the City, so this farm was a project, 'a bit of fun', and the Charolais were a way to show off. For Bourne, who was used to playing the market, the cattle were a new and very promising commodity; the first continental breed of cattle to be imported into Britain, they were rare and highly prized. 'It's like buying a cream carpet,' grumbled Hayes. 'These animals were never intended to get dirty.'

In the orchard Hayes had set his conker-coloured polished shoes carefully between the livid green goose-droppings, and now he must skirt the darker cowpats, walking with the deliberation of a mountaineer. Once they got to the road the Charolais lined the fence to see them off, sheeny nostrils flaring. Hayes and his children climbed the hill towards the church, other parishioners joining them in waves, so that all along there was a feeling of being on a kind of demonstration, although in the children's case it was more like a protest, and one they fully intended to keep up for the hour that the service would last.

As Hayes' conker-coloured shoes departed from the farm by the top road, a pair of gold thonged sandals were arriving by the bottom road. They belonged to Sheila Prince, who had recently moved to the village. A hundred years ago higglers and hawkers would have walked this same road, on their way to offer entertainment or miracle cures at fairs on the village green. Miss Prince had come hawking aromatherapy oils. She had once been a secretary in the Foreign Office, and aromatherapy was a hobby that she hoped to parlay into a small business, in her retirement. She had heard that Isabel Hayes might be a candidate for what she liked to refer to as her 'potions and lotions'.

Miss Prince's sandals were no match for the dusty farm road, giving negligible support to her fallen arches, so she made slow progress, pausing at the bottom of the hill to look up at the farmhouse and the barn that stood beside it. By the time she came to the top of the hill she was breathing hard, a light sweat at her temples and the nape of her neck. Still, she arrived at the house smiling like a saleswoman who plans to close a deal. Rather than knock on the kitchen window, like Mr Payne, she walked straight in at the back door, calling 'Hello-o! Hello-o!' in all directions.

Isabel heard the greeting and sprang up from her chair in the kitchen, hoping to head off this unwanted visitor before she could advance into the house. She was disconcerted to find that the woman, who was smart and looked to be in her late sixties, had penetrated as far as the gloom of the back corridor, where wellington boots were strewn all around – and then there was no alternative but to greet her and apologise for the mess and her red eyes.

'I've been cutting up onions, and they always make me cry!'

Miss Prince made sympathetic noises, but she was no fool: there was no smell of onions. Perhaps she knew there and then that Isabel Hayes was going to be easy prey. Anyway, her feet were killing her and she was damned if she was going to be sent off back down that farm track again so soon. So she stood her ground in the hallway and then, with the meaningful sigh of one who has been exerted and now plans to stay for a while and rest, plumped her box of oils onto the floor.

Isabel was left with no choice but to usher her guest into the drawing room, where Miss Prince took out her little bottles and arranged them on the coffee table. She explained to Isabel, who had never heard of aromatherapy before, how drops of different oils could be added to water in a special burner and how, when the mixture was warmed, these oils imparted a fragrance to the air that could literally alter one's mood.

'There are oils to cure exhaustion, bereavement, depression, loss.' She let the words go lightly, but, like a clairvoyant, was alert to any inadvertent response on Isabel's part, any clues. Isabel had an instinct, then, that her visitor must know about the miscarriage and she wondered if their paths had crossed before. Miss Prince did not look familiar, though, and it was quite possible that she could have heard about her misfortune from a mutual acquaintance; Isabel had been obviously pregnant when she lost the baby, and sometimes it felt as if the whole village knew what had happened. Mrs Lyall at the post office had even told her that it was 'Probably a blessing. It may have meant that there was something wrong with the baby.' Isabel sat on the sofa now, her legs tucked under her, smoothing the material of her denim skirt, and then smoothing the material of the loose covers. She let herself be lulled by Miss Prince's sing-song sales patter. She began to see the promise held within those little blue bottles.

'Speaking for myself,' said Miss Prince, her hand fluttering over her heart, 'I can honestly say that aromatherapy has had a profound effect on my life. Truly profound.'

Inside the medieval church of St Cuthbert the Hayes children were growing restive. Reverend Hollings, gazing heavenwards, nostrils flaring, was giving a sermon.

'He looks as though he's smelled a fart!' whispered Tom, and his face turned crimson with hilarity.

'I think Mrs Lyall's egged it,' said Mattie, and the two of them erupted into giggles, waving their hands in front of their noses and drawing a look of angry reproach from their father. The church was set up high, about a mile from the village green, not because its architects had wanted to make it distant, but because the villagers had shrunk away from the church, six hundred years ago, when the graveyard heaved with plague victims. Now, on Sundays, they returned and the Reverend Hollings was ready to greet them, standing at the church door, his hands clasped inside the long sleeves of his surplice. He watched them arriving on foot or descending from estate cars and, before they got close and he had a chance to see their dour expressions, could indulge in a fantasy of his own magnetism.

Geoff Hollings was tall, with thinning hair and a buoyant demeanour – aided by thick rubber-soled shoes – that would have better suited a younger man. People who saw him bounding around the village sometimes dismissed him as 'too keen'. He seemed to have a permanent spring in his step. His lips rose very high over his top gum when he smiled, giving him the look of a hungry, yet somewhat anxious wolf. Reverend Hollings had been ordained for only a few years, after a long career in social work and as a lay preacher. For years he had dreamed of the priest-hood as other men dream of early retirement and Spanish villas. He thought of himself as bringing new blood to an institution that had grown inert and, to that end, was trying to shrug off the old conventions associated with his posi-tion. Somehow, though, he could not help but adopt the pose and language of an Anglican priest. He kept saying that things were 'splendid', for example – and he hated himself for it.

As a younger man Geoff Hollings had worked in the inner cities, and that was really where his heart lay. He wanted to battle for justice, to rally the congregation to take up that battle. He dreamed of galvanising the parish, bigging up the brethren with grand themes. In sermons he had sometimes experimented with the fluting, faltering tone of Martin Luther King. And when he preached, it was not from the pulpit, but in the nave, to show the parishioners that he was one of them. As he strode up and down, he made it his business to smile at everyone: this was important. If only you could look into the eyes of a fellow human being – a brother or sister – could you not transfer to each one a gift of love? This is what he was thinking, at the end of the service, when he grasped each parishioner's hand as they filed out of the church and looked hungrily into their eyes.

To Reverend Hollings' dismay there were no black people in the village, so his job here was not to unite black and white; but he still would like to be uniting someone: perhaps the newcomers with older families? 'New folk' were very much resented in the village and that resentment was unremitting: you might still be regarded as 'new' ten or twenty years after your parents had arrived here. Second- and third-generation villagers, especially the wealthy ones, were no better than interlopers. It was partly with this *froideur* in mind that Reverend Hollings had introduced to his services the concept of 'exchanging the peace', even though he had been warned that people would not like it – and indeed they did not. They came to atone, to dispatch a weekly duty, not to clasp hands or embrace one another, murmuring platitudes. It was bad enough that they must keep craning their necks to follow his progress up and down the nave.

The parishioners mistrusted their priest; he was felt to be too chummy. They wished he would 'stay in the pulpit'. They did not like the way he swayed to the rhythm of the hymns, like some fey youth listening to pop music. They disapproved of the smiling emphasis he gave to certain phrases: 'Christ *loves* sinners. Alleluia!' He had removed the 1662 Prayer Book and introduced the Alternative Service (1970), to the chagrin of many parishioners, including the organist, who shot him baleful looks between the rows of pipes and deliberately included all the verses of hymns they had agreed, together, to curtail. So the hymns went on for ever, with their obscure and long-forgotten addenda, and became wars of attrition waged by the congregation. Their priest faced them, clinging on to his Alternative Service, and wishing it was all over.

The younger Hayeses – who were often the only children at this service – experimented with different ways to pass the time. They would, for instance, sing every other word of a hymn, or pick out certain words, conveying messages to one another in secret code. Tom was especially naughty: he could deliver the first line of the Creed entirely in belches. In the days when she had still gone with them to church, Isabel found this bad behaviour upsetting and was forever passing threats, in stage whispers, along the pew. But here, as elsewhere, she was notable nowadays for her absence. Over cups of tea in their kitchens, some of the other villagers gossiped about her, speculating among themselves about domestic ructions, crises of faith and nervous breakdowns at Hill Farm.

'She was never much good at the brasses, anyway,' someone or other said, smirking, of Isabel.

'Housework is not one of her strong points,' someone else replied.

* * *

Miss Prince, sitting on the sofa at Hill Farm, could have confirmed the fact. All the while she was making her sales pitch she was glancing around the sitting room, noting the heavy furniture, the dusty ornaments and the carpets that had been inexpertly cut and then cobbled together again, in order to fit the peculiar angles of the room. The books on the shelves looked shabby and old-fashioned. She would have cleared the lot of them away and freshened up this room with a more contemporary feel.

'Do you see anything here that might be helpful?' she asked in a voice of professional solicitude.

'Well,' Isabel cleared her throat. 'Perhaps this one. I'm sorry, I can't remember how you pronounce it.'

'The Ylang-Ylang?' Miss Prince allowed consternation to play on her lips and eyebrows. 'Life's been a bit on top of you lately?'

Isabel could not answer, but she nodded and this action tipped tears over the rims of both eyes.

'I'm so sorry to hear that,' said Miss Prince, moving closer on the sofa. 'Come, come, my shoulder's good for crying on.'

At St Cuthbert's they were singing about encircling gloom. *The way is dark and I am far from home.* The congregation at this church was much like any other in rural England: there were two lesbians among the bell-ringers, keen campanologists and stalwart in thick Aran jumpers. In the second pew sat a baritone who could be relied upon to provide the descant for Christmas carols, though he was unaccompanied in his personal life, because his wife had run away with a farmer from the next county. There were also a retired army general, a few closet racists, an aspiring novelist; some swingers, some failures, some binge-drinkers and a health nut. It was an elderly congregation. Reverend Hollings may once have hoped to bring succour to the victims of gun crime and drug abuse. Now he more often found himself listening to stories of dicky knees, dodgy bladders and faulty tickers.

The parishioners tended to occupy pews that reflected their standing in the village. In the front sat the county's High Sheriff, no less, as beaky and dignified as one would expect, and with two neat surnames, see-sawed over a hyphen to which he gave a Spanish touch with a calligraphy pen. His family coat of arms had been accredited by the Garter King of Arms. The same name was inscribed all over the church walls on plaques that commemorated the deaths, sacrifice and service of that one family, as though their service and sacrifice had been greater than that of the farm boys in the graveyard outside. They had been in the village for more than two centuries and exerted a concomitant influence, though all their actions came accompanied by a polite reluctance that must have been feigned. They regretted their superiority, one felt, and yet were bound by it. Who else would host the carollers at Christmas? Who would open the fête and organise the tug-o'-war? In summer they invited the public to visit their garden, in exchange for a donation to charity, and a light tea was served among the herbaceous borders.

The High Sheriff was High Church, too. He was discreet about that, but, since chief among his duties was the handing out of prayer books and hymnals at the church door, by the time he was ready to take his place in the pew there was usually a full congregation ready to admire the sheriff genuflecting and signing himself in the nave. Reading the lesson called for more displays of faith. He hated with a passion the Alternative Service. The High Sheriff's brother, visiting once from Winchester, had made an even greater play of his piety, genuflecting all the way up to the altar and back – though it was said afterwards that he suffered from arthritic knees.

Mrs Lyall, the postmistress, sat in front of the Hayes family, wearing a hair-piece that rose a good ten inches above her head and was made, in fact, of her own hair. For decades she had kept it in a growing and unkempt bun, the legacy of a youth spent in reckless spraying and backcombing, until finally her hair became such a worry to her that she had it cut off, and now she wore it as a hat.

At Hill Farm Miss Prince had taken Isabel's hand and pressed it between her own. Both women looked down at their hands together: Isabel's red, bitten fingers beside Miss Prince's manicured nails. 'Let me be a friend to you,' said the older woman. 'I think you need one.'

In the choir stalls at St Cuthbert's sat Mrs Smith and Miss Smith, sisters-in-law who were in their late eighties and had not spoken to one another for forty years. The source of their rift was so ancient it had become a mystery, but it was thought to revolve around the now-defunct Mr Smith – brother to one of the women and husband to the other – and an inheritance that had favoured him over his sister. The Smiths looked like a comedy double-act to Mattie's eye, even though there was absolutely nothing comic about their association. Miss Smith was tall and very thin and made angles whichever way she sat. She made them with her chin, her elbows and the mountain-range of her arthritic knuckles. She had a vituperative air and her mouth looked always to be straining closed over something sharp, or over some distasteful sentiments. Every so often these shot out just the same. Miss Smith could not help herself: she would shout out that someone was a bitch or a whore and, in the release that followed, she seemed to glow with a furious pleasure. Once, when her next-door neighbour was hanging up her underwear on the line to dry, Miss Smith had shouted 'Scarlet woman!' at her from an upstairs window. Only God knew if she atoned for the outbursts later. In church Miss Smith especially loved the psalms; it made her happy to sing about wickedness on a high, sustained note.

Mrs Smith, by contrast, was very small and worn smooth by years of hard work and the love of a kind, if ineffectual, husband. A curvature of the spine had bent her so far over now that people rarely saw her face, just her approaching hat and a curly laurel of white hair around its brim. Tom was the only one in the Hayes family small enough to look at Mrs Smith from underneath.

'What does she look like?' Mattie had asked him once, at supper.

Tom shrugged and said 'Don't know. Dreamy.'

'She's dreaming of Mr Smith,' said Jennifer.

You could sometimes glimpse that yonderly expression in church. Mrs Smith was very elderly now, and it was known that she never took baths because she preferred to use the bathtub for coal. She ate little, usually beans out of tins, and would not let anyone cook for her, for fear of being poisoned.

In spite of all the bad feeling between them, Miss Smith was damned if she would give up her place in the choir stall, and Mrs Smith must have felt the same way, because she had never given up hers, either. So they stood there together every week, and while everything Mrs Smith sang landed at her feet, Miss Smith – stiff with indignation – sang to the rafters. Miss Smith would not meet anyone's eye, and Mrs Smith could not. They were the only choristers, and neither of them could hold a tune.

The Sunday service was thus an hour for prayer, for recrimination, for lengthy hymns and for displays of faith. For some it was a time to sleep. At the end of it Reverend Hollings bestowed his blessing on them all. 'The Lord be with you,' he bade, from the step into the chancery and with his arms wide open, as if he wanted the parishioners to bound into them with the same doggy enthusiasm he applied to everything. The congregation dutifully responded, 'And also with you.' But the High Sheriff, who could not bring himself to utter anything so banal, chose this moment every week to make a rebellious stand.

'And with thy Spirit,' he intoned, not loudly, but clearly enough that his wife overheard and gave him a reproving prod.

'Go in peace, to love and serve the Lord.'

And off they went, though peace and love were not in every heart.

By the time Hayes and his children had reached the gate of Hill Farm, Miss Prince had gone, leaving Isabel with an oil burner and two bottles. One contained Ylang-Ylang, for melancholy, and the other Eucalyptus, for energy.

The children let their father walk on down to the house while they, still in their smart clothes, lay under the boughs of an oak watching leaves detach themselves and spin in the air before drifting to the ground. Autumn would soon be giving way to winter, its parting gift the vibrant colours sprayed across the year's last leaves. The oak's foliage had turned a fluorescent yellow, with patches of the sky showing through it as azure.

'Technically, Mrs Smith wouldn't be able to see the top of this tree at all,' said Tom, who had lately become preoccupied by all the things Mrs Smith could or could not see. 'Technically' was his favourite new word, a recent substitute for 'basically'.

'You're always going on about that,' said Jennifer. 'Anyway, she would be able to see it, because she would be lying on her back.'

'But her head would still point the wrong way,' said Mattie. 'Tom's right: she would be looking at her toes. For her to see the top of the tree you would have to hold her upside down, otherwise she would only see the lowest branches.'

'Poor Mrs Smith,' said Tom. 'Perhaps Jim could fix it for her to be straight.'

Jennifer sighed and rolled her eyes. 'Of course he couldn't, you idiot.'

There was not very much for the children to do on Sundays after church. On Saturday evenings they were allowed to watch television, which their father referred to as 'the box'. If it was summer, the trees in full leaf outside disrupted reception, and the children had to take it in turns to hold the aerial, for a better picture. Inevitably there were arguments about who had had the longest turn, and Tom was prone to whining that his arm hurt, but it was worth the discomfort to watch *Jim'll Fix It* or *Doctor Who*. Sundays, on the other hand, were unremittingly dreary. Villages on Sundays offered little in the way of entertainment; no paddle-boats, no ice-cream parlours, gallery trips or double-bills. These were times when parents felt no obligation to provide fun for their children, but expected them to conjure it up themselves. The Hayes children were good at that, though recently they had been developing separate interests. Jennifer had become fascinated by calories, and no longer much enjoyed being outside. After lunch she went up to her room to make charts about how many calories were contained in different foods. Mattie spread all of the *Sunday Express* out on the sitting-room floor, to look at the cartoons, then read about rapes and murders and the scandalous behaviour of people who lived in London.

Tom usually went down to the 'tank'. This was a large container of water beside the tractor shed at the bottom of the farm. It was some distance from the house and Tom was supposed to go there only in the company of his sisters, but they hated going, so Tom had persuaded his mother that he could be trusted to go alone, especially now that he knew how to swim. The tank had been there for twenty years or more, ostensibly as a precaution against fire, but, since it had never been used, the water had become stagnant and was covered in algae. It was unsightly and smelled bad. Tom loved it for those reasons, and also because the tank was home to a colony of newts. For hours he perched at the edge of the water, watching as the creatures darted across the murky depths, then emerged to scurry round the sides of the tank. He loved the miniature dimensions of their faces and elbows, their tails' languorous swish. It enthralled him to know that these were the descendants of dinosaurs. If he ignored questions of scale, he could imagine this algae-glazed water-world as a prehistoric scene, in which crested giants roamed among the rocks and plants. It was a living picture that entirely absorbed him.

Sometimes he tried to catch the newts with his fingers, dipping his hands in the water until they were raw and red from cold. At other times he pulled off their tails and watched them scurry away, discombobulated. He did this more in the pursuit of science than cruelty. His father had told him that newts could regenerate any part of their bodies – 'Limbs, eyes, spinal cords, hearts, intestines, jaws. Just imagine, Tom, if we could do that!'

'It would be really cool,' agreed Tom. 'We wouldn't have to be careful about anything. Technically, you could break your leg, or your arm, and get it back the next day. It would be like being a superhero!'

Isabel, meanwhile, took to her bedroom with her oil burner. And, after an hour spent lying in the cool sanctuary of her room, breathing in the aroma of Ylang-Ylang, she felt her nerves noticeably calmed. She wondered if this was the start of the 'profound change' of which Miss Prince had spoken. It was wonderful to feel a lightening in her mood and even to find herself able to cook supper without sarcasm that evening.

Isabel rarely made social calls, but, a few days after first meeting Sheila Prince, she decided that she would like to accept the invitation to drop round and buy some Lavender oil. Soon after that she became a regular visitor – less for the oils than for Miss Prince's camaraderie. The visits fell into a pattern: she would go on Tuesday afternoons after school, taking Mattie with her, while Tom stayed behind for Drama Club. Jennifer, who was twelve, came back from secondary school on the bus and made her own way home.

Mattie looked forward to this weekly chance to spend time alone with her mother. As they walked along the top village road, swinging their joined hands, she chattered about her day at school, talking as quickly as she could, so that she could squeeze everything in while she still had her mother's undivided attention. Miss Prince lived in the Old School House, a five-minute walk from the new one. The building was clad in forbidding grey stone, but if you looked up (as Mrs Smith would not have been able to do) you would see that it was topped by a charming Tyrolean clock tower, the clock's face painted blue. There were no windows on this, public, side of the house. Perhaps that had been by design: the children who came here to learn a hundred years earlier would not have been distracted by passers-by outside. The lack of windows made that house seem particularly mysterious, and when Miss Prince opened the door to them, she did it with a corresponding stealth, as though welcoming conspirators. 'Come in, come in,' she would say in a low voice that was almost a whisper, and they followed her inside, where the contrast with that austere exterior could not have been greater. Beyond a small hall was a bright, modern sitting room, with French doors leading to a garden full of plants and foliage.

You had to take off your shoes to go into Miss Prince's house and there was a rack in the hall for them. The novelty of that obligation, and the fact that the house was all on one level, made visits to Miss Prince's an exotic experience for Mattie. The most riveting detail was the floor-covering: deep-pile, shaggy cream carpets were laid throughout the house. Mattie thought they were like her father's sheep might have been, if they had never got dirty or been marked by the tupping ram.

Visits to Miss Prince's house were special not only because they represented a rare chance to spend time alone in adult company. This was the one time in the week when Mattie was allowed to have fizzy orange, produced by Miss Prince in shapely bottles from her kitchen, which was also fitted out in creamy colours. On the afternoon of their first visit Mattie heard the sigh of the cap being unscrewed in the kitchen and thought herself very lucky indeed. Returning from the kitchen, Miss Prince's toes, decorated with a vermilion nail-varnish, approached naked through the long tendrils of her carpet like some rare species of jungle insect. She and Isabel Hayes were going to drink not tea, but 'real' coffee with something Miss Prince called 'half-and-half', spooned from a tall dark jar. She placed the tray on a low table strewn with fashion magazines and sat down in an armchair next to it. Then, like a magician, Miss Prince produced from her sleeve a thin blue metal container, from which she coaxed a minute pill, which she dropped into her coffee. 'I'm watching my figure, you know,' she said to Mattie with an exaggerated wink. On the next visit she asked, 'Would you like to have a look in my rummage box?'

She did not know what that meant, but at her mother's behest Mattie nodded politely and watched as Miss Prince rose stiffly from her chair, walked to her bureau and produced from it a wooden box. She took off the lid, bent down and shook the box under Mattie's nose, as though offering treats to a dog.

'Go on, have a rummage, see what you find.'

Mattie took the box and withdrew with it to a shaggy corner of the carpet. It was a proper treasure box, inlaid with mother-of-pearl on the outside. Inside there were marbles, broken pieces of glittering jewellery, a magnifying glass, a compass, a miniature pack of cards, another packet – this time of postcards – and a tiny booklet with an attached pencil. Miss Prince said that this was for a lady at a ball to note down the names of men with whom she was going to dance. One or two names had been entered in the little book, but in too faint a hand to read. Mattie occupied herself for a time looking at the pieces of jewellery, examining them through the magnifying glass and pretending to herself that she was searching for flaws in gemstones. Then she laid them out among the carpet's soft tendrils and pretended to be discovering them, at some sacred spot in a South American jungle.

After a time she turned her attention to the packet of postcards. It was a motley collection, a batch picked up in a junk shop. Most of the pictures were in black and white and had been hand-tinted. There was one of a couple poised to ski, with 'Greetings from Austria' printed in a cursive hand across one corner. Others showed people waving from a cruise liner, or standing, smiling, beside a lake.

However, among the cards there was one that was not in keeping with the others. Its texture was quite different and Mattie realised that it was actually a photograph, old and discoloured. It was a studio shot of a young man and woman, dressed up for a fancy-dress party in pirate clothes.

When Miss Prince returned from the kitchen with more coffee, Isabel said, 'I love it here. It's so light compared with our house.'

'Well, colours do make a difference to our well-being,' said Miss Prince, accommodating herself in a winged armchair. 'Magnolia feeds the light.' Her own rings were directing light around the room.

Miss Prince had soft, lined pouches under her eyes, and surprised eyebrows that had been pencilled on, some distance above the place where one would have expected to find them. She was glamorous, with very tanned skin, but everywhere there were suggestions of misalignment. In her jacket, a smart tweed, from a good London shop, darts indicated the appointed place for her breasts, but these, making their own arrangement, came to their point an inch or two lower. Some of her consonants had an indistinct edge and that was because she wore several false teeth on an ill-fitting plate.

They would continue to visit Miss Prince through the rest of the autumn and winter. On arrival at Miss Prince's house, Mattie's great joy was to spend half an hour or so delving in the rummage box – which was occasionally replenished with new treasures. After that she was supposed to do her homework, while the two adults talked in low, mesmeric voices. A large, squashy cushion that Miss Prince called a 'pouf' was arranged on the shaggy carpet for her, and Mattie spread her books out around it. It was so easy, though, to be distracted by all the new stimuli to be found in Miss Prince's house: the perfume, called Riviera, in the bathroom, or the gleaming cleanliness of her kitchen – to which Mattie obediently returned her glass when she had finished the fizzy orange. In a corner of the kitchen a macramé pot-holder hung from a hook in the ceiling, and out of the pot spilled a magnificent spider plant. There was a wall-hanging in the sitting room also made from macramé, which Isabel had admired, and Mattie heard Miss Prince promising to teach her mother the technique. In the kitchen there was a wipe-clean board in the shape of a poodle, sometimes with a shopping list on it, but there were no framed photographs anywhere in the house. She wondered if Miss Prince had any children or friends to send her things.

In December the winter trees sent up shivering branches into a watery sky, and the rooks' nests, stranded at the top of them, seemed absurdly distant. At Christmas time Miss Prince gave Mattie a glass brooch in the shape of a butterfly, the first piece of jewellery she had ever owned.

'You are becoming a young woman,' Miss Prince told her with a smile and, from her position on the pouf, sitting low to the ground, Mattie certainly felt that she was gaining a new perspective on the adult world. Over the tops of her own grazed knees she admired her mother's legs shimmering in the fine-denier tights that so powerfully betokened womanhood. Mattie had seen her mother remove these delicate items from packets that bore the name 'Gypsy,' over photographs of women who were nearly naked and tossing manes of hair about – as though the experience of wearing tights had transformed them entirely, and not just their legs. More fascinating were Miss Prince's toes: on closer inspection they looked rather horny, and two digits had what Mattie supposed might be a corn or a bunion on them. The joint at the base of one of her big toes was so enlarged and swollen that it had forced the toe itself out of line. The skin was stretched tight and shiny over this protuberance.

On one occasion Miss Prince noticed Mattie looking at her feet. 'I'm afraid I'm an old crock, my dear.'

Mattie smiled politely, but said nothing; she had understood Miss Prince to be referring to herself as a 'crook'.

'Not at all, Sheila!' remonstrated Isabel. 'You're the best-dressed woman in the village and you have the most beautiful home. We have so much heavy, old furniture. It's demoralising. Sometimes I really feel that I would just like to get rid of it all.'

'Well, why not get rid of it? Chuck the old stuff out and get in something new!' cried Miss Prince. She laughed, and Isabel Hayes laughed too, in a proper, carefree way, as though she literally felt the weight of mahogany and chestnut lifting off her. Years later Mattie wondered if that was when the seed had been planted. Looking back on the events, she was often drawn to reconstruct a scenario that explained her mother's behaviour and the tragedy of the summer that followed. If she closed her eyes and cast her mind back, she could recapture the singular atmosphere of the house with the Tyrolean clock tower, smell the scent of Riviera and hear the sigh of the fizzy-orange bottle being opened. Mattie became convinced that Miss Prince had exerted some kind of influence on her mother and she wondered if a dangerous chain of events had been set in motion, starting with their first visit to the house, and later, when Miss Prince had urged her to chuck out her old stuff and her mother had laughed on the sofa. By then, of course, Miss Prince was long gone from the village – run away, as Mattie came to believe.

FOUR

In February it rained so much that the river burst its banks and flooded the bottom field, turning it into a water meadow. The flooding had some precedent and, for that reason, the strip of land by the river was not a part of Hill Farm's rotation system, but was permanently left to grass. This year, however, the field was colonised by a flock of fifty or so migrating swans. Hayes told the children that they were whooper swans on their way back home to breeding grounds in the sub-Arctic. Their journey might be two thousand miles long. From a shelf in the sitting room he took down an atlas and traced their route home with the cracked and dirty nail of his index finger. 'Siberia is extremely cold. Not many people live there, but the people who do have to wear fur from head to toe. It's at the top of the world.'

Entranced to think that they were hosting visitors from the top of the world, the children made regular trips down to the bottom field to study the birds as they glided in the shallow water, now and then upending frilly behinds in search of something succulent to eat beneath the water. Their mother went with them on one of those occasions, but Isabel's state of mind ill-disposed her to be uplifted by the visitation. She found the sight of so many myth-ical creatures in one place rare and alarming, as though it presaged a terrible event. In fact the swans had arrived in the same week that a man and woman had been killed in a car accident at the top of the village. At first no one knew anything about the young couple, or what had caused the car to veer into trees just short of the crossroad that marked the village boundary. In the pub there was speculation that a fox or a badger had run into the car's path and startled the driver, who may have been drunk. Later it was learned from the police that the couple had been married that day and were setting off on their honeymoon.

Soon after the swans appeared, Mr Payne came to the office door to enquire about the need to telephone the RSPB, or some other wildlife authority. Hayes had just been spending the morning with a sales rep from an agrochemical company, and had put in an order for one hundred tons of Promax. The rep had treated him to a demonstration of different grasses, principally a tetraploid Italian ryegrass that performed extremely well when top-dressed with high doses of nitrogen. It had been a thoroughly enjoyable hour. These bright young men arrived smartly dressed and were invariably charming. The figures they quoted were no less impressive: a field of winter wheat treated with the new fertiliser could be expected to yield 20 per cent more at harvest time. If this new ryegrass delivered on its promise, they would see quite an improvement in the quality of their livestock fodder in the coming year.

Isabel was also taken by the reps, who never forgot to smile and wave at her as they passed the kitchen window on their way to the farm office. She could not help but admire the way they looked so smart and efficient, like Mormons, in their pressed suits and white shirts. Nothing ever came out of her washing machine looking so clean. They left notepads and pens bearing the bright logos and zappy names of different agrochemical companies – promotional tools that were intended for the farm office, but ended up indoctrinating the children instead.

By comparison with the reps, Mr Payne struck Hayes as a pathetic and charmless specimen: who would want to buy anything he was selling? Thin and girlish, he was apparently unable to witness any sort of natural phenomenon without wanting it registered, logged or otherwise made official.

'I think that the swans will take themselves off once they have fed and rested,' said Hayes, standing at the outside door to the office. 'They have a long journey ahead of them.'

'But won't they get stranded when the water drains away?'

'Goodness no, they're perfectly capable of taking off from the ground. They may be bloody silly animals, but they know how to get themselves into the air.'

'Why silly? Don't you think they're rather glorious!' The pink tip of Mr Payne's nose began to glow.

'Not really.' Hayes rubbed the palm of his hand hard all over his face and head, making no secret of his weariness. 'They mess up the grass – they'll pull out great clumps of it. We've had a heron nesting by the river, and I expect they'll scare it off. And they're aggressive. A public footpath runs alongside the river. If someone gets injured, I get the blame. So forgive me if I do not share your sense of romanticism.'

He removed his hand from his face then and looked at Mr Payne, as though seeing him properly for the first time.

'Tell you what, why not come in for a coffee? I've just had a meeting, and Isabel was good enough to make a flask.'

'Oh, that's very kind,' said Mr Payne, hopping over the

threshold – but the invitation had not, in fact, been issued out of kindness. Ever since their encounter in the kitchen, Hayes' feelings about the tenant had been more complicated and time-consuming than he liked to admit. He was convinced that it was Mr Payne who had called out the fire brigade. He often found himself rehearsing arguments that were designed to ridicule or button up this tiresome fellow. Twice he had dreamed about him. It was as though he were suffering a small but chronic irritation in the digestive tract: he needed an antacid to neutralise Mr Payne.

Now, standing at the door with all the manly paraphernalia of the farm office at his back, Hayes saw his chance. He would place Mr Payne in his world, among the tools of his trade: his piles of invoices and records, the stacks of *Farmers Weekly* mouldering by the door, the thudding stapler and paper guillotine. Hayes would cut him down to size.

The farm office was a proper man's room, unheated, smelling of grease and farts. Some years ago it had reached such a state of chaos that Isabel refused to clean it any more. On one wall there was a map of the farm, showing each of the twenty-two fields and their current sowing arrangements. This year forty-five acres were down to winter wheat. The year's cropping plan had been modified slightly, because of the rain. Two fields should have been ploughed and drilled by now, ready for spring barley, but the rain was keeping Mikey off that job at the moment.

Notes pinned to the board around the map attested to a regime of chemical solutions to a range of different problems. There had been slug damage in three of the fields – the mild, rainy weather was probably to blame – but they had applied pellets and brought the slugs to heel. Hayes had more than twenty different kinds of spray in the store, pesticides with manly names like Titan and Checkmate, evoking battles and victories. The enemy would keep coming, of course. Last year's hot June had brought aphids in their droves, but Hayes was armed and ready for them. Sometimes, as he stood in the fields surveying the damage done by rabbits or insects, he could not help but strike a Churchillian pose. He would fight to the last can of pesticide. He would never surrender.

On his desk was a large diary marked with grubby finger-prints, as was everything else in the office. Here Hayes recorded activities on the farm at the close of every day. Yesterday's entry read: 'Fourteen steers dehorned. Fourteen to go. Dehorning subsidy applied for.' He was also encouraging Mikey to write his own weekly reports. Then they might have proper meetings, in the office, with coffee, rather than relying on the odd conversation snatched outside the tractor shed or the barn. Hayes found exchanges with his labourer awkward because of the difficulty of maintaining eye-contact. For some reason, whenever Hayes tried to reach Mikey's gaze, the other man's eyes slid away. The labourer had a surly demeanour: he was quick to blush, to stare at the ground as though enduring a rebuke, when Hayes was merely trying to give him instructions or advice. He was capable of working hard, though, and if he proved himself able enough, perhaps Hayes would be able to promote him to foreman. Martin, their farm manager, had left after the last harvest and Hayes had not been sorry to see him go. Just because he had some fancy degree in farming from Cirencester, he thought he could throw his weight about, demanding ludicrous pay rises.

Hayes took a cracked and grimy mug from the windowsill and pumped watery spurts of instant coffee into it from the flask. On the other side of the table Mr Payne blanched a little. He appeared very small, like a child called in to see the headmaster. The damp weather had caused one of his ringlets to detach itself from the topiary formation, and now it dangled over his forehead. The guillotine sat between them on the desk, with its blade raised. His pretty curls gave Mr Payne the look of a French aristocrat, waiting for the chop.

Averting his eyes from the rusty blade, Mr Payne found himself studying patches of damp on the wall above a high shelf that was laden with bulging files. A few of these had been forced to breaking point and documents spilled out of them. Elsewhere papers were strewn haphazardly around, some of them bearing the brown, circular record of coffee cups that may have been placed upon them months or even years ago. There was a wilful disorganisation about this room that posed a challenge to Mr Payne's own meticulous disposition. His fingers fumbled nervously with a paper clip.

Passing a cup to him, Hayes said, 'You're obviously very interested in the countryside – has it been a lifelong passion?'

'I was brought up in Bromley,' said Mr Payne, who was as discomfited as Hayes might have hoped by the cold, the dirt, the smell and the bitter brew that was now being passed to him (a cracked mug, he had read somewhere, could harbour up to a thousand different sorts of germ). 'There were some woods nearby, at the end of our street. I used to go there with my mother. Then later, well – my wife and I are ramblers.'

'Ah yes, ramblers.' Well, there was a bunch who had a lot to answer for! Hayes had read recently in *The Times* that tourism in the country had increased tenfold in the last twenty years. It was true that nowadays one often saw cars parked in the village lay-bys. A family of town-dwellers would be sitting on the verge, eating a picnic. They dared not move far from the car, it seemed. Perhaps they were frightened of cows and sheep, or of getting muck on their shoes. But they would become bolder, without a doubt. They would start running down the footpaths, and breaking the stiles, leaving litter and demanding 'better access'. There had already been one case of a farmer ending up in court because he had not kept a footpath clear. The thought of it enraged Hayes for a moment, as he contemplated the feeble creature sitting on the other side of his desk, and he foresaw how an honest countryman like himself might be brought down by some similarly meddlesome townie. In the corridor outside the farm office there was a large freezer with a whole lamb in it – but there would be room in it for Mr Payne, too, thought Hayes. Rambler Pie had rather an appealing ring to it.

'When we lived in London we helped campaign for the right to roam,' said Mr Payne, encouraged to see Hayes smile. He remembered the evenings spent in their north-London kitchen stuffing envelopes with flyers to be sent to members of the Ramblers' Association. After his break-down he had found this a soothing activity.

'I hope you're not one of these people who think the land should be nationalised and farmers stripped of everything?' said Hayes. 'Mind you, with the number of regulations they heap on us, we may as well be nationalised anyway.'

'No, no,' said Mr Payne hurriedly. He did not like to think of Hayes stripped of everything, or even to imagine what might lurk under the heaving green jumper. 'We simply want, you know, better access to the land. So that everyone can enjoy this wonderful countryside.'

'And you still like to – ramble?' Hayes left a pause before the word, to make it sound silly. 'Of course you do: I've seen you out and about rambling. You ramble and roam all over the place, don't you?'

The tip of Mr Payne's nose began to glow pinkish. The other man's expression, beyond the guillotine, was inscrutable now. He could not judge whether Hayes' tone was meant to be menacing or not. He looked down at his coffee, on the surface of which a slick of grime had formed. Then Hayes laughed so heartily it gave Mr Payne a start that sent the coffee slopping over the brim of the cup and onto his trousers.

'It's wonderful to see people really enjoying the countryside, the way you and your wife do!'

Mr Payne laughed too, with relief and, seeing how Hayes drained his own mug, gulped down as much of the coffee as he could.

'So, we'll see what we can do about the swans, all right? But don't go ringing anyone at the moment. I think they will take themselves off when they've had a good feed.'

Gratefully Mr Payne rose from his seat and moved towards the door. 'You'll let me know if someone is coming from the RSPB? I would like to see them at work. I admire them so much.'

'Yes, indeed. Of course I will,' said Hayes, ushering out his guest and thinking as he did so: 'Like hell I will.'

Hayes had no sympathy for the city view of the country, as embodied by Mr Payne. He did not make pretty excursions outside, to ramble and roam or to have picnics; he simply *was* outside, working, all the time. In late summer, during harvest, that might be for eighteen hours at a stretch. The exposure showed in his face: at harvest time his pale-blue eyes shone under a dirty brow. All day long he screwed his face up in the sun; when he finally relaxed his features at the end of the day, the creases around his eyes showed white, where the rays had not reached.

When he looked out at the land around him, Hayes saw a living medium encompassing a rich rural history, but the possibility of a rural future, too. A thousand years ago this part of the Weald had been one of England's most densely forested areas. When they had first moved to the farm, Hayes and Isabel spent hours walking around their four hundred acres. He remembered pointing out to her the greenways that marked the droving tracks used by the early Saxons. The Domesday Book made mention of herds a thousand or even two thousand strong passing this way.

'You have to picture,' he had said, 'the swineherds arriving here at the start of summer, after walking for weeks. Every year they brought their pigs up north from the coastal settlements to forage among the oaks and birches.' Encasing her shoulders with his arms, he held her chin with one of his hands and made her look where he wanted, re-creating the scene for his new wife in CinemaScope. 'All this, as far as you can see, would have been forest. They cleared patches and set up camp for the summer. Then in autumn they took their pigs back south again, stuffed full of wild mushrooms and ready to be turned into bacon.' It was easy, for him, to equate the love he felt for Isabel with his love of nature. He could not resist biting her ear-lobe and murmuring a soft 'oink' into her ear.

Isabel had laughed at the thought of that fat herd waddling home, and she had made some mischevious remark about the smell of swine not being so hard to imagine, what with Hayes standing nearby. He had pretended to lunge at her and she had pretended to fight him off. In the early days of their marriage they engaged in many mock-skirmishes. Isabel laughed readily and often. Her cheeks coloured so prettily when she laughed that it was tempting to keep plying her with jokes. So next he had told her about the bandits, who hid in the woods and jumped out on passing travellers, carrying off their wenches. And when Hayes grabbed her, and flung her over his shoulder, Isabel shrieked and begged him to put her down, but he ran with her right the way up the hill and back to the house, to the bedroom.

He wanted everything to stay the same. He wanted nothing to change. He wished that he could say that to Isabel: 'Please let us be as we were. Don't drift away.' He did not know how to put his fears into words.

The land was his solace. For this area had been cultivated thousands of years before Domesday – Hayes was sure of that. Once, while walking in a field, he had found two chipped flints that he believed to be tools dating from the Stone Age. He found the knowledge of this ancient presence extraordinarily comforting. For centuries, for millennia, even, men had been working here with the same aims he pursued now: to tend the land, to coax life from it and a livelihood. Often, as he sat on his tractor passing back and forth across a field, Hayes wondered, 'Who was here, one thousand years before me? Who will be here in a thousand years' time?'

The great forest that had once covered this area was hard to imagine now. Most of the oaks had been cut down in the thirteenth and fourteenth centuries to make ships for the English navy. Now only small areas of woodland and copse were left here and there; a token spinney denoted acres of vanished woodland. But the land still had a beauty, Hayes felt, precisely because of man's mark on it. It was a palimpsest on which the contribution of each generation could be read. Some fields on this farm still retained the distorted shape produced hundreds of years ago by the need to turn a plough and oxen at the end of a strip without creating too tight a turning circle. One or two of the sloping fields were curved at the bottom, reflecting the way the ploughman's team had drifted over the centuries. What he loved about this landscape was that it belonged to the people. The region had never been dominated by large landowners, but by yeoman farmers – men and women who worked for themselves rather than for aristocrats living in London. For centuries they mostly bred cattle, the Sussex herd, but the demand for corn during the Napoleonic Wars encouraged many farmers to plough up the land, the stiff, intractable soil that sometimes had to be broken up by hand. The same thing had happened again during the war years, and now land that was best suited to grazing cattle had been made over to cereals, by dint of the sheer determination of the people who worked it.

But it was madness, really, to try to cultivate this sort of soil. Apart from anything else, the drainage was so difficult. He had tried to explain this once to Isabel: 'You have to keep heavy clay drained, or the foot of the crop sits in water and rots away.' At the moment there were generous grants for improving drainage, but that was not the whole solution. The key was more powerful machinery: bigger kit. Anyone with money and sense was trying to upgrade now. In the last year they had bought a new cultivator drill and a new fertiliser drill. Now Hayes wanted to buy a new combine harvester. The John Deere had broken down more than once during the previous year's harvest; they had missed several crucial days' work and had had to call in contractors. It meant talking the bank manager round, and that meant asking Isabel to cook for them all. He did not know which of these petitions he dreaded more.

Hayes heaved a sigh. His eyes swept over the bulging hills. The hedgerows looked like the stitching and seams on an ancient landscape, one that had been scarred by plague, famine and changing patterns of ownership. In fact, the hedgerows were man-made and not, as people like Payne argued, part of an ancient legacy. In the Middle Ages farmers had cleared vast swathes of woodland in order to create giant fields, maybe as big as a thousand acres, for communal farming. The Enclosure movements of the eighteenth and nineteenth centuries parcelled the land into fields that might only be four or five acres in size. Their purpose had not been to promote diversity of flora, to provide nesting grounds for small birds or 'corridors' for wildlife, but to exclude the peasant farmers who had once worked the common lands together. In the House of Commons there was uproar about this 'brutal' alteration of the landscape. Hedges were planted up with hawthorn, not because it was pretty, but because it was prized for its inch-long thorns – 'quickthorn' they called it. One might as well have used barbed wire.

Men had made the hedgerows for the wrong reasons, to keep others out. Now, they were getting in the way for different reasons. A five-acre field was all but impossible to work with modern-day machinery – which was far too big – and crops could not flourish in the shade of an unruly hedge. Hayes had recently learned that a field on neighbouring land was for sale. A straggly, unkempt strip of hedgerow separated it from a small field on Hayes' land. If he could acquire the field and remove the intervening hedge, he had a piece of land that could yield some profit and facilitate the use of large machinery. Of course, one also avoided the need to take the machinery out onto the road – no small consideration, given that the top entrance to Hill Farm was on a blind corner. There had already been a fatal accident on that road this year. So why should a farmer not remove a hedge or two for the sake of agricultural progress?

Surely this was progressive thinking. Or was the countryside to become a pretty park, with all previous endeavours preserved and nothing new? This, to Hayes, was the real tragedy in the country. He had written to *The Times* about it. In fact he wrote often to *The Times*, on points of natural or agricultural interest. It was something of a ritual, before he slept at night, to plant new seeds of ideas for letters and let the soft rain of thought fall on them. And as he drifted off to sleep he would begin to formulate the first paragraph in his mind: 'Sir . . .'

He had never yet had a letter published.

*   *   *

'Look over here, children,' said Hayes, stooping to pick up something from the ground near the tractor shed. It was a weekend afternoon. Isabel was resting and had wanted the children out of the house.

The children ran to him.

'What do you think this is?'

'Poo! Urgh!' said Tom.

'No,' said Hayes, who had anticipated this reaction. 'Think again.'

'Is it a fossil?' asked Jennifer thoughtfully.

The object their father held in his hand was about an inch long, smooth and irregularly shaped. It was black, flecked with grey.

'Good guess, but it's too light for that,' said Hayes. 'It's called an owl pellet. Owls eat their prey whole but they can't digest the bones or fur, so they regurgitate the leftovers and spit them out, like this.'

Hayes gently broke the pellet open and inside, buried in the fur, the children saw fragments that revealed themselves as the bones of a rodent – a tiny skull and the minute vertebrae of its spine – curled in the fur.

'Gross,' murmured Jennifer, though she did not flinch, or look away.

'I think it looks lovely,' said Mattie. 'How could nature make something so tiny?'

'Is that what the baby was like in Mummy's tummy?' asked Tom.

'Don't be so stupid!' snapped Jennifer. She often dealt ferociously with Tom; she could not forgive him for being so much their mother's favourite.

'Steady on, Jennifer,' said Hayes. 'You would never

guess from looking at the surface what lay inside, would you? It looks so smooth on the outside.'

Then he directed their gaze upwards and into the tractor shed, and they could see the eyes of the barn owl glinting in the gloom of the rafters. It was just possible to make out the small, totemic face, like something lovingly carved out of bone.

'Poor things, they have a bad reputation, completely undeserved,' said Hayes.

'Why, Daddy?' asked Jennifer.

'Well, in centuries past, country people were very super-stitious – some of them still are. They used to call them "screech owls", and if you saw one it was a sign that someone was going to die. In *Macbeth* the owl announces Macduff's death. Do you remember, Jen?'

Jennifer nodded wisely. She had been studying *Macbeth* at school.

'They sound very scary,' said Tom.

'Nothing to be scared of, Tom,' said Hayes, giving his son's shoulder a rough squeeze. 'We should be very fond of owls. They can eat half a dozen rodents a night, which is always good news for a farmer. We don't like rodents much.'

'I like rodents,' protested Tom.

'You like everything that's disgusting,' said Jennifer, under her breath.

They were squinting up into the rafters for some time and, when they looked down again, it was to see a man striding along the road towards them, holding by the hand a small boy who had to trot to keep up. It was Mr Bourne, the hobby farmer.

'And now here comes the other pain,' murmured Hayes to himself.

'Good afternoon one and all!' cried Mr Bourne heartily. He was dressed as a city man dresses for the country, in red trousers that were tucked into expensive wellington boots, and a yellow jumper, with a waxed jacket over it. Bourne cast an eye over the broken pieces of farm machinery that lay around, the oil cans and empty fertiliser bags. To one side of the tractor shed was the silage clamp, its black plastic covering secured by tyres, pools of effluent around its base. 'Obviously you're not going in for this year's Best Kept Farm Award, eh, Hayes?' He began to laugh, but his laughter rang out alone in the shivering air.

Hayes felt irritation prick the nape of his neck. It was all very well for Bourne, who paid other people to look after his herd, but if you were going to keep cattle during the winter, you had to feed them, damn it.

'May I ask what you are inspecting so closely?' asked Bourne.

Hayes put a finger to his mouth, though Bourne did not look like a person who could easily be quietened. 'It's a barn owl,' he said softly. 'Can you see it?'

Bourne moved to stand beside Hayes, corduroy legs planted four-square amid the puddles. He looked up.

'Ah, look at that!' Craning upwards, Mr Bourne revealed to the children a pair of hairy nostrils and a thick neck that had chafed against many starched collars on countless commuter trains. He had a florid face, with a prominent nose on which thread-veins bolted away from one another, then sprang together again in knots, suggesting electromagnetic activity. In such a large face, his mouth looked small and rubbery. 'Isn't that cute!'

The word sounded wrong, both for the barn owl and for Mr Bourne.

'Now, now, to business – if you'll excuse me, ladies and gentlemen.' He motioned towards the children, all of whom were now looking very glum, as children so often do on occasions that require them to be friendly. 'I've been to look at the Charolais. They don't look right. They're not very alert.'

Hayes looked up suspiciously from the owl pellet. 'In what sense "not right"?'

'When I walked by just now, one or two of them were lying down.'

'They could be asleep.'

'Ha! Point taken. All the same – I'm wondering if maybe you brought them out of the shed too soon.'

'They have access to the shed at night. And I need the space in the barn, Harry. The sheep will be lambing soon. Our Herefords have gone outside, after all.'

'Your Herefords, yes. But the Charolais are a bit different, aren't they? Given that I plan to show them?' He was still smiling, but Bourne's stance – arms folded tight across his chest – suggested that he would have spoken more plainly had the children not been there. 'Do you think we can we go and have a look at them now?'

'By all means.'

'Tell you what: perhaps Peter could stick around and play with your lot for half an hour. Would you like that, Peter?'

The wheedling tone he used to address the boy was no

good; a look of horror flashed across Peter's face and he shook his head vigorously. Mattie knew the reason for this reaction and shared both his horror and his relief when Mr Bourne took Peter's hand and reluctantly bore the child away with him. She and Peter shared a terrible secret from school.

It was not until much later that afternoon that the children heard their father return. The back door slammed. Hayes marched into the house, removed his wellington boots and almost instantly banged his head on the low lintel between the hall and the dining room. The three children cowered in front of the television as a torrent of swearing followed, then they heard their mother's intervention.

'I'm going to turn up the television,' said Tom.

In the kitchen Hayes sat at the table holding a bag of frozen peas on his head, brooding on an inarticulate hatred of Bourne and his bloody Charolais. This method of cattle-rearing, as though stocking a cellar with fine imported wines, struck him as supremely self-indulgent. Cattle were for meat, for leather, for milk. But Bourne had made a packet in the City and wanted to throw his money about, so he alighted on this vanity project – and hobbies did not come much more expensive than Charolais. It would take the proceeds of twenty Hereford steers to buy one Charolais. By that measure, Bourne's ten heifers were more valuable than Hayes' entire herd.

When he had asked Bourne why he wanted to keep Charolais, Bourne had said it brought 'variety' to the countryside.

'Makes a change from fucking Friesians – if you'll pardon my French.'

That was the point, though: they *were* French. If Bourne was looking for variety, why not one of the traditional English breeds that were becoming so hard to find? Not so long ago you could drive the length of Britain and find a different breed in every region. If Bourne wanted to resist the insidious takeover of Friesians, why not establish a Sussex herd? They had been in this area even before the Romans. But you could tell that Bourne felt no romance about husbandry. He talked about his cattle as if they were racing cars.

'They can get to twelve hundred pounds in four hundred days. In beef terms, it's the Holy Grail – you know that, Hayes – the four-minute mile. And people's tastes are changing. They want leaner meat, less fat. Wait and see: these animals are going to change the face of British beef-farming.'

That was not Bourne's prediction, however, but the opinion of his agricultural adviser – for Bourne bought in everything, no matter what the price. He had bought his prize-winning heifers at a show in the autumn. Now he would try to scoop up more prizes, before selling the cattle on to foreign breeders and making himself a fat profit. Hayes could not help fuming about it. He wondered if the subject merited a letter to *The Times*.

'What is actually wrong with Bourne's cows, darling?' Isabel's voice retrieved him from his reverie and returned him to the dripping bag of peas.

'Nothing is wrong with them. They're a bit muddy, that's all. But he wants to parade them at the summer shows, and he thinks they aren't pretty enough.'

She looked questioningly at him and he thought, not

for the first time, that they really did not understand one another.

'Apparently they must have five-star treatment. They have to be kept clean and free of parasites. Their hooves must not get wet. The worst of it is that now I have to bring the bloody animals back indoors, when I need space in the barn for lambing.'

Hayes had stopped holding the frozen peas and let the bag sit on his head, water trickling down his forehead. What was particularly infuriating about this was that he had, for months now, been trying to get Bourne to admit responsibility for several ditches between their respective farms. In the autumn Hayes had paid contractors a handsome sum to clear all the ditches on the farm, mark the outfalls and apply a herbicide to keep the banks clear. But he was quite sure that at least half a dozen of those ditches belonged to Bourne, and he was damned if he was going to subsidise his neighbour's hobby. In retrospect, he wondered if it had been a mistake to take the Charolais.

'Surely the sheep only need to be in the barn if they've got complications,' said Isabel, who was cutting up vegetables and preparing to give them a good boiling.

'But there are always bloody complications! You know what sheep are like. The damn things drop dead at the drop of a hat! You'd think they actually want to die. Just in the last year we've had two heart attacks caused by low-flying fighter jets, and the ewe that got trapped in a fence and eaten alive by a fox. And last year it was contagious abortion ...'

Isabel, feeling that she should say something sympathetic and finding no immediate inspiration, took up her scourer and rubbed hard at a mark on the chopping board. She hoped by this to communicate solidarity and a resolve to labour, with her husband, against adversity. It was far too oblique and insufficient a gesture, though, conveying simply that she was not much interested in cows or sheep.

At least this new problem with the Charolais had yielded one benefit: Bourne had offered to help out with one of his own men. He was an Australian stockman in his early thirties who had come to work for a friend of Harry Bourne in order to gain experience of working on a British cattle farm. His work there had come to an end now, and he had time to fill before moving on. In the meantime Bourne proposed that he move into the tied cottage on Hayes' land. He could be on hand to keep an eye on the Charolais, and do any extra work that Hayes needed done. Bourne would pay his rent, Hayes would pay for any work not involving the Charolais. Ever since Martin had gone, Hayes had known that he would need to get more help, especially when lambing began. So this offer of casual labour with no commitment suited him very well.

They did not meet the new stockman until the following week, when both herds were due to be tested for tuberculosis. The children came to help bring Bourne's herd up. Like members of a Puritan cult, the white heifers moved gracefully up the hill with the children following their swinging haunches. Barricades had been put in place to form a corridor between an improvised pen and an area inside the barn where the cattle crush was waiting, looking like a medieval instrument of torture.

When all the cattle were in the pen, Jennifer turned to her brother and sister and said, 'Let's go up to the living room.' The other two knew immediately that she meant the area they had fashioned from bales of straw in the cowshed. You had to scramble up ten levels of bales to get there. At the top, under the rafters, was a reconstruction of Miss Prince's sitting room, as decribed in detail by Mattie to the other two. There was an armchair and a pouf (each made from a bale of straw) as well as a sofa (made from two bales). An upright bale represented the drinks cabinet, and another the 'music centre'. There was also a coffee table, on which the children had scattered old copies of the *Radio Times*. Sometimes they brought plastic beakers up to this room so that they could pretend to drink cocktails. And from here they had a perfect view of the shed, the crush and the cattle milling around their enclosure.

The low lighting in the shed created an air of anticipation and lent an artistic chiaroscuro to this interior, which was otherwise grimly utilitarian. The shed was twenty years old, but had been updated recently, with the aid of an agricultural grant, to improve ventilation. About a third of the available space was given over to bales of straw and hay. The children were not allowed to climb on the hay, because it too easily came free from its twine bindings, but the straw was fair game if they were careful. The rest of the shed could be partitioned according to the requirements of the season, to accommodate cattle or lambing sheep.

In this lighting the cattle crush was all the more ominous, throwing long bars of shadow that made a giant cage on the ground. The barricaded corridor grew similarly in importance, and the men standing around staked out their positions with a studied composure, as though they had been standing this way, bored and expectant, for hours, like groupies waiting for a rock star to emerge from his dressing room and dash to a limousine. Outside, the cattle had begun to move nervously in the pen, mounting one another as if to clamber out of the enclosure. Seen from the top of the hayloft, they gave a collective impression of wide eyes, flaring nostrils and urgently evacuated bowels. Mattie watched the white flanks jostle and push one another, a moving approximation of Miss Prince's carpet. She wondered if they already knew that some painful intervention was waiting for them.

'Fix me a Bloody Mary,' ordered Jennifer, and Tom sprang from his seat to oblige. Standing at the 'drinks cabinet', he produced a plastic beaker and made some appropriate glugging noises.

Meanwhile Mattie reclined on two bales laid end-to-end, with a copy of the *Radio Times*. 'I'm going to read about fashion shows now,' she said. 'Tom, please get me a Martini.' The straw pricked her legs and arms. Any time they rearranged the furniture their arms bore long red scratches the next day. They had once tried to bring a blanket up to the hayloft, to make the scene more comfortable, but were intercepted at the airing cupboard by their mother.

'Does Miss Prince wear high-heeled shoes?' asked Jennifer.

'No,' said Mattie. 'No one is *ever* allowed to wear shoes in her house. But you may wear nail polish. She's got bright-red toenails, like cherries.'

'Really?' exclaimed Jennifer with admiration. 'It's not fair only you ever get to go. I'd like to go to Miss Prince's.'

'Me too,' said Tom.

'Well, not everything in life is fair,' said Mattie, who had often been irritated to hear these words from her mother and was pleased to irritate someone else with them, in turn.

Down below, Hayes was manning the barricades, he and Bourne standing on one side of the improvised corridor: the 'race'. Mikey, looking lank and gormless in a dirty blue boiler suit, was on the other side together with a young man they thought must be the new stockman. They could not see this man's face, just that he was tall and slim, with broad shoulders. His blond hair, annointed with light from the bare bulb that hung above him, showed strands of gold and copper. The vet was waiting by the crush, wearing a belt slung around his hips onto which were attached the implements he was going to need. As they waited in the enclosure, the cattle grew more restive, jostling each other and sliding in their own shit. To the children up in the loft it now became apparent that the cause of their agitation was not so much the crush as the presence of Mikey's sheepdog Blue, which kept racing behind the pen, then swerving back again. These sudden movements were unnerving the cattle at the back, and their distress spread to those at the front. Blue – named for his eyes – was a young dog, with a tendency to get over-excited.

'Ready, Mikey?' called Hayes.

'Yeah. Ready,' shouted back Mikey, blushing. He gave an awkward thumbs up.

There was a commotion as Mikey and the other man struggled to open the gate of the pen to allow through just one heifer, without the others shoving in after it. Finally the gate was opened, the heifer was manhandled into the race and the rest held back. On finding herself separated from the herd, the animal immediately faltered and stumbled onto her knees, which looked as dirty and vulnerable as a schoolboy's, but the men goaded her back onto her feet, then prodded and pushed her towards the crush, where she staggered and flailed in her confinement, becoming with every second more confined. The vet secured the heifer with the belly-strap and pushed her head through the yoke. He took clippers from his belt, to remove the hair from two sections of skin on the neck, and then calipers to measure the thickness of the skin between these areas. With a syringe he injected into the white, shimmering neck two agents that could determine within three days whether the animal showed a reaction to avian or bovine tuberculosis. Then the heifer was released into a different area of the barn.

A doorway beyond the crush led to the milking parlour, which had not been used for many years. Its long-abandoned stalls were covered in cobwebs, the old milking apparatus suggestive of sinister surgical procedures. In the past the children had played hospitals here, before finally agreeing that the room gave them the creeps. Recently, though, they had been drawn back to the old dairy because a cat living wild on the farm had produced a litter of kittens in one of the bays. Sometimes the children came to see them and to leave little bowls of bread soaked in milk. Tom carried the bowls up the hill from the farmhouse, his tongue protruding from one side of his mouth as he concentrated on not spilling any milk.

Blue was now working some crazy circuit that involved darting behind the Charolais' enclosure, up through the door to the old dairy and back, tail low, hackles and ears raised, as though madly trying to follow the trail of several competing scents. The men, absorbed in their work, were oblivious to the dog's frenetic activity, but when a ball of fluff flashed out of the dairy and towards the back of the shed, Blue in pursuit, the children realised what was going on: Mikey's dog had smelt out the wild cats that lived in a corner of the dairy. They saw a cat leap up towards the frame of a window, but the dog jumped too and caught the cat's body in his mouth.

Jennifer screamed, 'Stop him!' and the men below all turned to look upwards; none of them had been aware of the young audience in the hayloft.

The blond man they did not know shaded his eyes from the bulb's naked glare and called, 'Who's that? Are you all right?'

'Please stop Blue. He's going to kill the cat!' screamed Jennifer.

After a moment's disorientation the man saw where they were pointing and ran towards the cattle enclosure. By now Blue had pulled the cat down from the ledge, but the blond man swiftly jumped over the bars and made for the dog, shouting and raising his hand as though he meant to wallop him. Blue dropped the cat and crouched on the ground, ears close to his head. The man picked up the cat by its scruff and examined it, then laid it down on the straw in an empty bay before taking Blue by the collar. He walked the dog round to Mikey.

'Your dog wants shutting up, mate.'

Mikey flushed. 'What harm was there?' But this was said more in sulky self-defence than as a challenge.

'Put him in my car for now,' said Hayes, so allying himself with the blond man, and then Mikey had little choice but to slink away, as his dog had, both of them aware of the rebuke.

Up in the loft, Tom began to sob.

'It's only nature,' Mattie said, to console him. 'Anyway, I think the cat will be all right.'

For a week the rain lashed down. Rain dimpling the surface of the river fooled the perch and brought them up gasping for insects. Meanwhile, the swans continued to glide point-lessly around each other on the field, like synchronised swimmers waiting for taped music to begin, dipping under-water from time to time, preening their muddied feathers.

In his stale office Hayes sat preparing his Cash Flow Forecast, in anticipation of the bank manager coming for dinner. He must make more than a hundred calculated guesses on what he might need to spend over the coming year. Then he must make it all add up, horizontally and vertically: it was a bloody nuisance.

On Monday evening the children watched from an upstairs window as the bank manager alighted from his car. He was a small man in a ruffled pink shirt, who seemed to pirouette between the puddles as he made his way to the back door; they had never before seen a man look so frothy. Perhaps the ruffles were intended to suggest a friv-olous side, to set debtors at ease. That day Isabel had tidied the household with a random zeal. There was so much to do that she did not know where to start, so she tackled everything that came to hand first, including the children, who were made to bathe and wash their hair, to give a good impression, should they happen to be spotted by the bank manager flitting up and down the creaking staircase. A soft lavatory roll had been put in the bathroom, in place of the customary sheets of medicated paper.

'You'd think the bloody Queen was coming, or something,' said Jennifer as they sat at the top of the stairs listening to the laughter rising from the dining room. Every now and then the door opened and noise cascaded out of it. Their mother would appear carrying a tray of empty plates. All afternoon she had been busy preparing the dinner: prawn cocktail, followed by moussaka and trifle. 'They are laughing a lot,' said Jennifer. 'Perhaps that means the bank manager is going to give them more money.'

'I don't really get it,' said Mattie, who was a thoughtful child and liked to understand things. 'Why does he have so much money and why would he give it to us? Does he feel sorry for us, or something?'

Tom began to cry. 'I don't want Mummy and Daddy to be poor.' And Jennifer rolled her eyes, but Mattie hugged her little brother.

On Tuesday, at Miss Prince's house, the rain was like smatterings of stones hurled against the windows by a fiercely determined hand. Mattie sat in the kitchen doing her homework and drinking fizzy orange. Miss Prince had suggested that she would be more comfortable there, with a table to work on, but Mattie felt her exclusion from the living room keenly. She missed the pouf and the shaggy carpet, though at least here there was consolation to be had in the ready availability of the biscuit tin. The door between the kitchen and living area was left barely ajar, so that Mattie could make out very little of the two women's conversation – and what she did pick up was not so much words as variations in volume and tempo. Sometimes her mother spoke very quietly. At intervals it would sound as though she was sobbing. Miss Prince spoke quickly and seemed to be saying a great deal, in a tone that was reassuring, but firm. After this had continued for a while Miss Prince came to the door and gently pressed it closed.

Now Mattie sat stock still, her pen above her homework, trying to quieten everything so that she could hear what was happening next door. But her thudding heart made a kind of ocean of noise while her mother's crying muffled the words, which seemed to come in waves of sound, as though issuing from an untuned radio. Sometimes her voice would rise, into a kind of wail. Then Mattie heard quite distinctly the words 'Can't remember what it's like to feel worthwhile,' and this burning information set her heart banging in her ears. She strained to be more attentive, and just as surely she heard Miss Prince's reply: 'Then you must feel worthwhile again, you must *be* worthwhile!'

FIVE

Two bodies swung from a beam in the utility room. They had been there for over a week, and could give you quite a shock if you went in to look for shoe polish. They were a present from the High Sheriff, who had given another brace of pheasants to the vicar, handing down advice about their preparation in silver tones: 'Tough old birds, I'm afraid, they'll need hanging for a few days.'

Hayes would have hung them for a long time anyway: he may have been Low Church, but he liked his game high. Having been brought up to think of animals as food, the children did not find the pheasants a sad sight. They were used to seeing their father bring his gun into the kitchen and shoot a pigeon clean out of the sky through an open window. Nobody felt bad about it, although Isabel disliked the disruption to mealtimes. Everything that was shot on the farm was eaten, even pigeons, which were fiddly to prepare and yielded little meat. During harvest Hayes liked to take potshots from the combine harvester – aiming at startled rabbits or pheasants as they fled the cutting blades. Their bodies, still warm, were hung from the hand-rail, where they swung limply as the combine advanced, a row of scalps to warn off the enemy.

They were used to the cycle of life and death on Hill

Farm. Even so, there was a poignancy about the pheasants' sleek heads – thought Isabel, as she loaded the washing machine – their necks entwined, the cock's bottle-green feathers close beside the hen's dun, as though their deaths had been down to some kind of lovers' pact, and not simply an unlucky pass at the end of the High Sheriff's shotgun. At the moment she was prone to seeing all life in tragiromantic terms. Even a withered plum sitting alone in the fruit bowl was sometimes too potent a metaphor for her. The Ylang-Ylang had not, after all, entirely banished Isabel's melancholy.

On a Saturday afternoon when there was nothing else to do Hayes sat down to pluck and gut the pheasants. Everyone was warned out of the kitchen, but the children kept bouncing back into it, determined not to miss out on any excitement. Hayes removed his woolly jumper – which was almost like removing a part of himself – and unbuttoned his shirt-cuffs with deliberation, rolling away the checks to reveal strong, scarred and freckled forearms. The whole kitchen table must be cleared, because Hayes planned to make a great mess of blood and feathers. Then the birds were laid out.

First Hayes plucked the feathers off both birds, until the table and floor were buried in plumage and fluff, and the kitchen looked like the scene of an improbably bloody pillow fight. He sent Jennifer for a rubbish bag and stuffed all the feathers in it before going further. When he wiped his hands over his face, little bits of feathers stuck under his nose. Next he cut off the birds' heads, still wearing their ruff of feathers like Elizabethan courtiers, and then their feet, those graceful talons that may once have strutted across the lawn of the High Sheriff.

When the belly of the bird was slit open, the smell of putrid flesh was so shocking that the children found it quite a thrill to catch the horror of it in their nostrils. As Hayes let the darkly bloodied guts spill over his fingers, they dared one another to approach the table, seeing how far they could advance without retching. Tom was the best at this. He could walk right up to his father's shoulder and look over it at the dissecting work in progress. Then he delighted in staying the course, licking his lips and making faces at his sisters, as if he relished the sight and smell of bloody birds.

Isabel came into the room in time to see her youngest child sticking a finger in the blood and pretending to lick it. An unholy fury came over her.

'That's a terrible, disgraceful way to treat an animal. You should be ashamed!' Then turning, she said to all of them, 'You have no respect. You understand nothing about life! You think of nobody but yourselves!'

The children froze. Hayes looked at his wife anxiously. Then Isabel turned on her heel and, with her cardigan pulled loosely over her shoulders, flew out of the farm-house like one of the feathered creatures that were considered fair game at Hill Farm. Down the hill she charged, sobbing with rage. Sheila Prince had told her that she could make changes in her life, but how would it ever be possible? She was trapped by circumstance and always would be: she had wasted her life and was too old now to change direction. She would end her days at Hill Farm without ever having worked, travelled or achieved anything of note. Rage could only carry Isabel so far, however; about halfway down the hill she let her pace slacken and chastised herself aloud. 'It's ridiculous, for Christ's sake, to cry over a pheasant.' But now that she was crying anyway she thought she might as well make the most of the tears – get her money's worth in a sense – and indulged herself in the sort of noisy, racking sobs she usually reserved for her bedroom when everyone was out. It was cathartic to make such a noise in the open air. At the bottom of the hill she turned right – and found herself face to face with the new stockman.

'Hello!' Isabel cried brightly, hoping to bamboozle him with a cheerful tone, even though he must have heard her snorting and wailing beyond the hedge. She raised her eyes in a brief greeting and prepared to walk on as though nothing were amiss. All kinds of embarrassments may happen among the English and be left safely unacknowledged. Jack was Australian, though, and not having been schooled in English techniques of evasion, he did not know that he ought to ignore her. Instead he stopped in his tracks and immediately asked her what was wrong.

'Are you all right, Mrs Hayes? Has something happened?' His face was full of concern, with none of the weary forbearance to which she had driven her husband.

She could have picked any one of a thousand answers, but for reasons she was afterwards unable to explain to herself, Isabel said, 'Oh, nothing. Well, the swans.' In the past she had cried about bombs, famines, her miscarriage and the state of the downstairs lavatory. The swans' plight, however, left her uniquely unmoved.

Jack looked puzzled. 'The swans? You mean down on the field by the river, right?'

'Yes, it's just that they've been there a long time, more

than two weeks now and, you know, the water's been draining away. I hate to think that they could get stuck there. But it's very silly – I'm sorry!'

'Perhaps there's something that can be done to resolve the problem.'

'Yes – well, I don't know. Let's hope so.' She shrugged, smiled and walked on. She had noticed Jack around the farm, striking elegant poses in his checked shirts and jeans, but was not yet sure that she liked him. He seemed to her to be suspiciously good-looking; Isabel was used to a more shambolic style of man. Briefly she felt flattered by his attention. But, once she had recovered her composure and returned home, Isabel did not give Jack another thought.

Her children, on the other hand, could think of little else. The episode in the cattle shed, and Jack's heroic rescue of the wild cat, had impressed them very much. They were mesmerised by his good looks and the unusual accent they had otherwise only ever heard on television. Besides, Jack was much more friendly to the children than Mikey had ever been, courting their approval by offering trailer rides or inviting them to help him with odd jobs.

Tom showed his admiration by attempting to emulate an Australian accent, while his sisters, who could not walk past Jack without collapsing into blushes, taunted each other to the point of tears about which one loved him more.

'Jennifer's wearing eyeshadow because she's in love with Jack,' observed Mattie after school, when they were meant to be doing their homework. She had to dodge out of range before her sister kicked her.

'Oh, is that what it is. I thought you must have been playing in the coal shed or something,' said Isabel, absently.

'Honestly, Mum,' Jennifer said. 'I haven't done that since I was about six!' Her eyes rolled in their dingy sockets. 'Anyway, I don't *play* any more. I'm not a child. You don't have to be so patronising!'

Isabel, who was pushing pieces of mutton through a meat-grinder, looked up with an expression of desperation. 'Well, what's wrong with being a child? You're only twelve, Jennifer. It's still very young to be thinking about make-up and diets . . .'

'Do you think you could just leave me alone for once?' shouted Jennifer. 'Let *Mattie* be your child. You love her more anyway! Plus she's a baby. She doesn't even know what a virgin is!'

'At least I don't have a verruca,' said Mattie, under her breath.

'Shut up! I hate you!' shouted Jennifer before storming out of the kitchen and slamming the door, which bounced against its ill-fitting frame, making for a less satisfying exit than she had intended.

Mattie went to her mother and put her arms around her waist. 'I don't mind still being a child, Mummy,' she said, looking up into Isabel's grey eyes and willing them not to fill with tears. She tended to think of herself as responsible for her mother's happiness, a caring nature so often being the badge of the middle child. Recently, though, Mattie had been hoping to devolve some of this responsibility to Miss Prince. It worried her to see that her mother's new friendship was not as sustaining as it had promised to be.

'I wish I could make you one hundred per cent happy,' said Mattie, and her mother turned away, covering her eyes.

'You couldn't make me happier, Mattie. This is my fault, not yours.'

Mikey, who was eating his sandwiches in the tractor shed, looked up one lunchtime to see the new stockman advancing towards him.

'Wotcha,' said Jack. 'Is this a private party – or can anyone pull up a tyre?'

Mikey reddened. He was used to eating alone and not experienced in lunchtime repartee.

'Yeah. Help yourself.'

Jack dragged a tyre over from the pile in the corner of the shed and positioned it close to Mikey's before sitting down. 'I'm starving,' he said, taking a bite out of his sandwich and, with his mouth full, 'Great view, by the way.'

From this vantage point the silage clamp and the water tank were away to the left, out of sight, and the tractor shed's open side faced onto a corn field, with no other buildings visible. Mikey often gazed out at this view when he was lounging against the tyres after finishing the paper, or picking at his teeth with a two-inch nail from the toolbox that was kept in the shed. If the sun was strong, the scene outside was lit up as bright as a cinema screen, which you could watch from the dark at the back of the tractor shed. It was like seeing a film in which nothing happened: no fights, no car-chases, no shoot-outs – just ripening wheat.

'Yeah, it's all right, I suppose,' he said, for the sake of saying something.

'So what have you got for lunch today?' asked Jack, leaning towards him.

Mikey held up a wodge of white bread in his dirty hands, prised it open and glanced inside. He shrugged. 'Dunno. Reckon it's either fish or ham.'

He had not intended the remark as a joke, but Jack evidently took it as one, because he laughed very abruptly, and looked for a second as if he was going to choke on a small piece of bread. 'Fish *or* ham?' Jack cleared his throat and wiped his mouth with the back of his hand. 'You mean you can't tell?'

'Well, they both come out of a jar!' Mikey remonstrated, laughing too, colour high in his cheeks. 'Fish paste or ham paste. They're both brown, right? They taste the same, give or take.'

'But don't you ever look at the jar when you're making them?'

'My mum makes them.'

'Oh, I see, your *mum* makes them. Lucky man.' Jack blew some strands of hair away from his eyes and surveyed the scene in front of them. 'This is a great spot, though. You know something else? Of all the buildings I've seen in this country, this is the most Australian.'

'Oh yeah? Why's that?' Mikey knew only that Australia was said to be full of sheep, but had no clear idea where it was, or what its buildings looked like.

'It's the roof.' Jack pointed up into the rafters and smiled at Mikey, while still chewing. 'The sound of rain on corrugated iron – man, that takes me straight back home. We have a shed just like this on our farm. When the wind blows it's like a giant instrument, like organ pipes playing – you know what I mean? When it rains, it's like percussion.'

Mikey nodded, although these observations were rather esoteric for him. At his school, anyone who had compared the rain to percussion would probably have been labelled 'queer'.

'What about Hayes: is he a good boss?'

'He's all right. Gets a bit shirty sometimes, if you don't do things his way, but I know more than him about tractor engines, so he can't touch me there.'

'Nice one,' said Jack with a wink. 'Always good to have something over the boss.'

Mikey smirked, still chewing his food, and thought that he and Jack could perhaps be mates. He pictured himself taking Jack down to the pub and introducing him to Dave and Tone, who would be impressed by Mikey's new friend and then think more highly of him. He wished he had not let on about his mother making his sandwiches, though.

From then on, whenever their paths crossed on the farm, there was more joshing about sandwiches. Mikey smiled at Jack's jokes, though they caused him some apprehension. For Jack, the jokiness was shorthand for a willingness to get on; if they had both been English, he would have ribbed Mikey about football. He could not have known about the other man's defensiveness; Mikey's wariness of jokes dated from school, where humour had been a weapon – and very often he had been skewered at the end of it. As the weeks passed, Mikey watched as his Australian co-worker became established as a senior authority on the farm. Any time Hayes required the men to work together, the more complicated instruction was given to Jack, while Mikey might be relegated to manning gates or hefting sacks of fertiliser. Although he was younger, he still should have had seniority, Mikey felt, as an employee of longer standing.

Jack's status on the farm grew, and with it Mikey's resentment, and the labourer began to feel a return of his old compulsion. Setting fires had been an outlet for the frustrations of his early teenage years, after his father left home. By the time he was fifteen, he had four arson attacks to his name, but the police had suspected his involvement in the last and that had been enough to stop him attempting a fifth. Still, these days, there were times when he felt an itch in his fingers and rattled the matchbox in his pocket. Walking past the fertiliser shed he thought of all that ammonium nitrate packed together and fantasised about explosions. Sometimes, sitting at the back of the tractor shed, he struck a match and let the flame burn itself out, stinging his fingers, and that was enough to quell the desire. Other times he had to put the matchbox on a high shelf, to stop himself thinking about fire.

Jack had been hired for his expertise with cattle, but his experience on a large farm in Australia more than equipped him for sheep husbandry, too. He knew how to move the animals around gently but firmly, holding them by the scruff of the neck, or pinning would-be escapees against the pen with his thigh. In March, as the time for lambing approached, he prepared a nursery field, close to the house and to his cottage, with pens improvised out of bales of straw. Several times a day he moved among the sheep, sizing them up, prodding them with his hands to see which was ready to 'drop'. He had a knack for predicting multiple births or complicated deliveries.

Back in the autumn Hayes had identified a suitable tupping ram through the small ads in a farming magazine. Mattie and Tom had been there to see the beast arrive in a van one cold afternoon in October. Its owner was a small, wiry fellow who seemed to have relinquished his own virility in favour of the ram's. When the ramp was put in place and the doors opened, there stood the animal, glowering and steaming in his own heat.

'Blimey,' said Tom, 'he looks cross.'

The ram had lowered his head as if to charge, then stayed mysteriously immobile, surveying the waiting pasture and the many available sexual partners with contempt. He was a Jacob, with a black face and horns neatly coiled on either side of it. Strapped around his middle he wore a harness, like a sort of leather chastity belt, except that in this case the desired outcome was the opposite. Fixed to the harness was a raddle, or wax crayon, so that any ewes the ram inseminated would later bear the mark of their shame. At that moment, however, the ewes appeared dismissive of their would-be inseminator, huddling like sulking sixth formers in the opposite corner of the field. Over the following days Tom and Mattie had found many spurious reasons to walk past the sheep. On the pretext of collecting herbs or 'getting fresh air', they set off for the field hoping to find it rampant with sex. Invariably they found the ram in one corner and the ewes in another.

'When do you think they actually *do* it?' asked Mattie. She dared not put this question to Jennifer for fear of being scorned, but Tom was both kinder and less worldly.

'They probably want to be private,' Tom said. 'I think

they're embarrassed. They probably wait until everyone's gone.'

Five months on, all the ewes were marked and the first offspring of these grudging unions were arriving. Jack was often in the field, helping with the difficult deliveries, encouraging the new lambs to latch on to their mothers, rescuing others that were rejected by the ewe.

In the evening, while bathing and getting ready for bed, the children regaled their mother with stories of Jack's quiet heroism. If Isabel paid scant attention to their anecdotes it was partly because it made her uncomfortable to remember meeting Jack on the farm road. She did not herself have cause to speak to him again until a week or so after that, when he appeared at the kitchen door one evening, with a bundle and a request to 'warm up this little fella'.

Inside the bundle was a premature lamb, shivering and breathing hard. 'He's one of triplets and his mother doesn't want him. But if we can just put him by the oven for a bit, he'll be right as rain.'

'Of course.' Isabel opened the door to the lower, cooler oven in the range and Jack stooped to place the lamb inside. She warmed, as any woman would, to the sight of a man taking care of something fragile, at the same time noting that her predominant response was not maternal. As he bent down beside her she had noticed his lean, brown neck and the whiter skin revealed below his collar. She felt she ought to avert her eyes from this private territory, and yet did not. The unwitting exposure endeared him to her.

'If his mother doesn't want him, who is going to look

after him?' asked Tom, who was preparing to be upset on the lamb's account.

'Well, what about you, mate?'

Tom's eyes lit up. 'Can I really?'

A rumble of background rebellion rose from his sisters, but Isabel ignored it: 'If Jack says that it's all right, and you won't be a nuisance, then of course you can.'

'I say that it's all right, and you won't be a nuisance,' Jack said to the children, then turned to her with a smile that seemed to burn up the oxygen in the air between them and leave her light-headed. Blushing to hear herself parodied, Isabel could manage only a prim smile in return. She could barely meet his eye, even though she wanted very much to look at him. Her girls had been right: he was handsome after all.

After that, Tom attached himself to Jack as a kind of apprentice shepherd, trailing after him through the fields when he got back from school, to see if any lambs had been born. He watched, unflinching, as Jack skinned a dead lamb, then draped its fleece over an orphan so that it would be fostered by the mother of the dead one. 'Now she thinks he smells like hers, and she'll look after him,' he explained to Tom. 'You can try to fool them by rubbing some ointment under their noses, so they can't smell so well, but this way works much better.'

Jennifer and Isabel followed him too, though they were too squeamish to watch the newborn lambs slipping in afterbirth as they took their first steps, or the dead ones being skinned to make coats for orphans.

If the children were besotted with the new stockman, Hayes also liked Jack much better than he cared to admit:

it was galling to acknowledge that a gentleman farmer of Bourne's ilk had shown such good judgement in his choice of employee. Jack worked quickly and efficiently and, when a job was finished, he instinctively knew what to do next. Mikey, on the other hand, tended to wait for instructions and was often to be found lolling in the tractor shed, drinking tea from a flask and smoking roll-up cigarettes. Impressed by Jack's energy and expertise, Hayes decided to put him in charge of all the livestock. He broke the news to Mikey one afternoon as the younger man was attaching a set of disc harrows to one of the tractors. The announcement was presented as a kind of promotion: this new arrangement would free up Mikey to concentrate on the arable aspect of the farm, said Hayes, 'and develop that side of things somewhat'. Mikey, squatting between the back tyres of the Massey Ferguson tractor, did not look up from his work as he listened to his employer and, while that would usually have irked Hayes, this time it came as a relief, given that eye-contact with the labourer was so awkward. 'I'll let you get on then,' he said, pleased to see Mikey diligently applied to the task in hand and then, because some closing gesture seemed necessary, he patted one of the Massey's great back tyres, as though it were the flank of a much-loved horse, before trudging back across the field.

Mikey watched Hayes' retreating figure until it was lost from view, then he stood up and kicked the tractor's wheel hub so hard it hurt his toes inside his boot. He knew that he was being moved aside and the rejection struck at his core, because it came from the person whose opinion he valued most. There was only one place he wanted to be:

when his work was finished, he took his rejection, and his dog, down to the pub.

The pub was a refuge, even though it was so close to his own house, on the other side of the village green. Mikey usually came here after lunch on Sundays, with his mother's recriminations about dirty dishes ringing in his ears. This was where he met his old school friends, Dave and Tone. Tone was the quiet one and Dave was a laugh – everyone said as much. You knew that from the moment Dave pushed through the swing door into the bar, staggering like a desperado, eyes rolling, arms stretched out towards an imaginary pint. With Dave every physical gesture was magnified. Every anecdote required him to come down off his stool – drawing a sticky sigh from the faux leather seat – so that he could enact parts of his story, what someone had said, how someone else had reacted. If he was imitating the manager at the chicken-processing plant where he and Tone worked, he used a ridiculous, falsetto voice.

Dave liked to play to an audience – the bigger, the better – but the person he most wanted to impress was Hazel, who worked behind the bar. Place a counter in front of any man or woman and you instantly bestow on him or her an alluring authority. Hazel had this in some measure, in spite of the rather sulky way she scuffed up and down behind the bar doling out snakebites and lager tops. When she was not serving she was usually at her station beside the glass-washing machine, caught in the perpetual motion of drying off the glasses and returning them to a low shelf behind her. The men instinctively gathered at this point in the bar because, when Hazel stooped to pick up the glasses, her low-cut top drooped open and they could see the tops of her breasts, encased in pastel-coloured lace. Then, when she turned and bent down to put the glasses on the shelf, her skirt tightened across her backside, and she sometimes appeared to be wearing no underwear.

But when Dave came in, it was a different story: Hazel's eyes shone. Apparently she never tired of the staggering 'Where's my pint?' routine, but found it funnier on each occasion. Dave knew that there was an opportunity for him in this, but seemed unsure how to pursue it, except by giving Hazel more of the same. So now it was a given that the only kind of entrance Dave would ever make into the bar was the one of a staggering lunatic. In pursuit of Hazel's happiness Dave worked on his anecdotes, making his gestures progressively theatrical, while Tone's, on the other hand, became ever more oblique. He was happy to let Dave hog the limelight – but this was not to say that he lacked expression. By minutely altering the positions of the lip and eyebrow he denoted a range of attitudes, but especially scepticism, which seemed the correct rejoinder to Dave's excesses. A summary of small movements, that was Tone.

Dave and Tone. Tone and Dave. In scale and scope they were very different, but both were magically alert to the movement and exposure of female flesh. This seemed to be a kinetic process – or perhaps they picked up pheromones. A tight-fitting skirt passed behind them and they instantly knew about it. Dave's great shaven head swivelled round to take in the view, while Tone looked askance and raised an appreciative eyebrow. A fit of giggles in one corner of the pub caused a pair of breasts to bob, and Dave's eyes were there in a shot to drink in the action, with Tone's narrowed ones following half a second behind. It was only their murmured comments and snuffled laughter that tipped Mikey off and, once he had turned to get his own eyeful, the spectacle was all too often over. They had an instinct for these things that he lacked. And they knew about women or, at least, that was the impression Mikey had, while he knew nothing. That much had been made plain to him, by Karen, behind the cricket pavilion.

The evening of his demotion Mikey found Hazel alone at the bar cleaning the counter and polishing the brass beer pumps. There was a crackling fire in the grate and Blue instinctively curled up in front of it. Mikey took in the framed pictures on the wall, the hoovered carpet and the tang of floral room-spray, and felt comforted. On the wall a board announced the evening's special dishes, each of which was to be accompanied by 'garnishing'. Mikey did not know what that was, but it sounded sophisticated. This was exactly what a pub should be, he thought: a home for people whose real homes are not inviting. He settled himself on a bar stool and asked for a pint.

'Are you all right then?' asked Hazel. Recognising the therapeutic element of her job in the pub, she always asked the men if they were all right. Mostly they would grumble a bit, before conceding that, all things considered, they probably were all right.

But Mikey said, 'I've just about had it up to here, if you want the honest truth.'

'Why's that then?'

Mikey told her then about the new stockman, and how

he thought the sun shone out of his rear end. Hazel laughed and said she knew how frustrating it was to work with a wanker. She glanced theatrically at the door to the kitchen, where the landlord and his wife were arguing about the evening's menu. Then they both laughed, and Mikey thought how good it was to feel understood. The beer agreed with him very nicely, too. Blue stretched out in front of the fire and fell into a quivering dream. Mikey asked Hazel if she would like a drink too and she served herself some kind of woman's drink from a small bottle. He thought then that she was very feminine, very pretty. He watched her hand moving up and down the brass pump and felt desire pricking in his groin.

Behind the bar, bags of peanuts hung from a display card that was printed with a picture of a topless woman. This was a marketing ruse to encourage sales of peanuts: as the bags were removed, more of the woman's body was revealed. All you could see at the moment was the woman's face, the top of her chest and her bare arms. She was obviously somewhere very hot, though, because beads of sweat were on her forehead and she was squeezing water onto her face from a sponge. Mikey had never been abroad; probably the hottest he had ever got was when standing in close proximity to illegal fires. In a few weeks his mother was going to Spain; he could not remember if it was to the 'Costa del Sol' or the 'Costa del Crime' – he got them mixed up – anyway, it was somewhere very sunny. She had been driving him round the bend singing 'Viva España' all around the house. For the first time in his life he was going to be on his own for two weeks and would have to do all his own laundry and cooking. His mother seemed not to mind leaving him alone, though. She said it would do them both good to have some time apart and that she was looking forward to the break. Any normal man his age would use the opportunity to have a few parties, get some girls round, but Mikey did not know how to do anything like that, nor did he know any girls to invite. Karen, his ex, would laugh in his face, probably. Anyway, she did not live around here any more. He looked again at the peanuts girl and wondered about buying a bag.

'This bloke you work with's been getting on your tits, then?' asked Hazel.

Mikey felt himself flush. 'He's been here five minutes and he thinks he owns the place.'

'Where's he from?'

'He's Australian. They love a bit of sheep-shagging, don't they? He's never happier than when he's got his hand halfway up some sheep's doo-dah.'

Hazel laughed again, causing different parts of her anatomy to jiggle about. Mikey gloried in his luck. All too soon, though, the door swung open, and in came Dave, staggering, cross-eyed, a desperado with his tongue protruding from one side of his mouth and both arms stretched out towards his pint. Tone sauntered behind him, shaking his head and tutting as usual, and wearing the accustomed expression of forbearance. Mikey resigned himself to losing Hazel's attention.

Hazel registered the routine and, appreciating that it was all for her benefit, raised a smile, but then she turned back to Mikey. 'Go on, then, tell us more about this sheep-shagging Aussie bloke.'

'Yeah? OK then.' It was the first time that Hazel had

shown more interest in him than in Dave, and Mikey was temporarily lost for words. His eyes rolled upwards, as though he hoped to catch sight of something inspiring in his own brain. 'Well, you know what Aussies get their girlfriends for Valentine's, don't you?'

'No?'

'A bale of hay.'

Hazel shook with laughter again. She had to put her drink down so that she could support herself on the bar as she laughed. Mikey felt a warmth spreading across his chest and shoulders and realised that it was stoked by Hazel's laughter. 'You know what they do when they want to do the business, right?'

Hazel was pink with laughing. She could barely get the words out. 'No, go on, tell us,' she said in a squeak.

Mikey slipped off the bar stool as he had watched Dave do so often in the past. 'They walk around the field to see which sheep they fancy the most, then they grab her, tuck her back legs into their wellies and away they go – ease of access, see.'

With that, Mikey began to make jerky pelvic thrusts, grasping with his hands an imaginary woolly rump. Hazel was laughing so much that tears had appeared in her eyes. Dave was laughing, too, in spite of himself, and Tone had allowed himself a wry smirk. This was too good: he could not stop now, so Mikey threw in an assortment of X-rated sound effects and kept rutting away, all the while imagining a future in which he could be the funny bloke down the pub, no longer merely a spectator to Dave's antics.

He was in his element and, when the swing door opened

behind him, Mikey did not hear it, nor did he see anyone enter, before he felt the pressure of a hand on his shoulder.

'What are you up to, mate? What's the big joke?' Jack was beside him, smiling benignly.

Mikey flushed again, violently. He had the uncomfortable sensation of his blood running hot and cold at the same time, and his heart pounded so hard he thought he might vomit. His hands froze. The others, who had recognised Jack by his accent, were delighted by this unexpected turn of events.

Hazel said, 'Are you Jack, by any chance?'

'Yeah,' said the Australian, looking puzzled. 'Why?'

'Mikey was just telling us how you Australians like to do the business – with your sheep . . .' Her voice trailed off in another squeak.

Jack looked blankly at her for a moment, then registered that he was the butt of some national stereotyping. 'Oh, I see. So that's what you were doing! Nah, we don't do it like that, Mikey. We don't roger her from behind. We like to turn her over so we can give her a nice kiss on the muzzle. It's more romantic.'

At that, Dave threw his great head back and exploded with laughter. Then in one action he slapped his thigh, slipped off his stool and began to reach into his back pocket for his wallet.

'Good man! Good man! Here, get this fellow a drink, Hazel.' And to Jack he said, 'You probably want a *cold* beer – am I right?' And just like that, the Australian was incorporated into the group at the bar, which now seemed to close around him.

Mikey, whose hands had remained frozen in the air in

front of his pelvis, allowed them to drop limp at his sides. He could see that Hazel found Jack good-looking: she had begun to bat her eyelids and move her head in a different way from normal. Dave and Tone liked him, too. It seemed that Mikey had unwittingly eased his rival's entry into this enchanted circle, and at his own expense. In all the years they had known each other, Dave had never offered to buy him a drink; they always paid their own way.

After he had finished his pint Mikey slipped away. His friends at the pub did not notice him go. They were indifferent to him. Yet no one, it seemed, was indifferent to Jack. Wherever he went in the village he was noticed and admired for his good looks and easy manner. Mrs Lyall, who sold him aerogrammes, thought he looked like Robert Redford. The High Sheriff's wife asked him for help releasing her hand-brake, just for the pleasure of having this handsome stranger lean into her car. He held the people at Hill Farm in his sway, because he was different and they had not met anyone like him before. 'He's a breath of fresh air,' Isabel confessed, on the telephone, when her mother enquired about the new stockman. With his grace, his humour and his new way of doing things, Jack had brought change to their lives.

When he appeared unannounced at the kitchen door one afternoon, Isabel seemed to discern some magic alteration in the air before registering the presence of the visitor himself. She had been ironing, tackling some tough creases in Hayes' trousers and noticing, with dismay, a spray of oil stains down one leg. She saw Jack first through a cloud of steam and started, almost dropping the iron.

'Sorry if I gave you a shock,' Jack said. 'I was just wondering if you were still worried about the swans.'

'The what? Oh, that!' Carefully she placed the iron down. 'I should explain. You see, the other day, I was feeling under the weather; I had been suffering from insomnia.' Isabel paused, then added. 'Also a sort of the virus.' The addition of the virus, she realised, was overdoing things. 'I'm feeling a lot better now,' she concluded and took up the iron again.

'I'm glad to hear it,' said Jack, 'but I've had an idea. I've thought of our solution. Can you spare ten minutes?'

The children would not be home for more than an hour, but all the same, Isabel made preparatory moves to decline this invitation, working up a polite smile. In the last six months her sphere of movement had become ever more circumscribed. Nowadays she was nervous to venture far from the house, unless it was to go to the school or to Miss Prince's house. Any kind of spontaneity alarmed her. Nevertheless, there was something so winning about the way he had spoken of 'our' solution.

'I don't think I can . . .'

'Sure you can – can't you?' He stepped into the room, approaching the ironing board and, with this bold assurance, it was as though Jack had dared to cross an imaginary line into her secret world of shame and fear. He saw these deficiencies, she felt, and did not flinch from them. 'I promise it won't take long.'

Isabel stood, revealed, in the kitchen. And now she felt she must say 'yes', because she was too embarrassed to say 'no'. She thought for a few seconds, then made a decisive move: she switched off the iron and stepped out from behind the ironing board.

'Well, if it's not for long . . .'

Five minutes later they were rattling down the hill in the farm Land Rover. 'This isn't going to involve guns, is it?' she asked.

'No, it's not, Mrs Hayes.'

She could not tell if he was being respectful or mocking her. 'It's fine to call me Isabel.'

He shrugged and smiled.

'You know all swans belong to the Queen?'

'And, as an Australian, I hold the Queen in very high regard.'

They had come now to the end of the paved road and continued onto the track. The Land Rover swung from side to side as Jack negotiated the larger rocks and ruts. She held onto the door handle, anxious not to be jostled against him. The river was not much more than a mile from the house – all the same, she felt as though she had travelled dangerously far from home. Looking back over her shoulder, she could see the sun glinting on one of its upstairs windows, turning it into a bar of molten gold. The same light blazed for a moment on a silver buckle at Jack's waist.

'The thing is,' said Jack with a frown, 'I don't know if these swans really count as the Queen's. Didn't they come from Siberia? They're more likely to be communists, aren't they?'

She looked at him, trying to gauge from this sideways angle the degree of seriousness in his enquiry.

'I really wouldn't know,' she said carefully, 'about their affiliation.'

'Only one way to find out, I suppose. Do you know the words to "The Internationale"?'

'No, I can't say . . .'

'That's a shame. Well, I'll give it my best shot.'

Then he wound down the window and sang lustily: 'So, comrades, come rally, and the last fight let us face. The Internationale unites the human race!'

Isabel, as embarrassed as she was delighted, burst out laughing. The sound of her laughter rang in the air like something foreign to her own ears.

'I think you really must be mad,' she said, but she loosened her grip on the door handle. When they had reached the edge of the field, Jack said, 'Now hold on tight.' He put the car in gear, revved up the engine and drove fast, following the track's curve around the edge of the field. She thought that he would stop a safe distance from the swans, but instead he drove onto the grass towards the flooded area, then leaned hard on the horn.

What followed took no more than a few seconds: first, a few of the swans rose, threatening and hissing, making arrogant curves with their necks. Then they began to extend their necks and unfold their wings, and with this transformation they seemed to disavow all their pretty associations with the Crown, with country pubs and ballets, in order to rekindle a more alien blood-tie. Together they revived a Jurassic scene of pterodactyls and swamps. Hearing the beating of these great wings very close to her, Isabel feared for a moment that the birds might attack the car, that they could even break through the windscreen.

Then one or two of the birds lumbered into the air, and before long the outlook was filled with skeins of grey and white, weaving a darker texture into the sky. The birds' flapping moved the air around the Land Rover, and there was a great sound of thudding motion and of trumpeting cries as the whole flock took off.

Jack leaned forward on the steering wheel, then turned, smiling, to her: 'How about that?'

She felt a knot in her stomach of fear and elation and a sense – the kind some people only experience a few times in their lives – of having witnessed a scene with the power to change her. This landscape, which had been familiar for so many years, which had become routinely pretty, had been made new and strange by the presence of these preternatural creatures. Perhaps there was a part of her that wondered, subconsciously, if all outlooks might not be transformed by a foreign element. She had been stuck in life, but here was something to fetch her out of the doldrums. For the moment she could not think how to put such feelings into words, nor would she have wanted to do so in front of a man she barely knew, so she took the English way out, and made light of the situation.

'Are we stuck in the mud? I hope you're not going to make me get out and push . . . ?'

'Oh, come on! Is that all the gratitude I get?' He knocked her arm with his in mock-reproof. It was the slightest of gestures, but Isabel was rarely touched by anyone other than her children, and this unexpected contact was like a mild electric shock.

'I am grateful,' she said. 'Thank you.'

For all that she played it down, the experience affected

Isabel deeply. It was a silly thing, to be so impressed by a man's looks and charm, but she could not help but feel flattered that Jack had gone to so much trouble on her account. It showed that she had been – however briefly – on his mind, and Isabel did not consider herself the sort of person to occupy another's thoughts. She was still thinking about it that evening, and the following after-noon when the incident with the swans was re-created above the snowy landscape of Miss Prince's carpet. Enrap-tured, Miss Prince clasped her hands together as she listened to the story unfold, and all the while her diamond rings sent shards of light shooting around the room. 'It's a sign,' she said, 'a sign that things will change.'

SIX

In a field at the top of the farm a pair of boat shoes lay in the grass. Neat in navy blue and trimmed with a leather cord, they gave onto a pair of ankles, calves, knees and thighs – very white, very thin and sparsely haired – quivering in the weak sunshine of an English spring. It was Mr Payne, lying beside a hedgerow, in ecstasy. Around him were scattered books on British fauna and flora, and a notebook in which Mr Payne had made a series of annotations in a tiny, ornate hand. The words evoked a centuries-old litany: hawthorn, blackthorn, ash, hazel and briar, the components of an ancient English woodland.

Mr Payne sat up suddenly, blinking in the spring sunshine, the blood rushing to the tip of his nose. 'Dogwood. I am sure that it is dogwood. I am sure that it is.'

His first thought was to tell Debbie. He got quickly to his feet, gathered his things into his satchel and set off at a trot back to the cottage, where he found his wife cutting up potatoes.

The kitchen was at the back of their cottage and looked onto a small garden and, beyond that, an uncultivated field, which the Paynes could not help referring to as 'our field'. Perhaps it is in the nature of couples with no children to become proprietorial about other things. Since moving here last summer they had grown to love this home in the country. Considering that it was rented accommodation, the house was not at all bad. In the kitchen they had put down new linoleum – a brighter and more hygienic alternative to the old, cracked tiles they had found when they arrived. Mr Payne had worked hard to clean the cooker which was rather antiquated, with an eye-level grill that spat fat at you if you tried to do bacon on a high heat. He rarely attempted such a thing; he was nervous of grills, or any heated activity. Debbie had made the room look cheerful with garlands of dried flowers hanging on the walls and a few framed photographs of kittens. All her friends and relations knew that Debbie loved kittens, and often sent her the kind of feline-themed cards and gifts that are designed to extract sighs and exclamations. Her mother had even offered to give her one as a pet, but Debbie preferred the idea of kittens to the reality; she did not like the odour and mess associated with real animals.

'I'm making curry,' said Debbie, as her husband came in at the back door. 'I thought we could do with something spicy.'

Mr Payne paused as he slipped off his boat shoes and looked for his house slippers. He wondered uneasily if this were a sexual innuendo – Saturday was their usual night for amorous activity, and sometimes Debbie tried to foster the right atmosphere with interesting underwear, alcohol or candlelight. He did not dare tell her that these efforts made it even harder for him to perform. Candles, for instance, entailed a risk of fire that quite distracted him. Anyway, this was not the moment to start worrying about that. He took a few steps into the kitchen, then stopped with deliberation, ready to deliver his news. He cleared his throat.

'Something very exciting has happened, Debbie. I have just counted five kinds of wild flower in the hedgerow at the bottom of our field.' He stopped, beaming, to allow this information its moment. When Debbie said nothing he continued, 'According to the Hooper method of ageing a hedge, each wild flower stands for one hundred years. Five species of flower equals five hundred years, Debbie – do you see? It means that that hedgerow, although it may not look like much, is a monument to our heritage. It has been standing there longer than Westminster Abbey.'

'That's wonderful, dear,' said Debbie. 'I don't think I've ever seen you so excited about something.' She put some spices in a heavy stone mortar and began to grind them with the pestle in a meaningful way.

'Well, it is exciting. It's a connection with our past. It's all the more important when you think of what's been going on. In the last thirty years a quarter of all the hedgerows in England have been torn up. In Cambridgeshire it's nearly half!'

Mr Payne slung his satchel over the back of a chair and switched on the kettle. Standing beside the counter, he found himself looking musingly into the eyes of a kitten, which looked musingly back.

'This is something worth fighting for, Debs. It's part of our natural heritage.'

Debbie was right. Rarely in his life had Mr Payne felt so excited about anything. There had been times when he had even wondered if a predisposition towards excitement was lacking in him. At school he had been bullied for being thin and small, and was neither funny nor intelligent enough to rise above the bullies. At college he had struggled, and failed, to lose his virginity, and that failure overshadowed his meagre academic achievements. He had never been able to find much enthusiasm for the traditional male pleasures: football, sex or getting drunk. At Hackney Council his job had been to deal with customer complaints – if only they had restricted themselves to complaining. All too often the callers were abusive and threatening, or they harped on hysterically about their status as rate-payers. Mr Payne had never developed a strategy for dealing with the tirades, nor could he let them go afterwards. He bore the verbal bruisings on his psychic person for days.

After two years in Customer Complaints Mr Payne had been moved sideways to Bulky Refuse Collection. Here, at least, the complaints were all on one theme – but perhaps there was no other theme that exercised people to such a degree. Nevertheless, he had begun the new job in Bulky Refuse with a willingness to find it interesting. It was a promotion of sorts: he was to have his own desk with a typewriter and a smart new telephone that used buttons instead of a dial.

After all, the job was not devoid of interest. There was something magical about the way sofas appeared on the corners of Hackney's streets overnight, as though some divine authority placed them there, offering repose to the borough's weary housewives, to the tramps and to the Jehovah's Witnesses who totted up miles every day in the service of their faith. Who deposited these unwieldy objects, and when? Did people get up in the night to do it unobserved? Did they go out late after bingeing on drink and drugs, somehow contriving to manoeuvre three-piece suites into council lifts? Their journeys and provenance were a mystery, but once the bulky items had arrived at their destination, they became the responsibility of Mr Payne's department. A friendly phone call from a member of the public would have been enough to get him on the case, but usually the first he heard of it was an abusive rant from a 'rate-payer'. Of course the sofas must be removed quickly, because otherwise children set fire to them – making a mockery of the so-called 'flame-retardant' covers. A burned-out sofa then became a magnet for other kinds of rubbish, both large items, which were the responsibility of his department, and general household detritus, which was not.

Ron, who headed the small team charged with picking up bulky refuse, was adamant that his men had 'no mandate' to collect bagged rubbish. He was a unionist and knew his rights. If rubbish was able to be bagged, it was, by definition, not bulky. So, while the men who went out with a truck in the morning removed the sofas and other large objects, anything smaller they left on the street for the Refuse Collection. The problem did not end there, because the bin-men would then decide not to collect it either: in their view, bags that were not left outside a specific house fell into the category of fly-tipping, and they had 'no mandate' to deal with that. There were men who did deal with fly-tipping, but unfortunately they worked for Ron. All too often these intractable disputes ended in stalemate, and private contractors had to be called in to dispose of the waste before it compromised public health regulations.

In all the years Mr Payne worked in Bulky Refuse, he never found the correct tone for dealing with Ron. He tried cajoling, even begging, but he could not bring himself simply to insist that Ron do his job, and so the rubbish removal became every week a greater headache – now with the involvement of contractors, too – and he felt himself increasingly powerless to deal with its pressures. The violence of his telephone callers overwhelmed him, until he had nightmares about bulky refuse and pictured himself crushed beneath three-piece suites. To sit in the ghoulish glow of that fluorescent light every day, drinking insipid coffee while someone on the telephone called you a 'moron', was more than he could bear. Things might have been different if even one person had ever rung to thank him for the prompt way in which he had organised disposal of their mattresses, sofas, unwanted carpets and ping-pong tables, pianos, exercise bicycles and trampolines. No one ever did, and after ten years Mr Payne woke up one morning and found that he could not move – he literally could not sit up – and also that he did not care about anything at all.

Mr Payne's mother came from Bromley to help him recover from the breakdown and soothed him with stories of his childhood and their walks together in the wood at the end of the street. It was she who suggested he join the Ramblers as part of his recuperation, and that was where he met Debbie, a community nurse who was four years older than him, large, welcoming and undemanding. He lost his virginity at the age of thirty-two. Sometimes the fact of it still amazed him, and he wandered about Hill

Farm thinking to himself, 'I am not a virgin. I know about sex.'

It was a week since the swans had departed. When Mattie and her mother arrived at Miss Prince's house that Tuesday, she opened the door just a crack and peered around it. Her hair appeared to be wrapped in some kind of elaborate turban and, as far as Mattie could see, she was wearing nothing else. 'Give me a moment, my darlings,' she said. 'I'm just gilding the lily.'

They waited for a few minutes on the step before the door opened fully and there was Miss Prince, wearing a velour track suit that gave her the appearance of a giant soft toy. There was an unctuous quality to her skin that suggested she had just now finished rubbing creams into it, and the thin arch of her eyebrows was freshly applied.

'Come, come, come,' she murmured, and then, 'Shoes, Mattie.'

Mattie sat on the floor and struggled with the many knots of her school shoes' laces, while her mother followed Miss Prince to the bedroom; through its open door she heard gasps of wonder and surprise. After she had put her shoes on the rack, next to her mother's, she tiptoed through the carpet's silky fronds to the bedroom, where the women were sitting on Miss Prince's bed looking at piles of clothes. An old trunk was open on the bed, too, revealing yet more clothes and jewellery.

'This is all gorgeous, Sheila,' Isabel said softly. As she settled herself on the bed, Mattie wondered if her mother had deliberately chosen a pretty tone to match the room.

The room's opulence reminded Mattie of photographs she had seen in the French magazines that were piled on a table in Miss Prince's lavatory. The satin counterpane on Miss Prince's bed was cool and slippery under her fingers. The walls bore a pattern of roses climbing up trellises. The curtains – which were closed and hung to the floor in heavy, undulating swags – showed the same pattern, this time with light shining through it. Mattie had never seen such a thing before; it was like watching some solid entity vaporise before one's eyes. Indeed the overall atmosphere in the room was one of sheeny liquidity, as she watched her mother draw streams of bright silks before her, and streaks of light, escaping between the curtains, caused them to blaze for a moment in her hands – fierce elements in a colour experiment presided over by Miss Prince.

Mattie laid her head down on the cool counterpane and let her eyes lose focus – as she sometimes did in Maths lessons – so that the silks and jewellery swam before her in a kaleidoscope of undefined colours. The absence of air in the room and Miss Prince's heady perfume made her feel sleepy, and she swallowed a yawn. At school, yawning provoked a tart response from the teachers, but she had been tired recently because she found it hard to sleep, knowing that her mother might be crying in her bedroom down the corridor. It was evidently making her mother happy to look at Miss Prince's things, though, so she felt able to relax. She hoped, in a dreamy way, for her mother's hand to rest against her cheek, or for Miss Prince to offer her a biscuit.

'Such beautiful fabrics,' Isabel was saying to Miss Prince. 'Why don't you wear any of these things?'

'You must be joking! I've gone up three dress sizes since I last wore this lot. On the other hand, you, my dear, would look lovely in them. And you must have them. Take everything! I've got no use for any of it.'

Mattie studied her mother's face, wondering what she would say to this. In her experience, adults often made rather grand gestures in the expectation that they would be refused, and trouble sometimes ensued if they were not.

As she had expected, Isabel frowned and shook her head. 'I can't take it all. What about the jewellery? And these scarves? You can still wear them.'

'Darling, it's paste. And I have no use for it – or the scarves. All this stuff reminds me of everything that used to be, things that are over and done with. I had a lot of fun with it at the time, but I've no wish to think about any of that again. It's your turn to have a bit of fun. Doll yourself up and make yourself look lovely.' She laughed theatrically and Mattie noticed how the velour bosom shuddered up and down with her laughter. She felt some consternation. Her mother was lovely the way she was. Why did Miss Prince think she needed any enhancement?

Then Miss Prince sat down beside Isabel and took her hand. 'If you won't do me the favour of taking the whole lot away, then at least choose some of it.' She pinched Isabel's arm playfully. 'It's your turn now – you deserve a bit of fun. Make yourself look pretty. This is *your time*.'

Mattie saw her mother look up rather sharply to meet Miss Prince's eyes, but she seemed to find no extra meaning there, or at least nothing that she registered openly.

'Now, pick some things out – but remember, anything you don't take is off to the jumble sale next week. Mattie and I are going next door to get a drink and a biscuit, aren't we dear? We'll leave you to it.'

And Mattie, who was learning to equate biscuits with conspiracy, followed Miss Prince out of the room with barely a glance back at her mother.

The jumble sale to which Miss Prince referred was an annual event held in aid of various charities, but especially the church roof, which was imperilled, as it always is, in all English villages. It took place in the church hall and was an occasion for the villagers to gather behind trestle tables bearing home-made food, bric-a-brac and pile upon pile of woollen objects: jumpers, cosies, mittens, bootees and bedsocks. You would think this farming community wanted to emulate its own sheep, and gather itself into a woolly fold, safe against the predation of a prowling fox.

Now their pastor arrived, Reverend Hollings, lean and with a wolfish smile suggesting an appetite that could not be sated by jams and cakes alone. He bounded into the hall, arms outstretched, wanting not to shake hands, but to embrace his parishioners, devour them, almost, with his love and his desire to serve and cherish them. They shrank from his love into their cardigans and turtle-necks, letting intervening cups of tea frustrate his attempts at bodily contact. All this hugging and kissing might suit Londoners, some felt, but it was not right for a country parish; it made them feel queasy. Unfortunately, Reverend Hollings' chosen outfit of jeans and a dog-collar damned him as 'trendy' in the eyes of his detractors. They did not know how he had agonised in the vestry that afternoon, wondering whether or not to wear his cassock.

Tea and wool. Wool and tea. Here were comfort and safety. Here was an opportunity for the villagers to meet and tell each other stories of operations and other misfortunes, of rheumatism, aneurisms, varicose veins and irritable bowels. After such pleasurable exchanges, they browsed among the stalls. Anne and Jean, the lesbian couple, were selling home-made preserves and chutneys made from historical recipes they had picked up while on a campanologists' tour of Italy. The divorced baritone had a stall of second-hand books. Mrs Lyall from the post office sat behind an array of knitted toys she had made herself. And there was bric-a-brac as far as the eye could see: clusters of artificial grapes, china shepherdesses, collectable thimbles and Royal Family ashtrays. Isabel always volunteered to help sort the jumble, and it seemed to her that exactly the same garments, knick-knacks and books appeared each year, only in different arrangements. This year, although she had abdicated from so many other community duties, she was helping out again, serving teas. She was stationed at the back of the hall between two giant, shining urns and behind plates of scones laden with cream and jam.

Around the tables the villagers enacted their woolly choreography while the High Sheriff stood to one side of the action, not actually genuflecting – though he may have bent his knees now and then to relieve lower back pain. He watched with his hands clasped behind his back, nodding wordless greetings or expressions of approval as though directing actors in a play about jumble sales. This stance – clasped hands, soft knees – was one he had learned from the Duke of Edinburgh, whom he had had the pleasure of meeting when His Royal Highness came to the Weald to open a museum on hop-picking. It was a useful pose at Christmas, too, when the carollers gathered in the manor house to sing 'Ding Dong Merrily' before a blazing fire in the drawing room. On these occasions the High Sheriff would look around him, thinking what a marvellous impression he must make. Here were all the accoutrements of his standing: his Persian rugs, his Labradors, his handsome wife – singing 'Hosanna in Excelsis' beside him now – and their good-looking offspring recorded in photographs here and there. On a low table beside the sofa there was a framed photograph of the sheriff meeting the Duke of Edinburgh, and another frame showing his letter of appointment: 'Whereas Her Majesty was this day pleased, by and with the advice of Her Privy Council, to nominate you for, and appoint you to be, High Sheriff of the County of East Sussex during Her Majesty's pleasure.' He and his wife slept in a four-poster bed; they had an en-suite bathroom, and he could hazard, with some authority, that theirs was the only bidet in the village. But was that all there was to life? A keen observer might have detected a far-away look in the High Sheriff's eye and perhaps a kind of resignation in the set of his mouth, as though he would have liked to play a part on some bigger stage even than the shrievalty afforded.

Now the hall was full of people and the clattering noise of cups meeting saucers. Arriving in the midst of the hubbub, Jack experienced a moment of perfect cultural dislocation, disorienting him for a minute or two. He had come looking for useful things with which to furnish the cottage, but this was unfamiliar territory and, at first glance, he could see nothing here that would be useful to anyone.

He was lost until he caught sight of Isabel at the other end of the room, framed between the two great steaming, chugging urns, like a 1950s film star waiting for a brief encounter. She was wearing red lipstick and one of Miss Prince's jackets. Seeing her made him feel nervous and he could not explain that nervousness to himself.

The High Sheriff noticed the arrival of a young man he had never seen before, and registered with interest the way Isabel's face lit up as he approached her. He was an attractive-looking fellow, tall and rangy, and apparently with a ready smile; perhaps he was a relation of hers, although he did not look very English. The sheriff was not standing far from them, but these days his hearing was frustratingly poor, especially when he tried to pick out conversation against competing background sounds. What with the people, the clattering noise of teacups and the sound-absorbing properties of wool, he could not hear what Isabel and Jack said to one another. Tinkering with his hearing aid merely produced a high-pitched whine. Now here came Mrs Lyall, from the post office, carrying coffee and walnut cake, her cheeks flushed and her hair on askew; reluctantly he resigned himself to a less interesting exchange than the one on which he had hoped to eavesdrop.

What the High Sheriff failed to hear was not all that significant: it was the stuff of countless flirtations. Jack, playing up his foreign helplessness, had asked Isabel to rescue him: he was lost in this jumble jungle. He did not speaka da language. She must interpret for him. She went along with the game, blushing with pleasure. 'Nearly new' she explained, was a nice way to say 'second-hand'. A 'tombola' was a quaint way to lose money. 'Bric-a-brac' meant 'junk'. They had both laughed. In fact Isabel, hiding behind the urns, had found herself embarrassingly unable to stop laughing. It was as though she had been such a long time without using this mechanism that she had forgotten how to calibrate it. The High Sheriff was not the only one to notice the high colour in her cheeks. Several people heard the unusually youthful laughter and looked over to ascertain its source, though not Mrs Smith, whose eyes, perforce, were fixed on the contents of her plate.

Miss Smith, picking critically over second-hand cardigans, looked up from the other side of the hall and questioned whether it was appropriate for a married woman to smile and laugh so much. Even Isabel knew that her reaction was over-ebullient, but she was unable to help it. She could not remember the last time she had liked someone as much as Jack. He charmed her to pieces.

Once Mrs Lyall had communicated her message to the High Sheriff she scurried away, leaving him to make his way to a stage at the front of the hall. If he had been a sheriff in the Wild West, perhaps he would have swaggered through the crowd, hand on holster, but he was British, he was old and his back hurt. When he got to the podium he patted his jacket pockets and fretted, for a moment, that he had lost his glasses. At the foot of the stairs Mrs Lyall pointed at her own towering hat of hair, alerting him to their presence on the top of his head. He was, as so often, confounded and then relieved in the space of a few seconds. One could take pleasure, nowadays, in these ready comforts: nearly every day the High Sheriff fielded despair and relief in short order, usually in matters related to his glasses or his bladder.

'Quiet, please!' trilled Mrs Lyall across the hall.

The sheriff donned his bifocals and looked up and down through them at the people gathered in front of him, as though preparing to discipline unruly school children. Mrs Lyall passed him a note.

'Ah yes,' he said. The microphone, which was wrongly adjusted, screeched feedback through the speakers into the hall, forcing everyone to wince and make protestations. That always happened: it was as much a part of the proceedings as the tombola and bric-a-brac.

'Can someone sort that out? Thank you. Now, during the afternoon many of you will have visited the cake stall and admired the quite splendid cake contributed by Mrs Lyall, and many of you have also paid twenty pence for the honour of guessing its weight.'

At the back of the hall Jack's eyes met Isabel's with an expression of aghast bewilderment. He was playing this up, of course – they have jumble sales in Australian church halls, too – but the opportunity to make Isabel laugh again was too good to miss. She had to look away from him and take cover again behind the urn, laughing so much that her shoulders shook. The sheriff, oblivious to their antics, soldiered on.

'So, it is now my duty to announce the winner of the competition, and indeed of the prize itself, which is indeed, indeed – ah, the cake itself.'

That evening, after she had said goodnight to the children, Isabel poured herself a gin and tonic and lay on the sofa; that she should desire to do such a thing was, in itself, a marvel. Usually it was her habit to settle the children down before either watching television or going to bed herself, to read, before turning the light out early.

An hour or two later Tom found her there on the sofa, still in Miss Prince's jacket, when he came downstairs after waking from a nightmare.

'What is it, my love?'

'I dreamed you'd gone to prison.'

Tom's dreams were always extreme. Before this she had suffered poisoning, strangulation and abduction by aliens. He was an anxious child, one of the kind who follow their mothers to the lavatory and then stand outside, waiting to unburden some new worry or grievance.

He joined her on the sofa and she kissed the top of his head. 'I'm perfectly all right, darling.'

'I went looking for you in your room, and you weren't there and I got frightened.'

Recently there had been a pattern to these night-scares: Tom would wake and go to find Isabel and she, gratefully, took him into bed with her, wrapping him in her arms and breathing in the smell of his hair. She would have held him all night, but when Hayes came upstairs he always moved the child back to his own bed. By being downstairs, she realised now, she had disrupted the pattern. She felt a pang of regret. Tom was no longer the one she desired to hold in bed.

'But now that you're here, you can be the lucky one to come outside with me and look at the stars.' By the back door she bundled him into one of her coats and carried him outside. 'Look: you can see thousands of them tonight – I don't think I've ever seen so many. If

I were clever, I could point out the constellations for you.'

'You are clever, Mummy,' said Tom, still sniffing. He could not bear his mother to be disparaged.

It was a clear and very cold night and the sky was a black expanse pricked all over with lights. Isabel thought she could identify the Plough and beyond it the Milky Way, and the North Star.

'Do you think that could be the Archer, there? We really should get ourselves a map of the constellations. Shall we do that next time we go to the bookshop in town?'

Tom nodded, but, instead of cheering him, the sight produced racking sobs.

'What's wrong, darling? What could possibly be wrong with a sky full of stars?'

'It's not fair. Mrs Smith can't see any of this.'

'What? You are a worrier! Well, you know, perhaps she could, if she lay down.'

'No, she couldn't,' said Tom, whose nose was running now. 'We thought about that, but technically she would just be looking at her feet. The world is very unfair.'

'The world is unfair,' agreed Isabel. 'But there are compensations. And if Mrs Smith really wants to see the stars, she can hold a mirror in her lap and see them reflected.'

That thought seemed to cheer Tom a little. He pressed his sticky cheek against his mother's face and looked up with her into the sky.

'Will we have to go and live on another planet if this one runs out?'

'I don't think that will happen.'

'But maybe it will, if there's an explosion.'

'What do you mean? What explosion?' She hated to think that, in spite of all she did to shield the children from news reports, he might have heard about some bombing or other disaster.

'Daddy says there will be a population explosion.'

'Oh – well, I'm sure it won't be that bad. The world is a big place.'

'I wish Mrs Smith was a newt.'

'What? Goodness, Tom, you do say some funny things! Whatever should she be a newt for?'

'Because she could regenerate,' said Tom. 'And then she could look at the stars.'

The day after the bring-and-buy Isabel loaded a box full of items for Jack: old sets of crockery hunted out from the attic, a spare kettle that was kept in the office but never used, a chipped teapot, some blankets and a rug. In the evening, when his work on the farm was finished, she took them over to him.

They bantered a little on the doorstep, before she handed over the box. Then he asked her in for a cup of tea. She sat down at the fold-out kitchen table – made cheerful now by the checked tablecloth she had brought – and watched as he poured boiling water into the mugs, then dropped the used tea bags into the sink. It infuriated her when Hayes did this at home, but somehow, in Jack, the same action seemed dashing and cavalier. For half an hour or more they talked. He told her that he had grown up on a cattle farm in New South Wales, then studied agriculture at university. His mother had died a few years ago and soon he would be taking over responsibility for his father's farm, but he had wanted some time away first. After the harvest he was going to spend a few months travelling on the continent before returning to Australia. 'I want to see something of France, Italy and Spain before I go home.' He had been reading about the anarchist uprisings in 1930s Barcelona, and liked the idea of going there. 'So much to see and so little time to see it in,' he said with a grin. 'Maybe I can pick up some casual work along the way. That's the plan, anyway.'

He asked her if she had travelled much, and Isabel, wanting to say something, alighted on a childhood anecdote about camping in France, how her father had worn a suit at all times and her mother had been reduced to tears by the communal shower. Jack laughed to hear it.

'What were your parents like, when you were growing up?' he asked.

'They meant well, but,' she hesitated, surprised to find herself talking in this way to a stranger, 'perhaps they were scared. They didn't really give me a chance to find out anything about the world – you know, to stretch my wings.'

She had not been brought up to talk about her feelings, for Isabel's mother believed that it was 'vulgar' to expose oneself in conversation. Indeed her mother's philosophy of life was largely staked on an opposition to vulgarity. The adolescent Isabel had been persuaded that emotional turmoil was best sublimated into physical activity, especially country walks.

It made Isabel feel giddy to think of her mother, and

for a moment she wondered if there was something dangerous about this kitchen coterie. But the cheeriness of the tablecloth, the tea and the biscuits argued against danger, and it was such a pleasure to have someone listen to her the way Jack did. Isabel could not remember having provoked so much interest in anyone for a long time. Wanting her fill of his attention, she found herself talking about subjects she rarely broached with anyone else: the thwarted ambitions of her youth; her thirst for some sort of adventure beyond the farm.

'I'm the same,' he said. 'I've always wanted to go out and see the world. In the past I think I've been guilty of wanting to escape things. You know, maybe I was afraid of getting bored. I was scared I was going to get trapped on my dad's farm and I was always thinking about ways to move on and see new stuff. Whatever I was doing, my mind kept racing on to the next place. I don't know if you understand?'

Yes, she nodded.

'I told my father that I wasn't going to take on the farm when he retired, and he was devastated. So he gave me some time to come away and think about it. And since I came here I've realised – I don't know, I must be getting old, or something.' He glanced at her and then, abashed, into his cup.

'Go on,' prompted Isabel, 'what have you realised?'

'Just that change doesn't have to be about moving on. It can be about bringing new ideas to what you're already doing. I've decided that when I get back home I'm going to take on the farm and change things around. I'll put into practice some of the things I'm learning here: innovate, maybe even introduce our own specialist herd. I don't know why I'm telling you this – it's pretty boring.'

'No, it's not!' To be a party to his confidences delighted Isabel, in fact, and she felt that she could have listened to him for hours, cheerfully disowning the family that was waiting for her at home. He had said 'I'm the same' and, with these words, had seemed to create a bond between them. All the time they were talking she was thinking about how much she would like to touch him. Her eyes followed the lines of his cheekbones and jaw, and the curve of his neck down to his shoulder. She could tell that his body was strong, that it would feel good under her fingers. Suddenly she regretted her over-helpful urge: instead of bringing so many things to the cottage all at once, she should have spun this charity out over more days and seen more of the handsome new stockman. So when she left she said, on an impulse, 'You know, we probably have other things that could be useful. There's loads of stuff in the attic, and I think there's an electric heater somewhere. After all, it does get quite chilly in the evenings.'

'That would be great,' said Jack, and it seemed to her that he had agreed very quickly, and that must be because he wanted her to come back.

Lying awake in bed that night, however, she wondered if she had read things the wrong way round: he had agreed quickly, in fact, because he wanted to get rid of her. These are the kinds of quandaries that more often occupy the minds of much younger people, but, not having experienced the hurly-burly of a romantic youth, Isabel had some catching up to do. She had known Hayes since she was a teenager and, though she had thought she was in love with him when they married, her physical feelings for him were pale sensations compared to the tumult she felt now – when she thought of Jack's unbuttoned collar, when she remembered his arm brushing against hers in the Land Rover.

Putting her anxieties to one side, the next day she returned to the cottage with the heater, and the day after that she brought extra blankets. Later she dug out a few framed pictures 'to cheer the place up'. Each time she found something to take to Jack there was a delight in seeing him again, and then the regret – absurdly intense – of having to leave. After a week the cottage was looking finished in every detail, and that dismayed Isabel because it meant that she had no further excuses to return.

'I think you must have everything you need, now. At any rate, I've got nothing left in the attic.'

She laughed ruefully, lingering on the doorstep for a few seconds longer than was necessary. She allowed a melancholic cast to shape her lips, conveying – if he chose to notice it – how much of a disappointment it was to have run out of reasons to visit. Just as she had wondered how to interpret the speed of Jack's response the other night, he must now interpret her delay on his doorstep. When love is at stake, these minute infractions need to be scrutinised with scientific care. Metaphorical lab gloves may be donned; microscopes, calipers and a range of precision measuring implements come into play. Of such a mysterious and fragile substance is human attraction made.

On this occasion, as it happens, Jack read into her hesitation all that Isabel had intended to convey.

'It isn't everything I need, though,' he said, and he pulled her inside and then he kissed her.

For days afterwards Isabel could think of nothing else. Jack's kiss ignited in her an unimagined euphoria and sent spinning into motion a thousand clichés. For the first time in her life she knew what it was like to walk on air. She was over the moon, knocked for six, head-over-heels. The trite lyrics of pop songs seemed full of wisdom to her; they spoke straight to her heart.

Knowing what an effect he had on her made it quite wrong to go back to the cottage after that, of course – but Isabel went back all the same, and kept on going back. Each time they kissed was a revelation. To touch his body, firm beneath the shirt, after Hayes' hilly frontage, made Isabel feel more desire than she had ever imagined possible. When her fingers crept through a gap between the buttons of his shirt, the warmth of his skin induced a delicious vertigo in her. Jack whispered that she was beautiful, that he would take her to Barcelona to live in a garret among anarchists, and she could not help laughing with delight.

The women's magazines she read promised a 'new you', but were powerless to deliver such a thing. However, this infatuation really did make Isabel feel like a new person, newly alive. Her trips to the cottage were made easier precisely because she did not feel herself. She was no longer the woman she had been, but something better: Isabel regenerated. When she walked over to the cottage, it was in Miss Prince's fabrics and jewellery, armed with Miss Prince's bravado. If she had ever stopped to ponder the legitimacy of such a transformation it would probably not have troubled her: the woman she had been before was so pained and unhappy, it was a joy to be set free. In fact she did not worry about any of it. It was such a relief not to be crying any more. When Jack took her face in his hands and kissed her eyes, it seemed to her the most precious gift of love.

Meanwhile she was continuing to visit Miss Prince and, each week, her friend pressed her for information about the dashing Australian. At first Isabel demurred, enjoying the secret of her trysts. She did not want to talk about Jack, yet on the other hand she wanted very much to talk about him. Finally Isabel could not contain her secret any longer: she confessed to having kissed Jack, more than once. 'Perhaps six times.'

'Six! And you never told me! I *demand* to know the details.' Miss Prince thumped the arm of her chair, raising a miniature cloud of dust. It was a long time since her sitting room had witnessed such exciting revelations.

Her jokes, the mock-outrage and exclamations were a ploy to break down Isabel's reserve and encourage a flow of confidences. For, now that Isabel was visiting during school hours and without Mattie, the timbre of their conversations had changed. After she had brought in the coffee pot and the jar of half-and-half, Miss Prince settled in her chair to deliver forthright opinions on sex and love, the strictures of marriage, the need, on occasion, for infidelity. As she talked, she got up every now and then to straighten a painting, or polish the leaves of her rubber plant, so creating an atmosphere where the trade in such ideas was as innocuous – as routine, almost – as housework. Isabel grew comfortable with this style of conversation; then the sweet indulgence of talking about Jack proved irresistible to her, and Miss Prince's sitting room, plush with soft fabrics, became a seductive confessional. Surely nothing said in such a soft setting could have hard resonance in the outside world? Casting aside her better instincts as though kicking off uncomfortable shoes, Isabel let herself talk about the man who had come to dominate her thoughts. She grew poetic on her subject, making a summary for her friend of Jack's physical attributes: his broad shoulders, the dark-blue circumference of his startling light-blue eyes, his arms, rippling with muscles. They both burst out laughing when she used the word 'rippling'.

'Well, maybe I'm exaggerating . . .'

'Never mind! Never mind! Tell me more.'

Isabel had not indulged in so much nonsense about the opposite sex since whispering confidences to her best friend in a shared lavatory cubicle at school. It could have been a cause for embarrassment, except that Miss Prince played the corresponding part so well – making herself girlishly receptive to all of Isabel's disclosures. Perhaps the affair with Jack would have stayed at that cubicle-level of giggles and breathless revelation, had Miss Prince not found ways to push it further. 'It would be lovely for you to be with him for longer,' she suggested. And when Isabel regretted, with a sigh, that their romance could not continue, Miss Prince grew indignant. 'You cannnot take a step towards something and then walk away from it again. This is life's gift to you – it is wrong to refuse a gift.' Invoking a curious mixture of women's rights, New Age philosophies and aromatherapy, she encouraged Isabel to feel that Jack's courtship was her due. This was merely the first step. To spurn him now would be to contradict some universal law. So it was that what had seemed to Isabel an aberration, albeit a wonderful one, became, under Miss Prince's tutelage, meant to be.

She began to seek him out with the excuse of giving him tea: a perfect alibi. Everyone knows that tea is an essential, as fundamental as food and water, especially to the working man. So long as she was carrying tea, Isabel looked as though she was doing her job. Was it not the duty of a farmer's wife to provide refreshments and cheer? And Isabel did seem much more cheerful than she had of late. Hayes noticed the change and the children were grateful for a lighter atmosphere in the kitchen, especially when meals were being prepared.

One afternoon she took a cup of tea up to the barn where Jack was checking on some of the new lambs.

'All day I've wanted to see you,' he said. The light-blue eyes fixed on her with intent. 'I want to see you all the time. I wish that we could have more time together.' Glancing around to be sure that they were alone, he laid the tip of his finger on the nape of Isabel's neck and drew a sinuous line down beneath her collar.

In Miss Prince's kitchen, where all was cream except for ten vermilion toenails like splashes of blood on the white tiles, steam billowed around the women as Isabel touched, with the tip of her finger, the nape of her friend's older neck, conveying, across the generations, the shivering intimacy of that moment in the barn. Miss Prince took the kettle off the hob, turned to her and said, 'He's getting serious!' She raised her eyebrows and asked, with false innocence, 'Where will it all end?'

'I don't know,' Isabel whispered. She leaned back against the counter, twisting in her hands a handkerchief that she had just now found in her pocket. It was a child's one, with a panda embroidered on it, that Isabel had meant to give Tom that morning as an incentive not to wipe his nose on his sleeves. Now, the picture of him in his school jumper, with its mucus-stiffened cuffs, filled her with pathos. 'It's difficult. I don't know,' she said again, with a shrug. To think of any member of her family being hurt by her behaviour was agonising. So she tried not to think of them. As she tucked the handkerchief back, deeper into her pocket, she wondered if it might be better not to see Miss Prince for a time, and not to discuss Jack with her any more.

As though intuiting this distance that Isabel was just now planning to put between them, Miss Prince placed her hand on her friend's shoulder. 'You mustn't let this go. These chances in life rarely come by more than once, my dear. Don't settle for half-measures.'

And, as Isabel averted her face, preparing to go into the other room, Miss Prince murmured, 'Just think how wonderful it would be.'

SEVEN

The year was still young, but the villagers felt old. Every-thing ailed them. Across the valley they were waking up now, to a chorus of creaking bones and bedsprings. The High Sheriff's knees hurt. Miss Prince's hips hurt. The divorced baritone's back hurt. Miss Lyall's neck hurt. Miss Smith had slept badly, as always, tossing and turning, chewing over all the injustices that had been done to her in life. They were rolling over in bed now, reaching for spectacles and pill boxes, sitting up and rising uncertainly onto arthritic feet.

At Hill Farm, Isabel woke and rose from her bed like a phoenix from the ashes. Every part of her body felt young, strong and supercharged. She opened the windows, pulled off her nightdress and let the breeze lick at her body, before walking naked into the annexe next to the bedroom she shared with Hayes.

Each of the children had slept in this room as a baby. It was a dressing room, incommodious thanks to the clunking presence of a mahogany tallboy. She could not look at this object without dread; inside it were piles of linen tablecloths that her mother had given her, and that she never used. They seemed to symbolise the constraints her parents had put on all things in their effort to make life tidy and safe. The room itself discomfited her because she had expected to use it as a nursery again, for her fourth child. For months she had been unable to enter the annexe at all, but in the last few weeks she had found the strength to dismantle the cot that had stood waiting in a corner of the room, and to reimagine this room as a kind of boudoir, strewing some of Miss Prince's scarves around it. Several of the prettier dresses given to her by Miss Prince she put on hangers to decorate the tallboy. Propped against one wall was a large, gilt-framed mirror. Now she stood naked in front of this mirror and found herself to be beautiful. She still had the poise and good posture bestowed on her by childhood ballet classes. The curve of her breasts and hips was accentuated by a small waist. Her eyes, grey leaning towards green, were widely spaced, and the downward sweep of her hair made a graceful partner to the upward sweep of her cheekbones, bestowing on her face an open regard and an appealing innocence. People sometimes said that Isabel was pretty, but not in her hearing, and she had not realised it herself until now.

The day before, she had made love with Jack. She had been waiting for him, sitting on a grassy bank beside the cottage, when he returned at lunchtime to make himself something to eat. Hayes was away, arranging the purchase of a field that bordered their land, so she had not needed to bring a cup of tea with her. When Jack had arrived at the cottage he had been delighted to find Isabel there and, without asking questions, knew why she had come. Sex is a less complicated science than love, requiring fewer tools of deduction. He had taken her into the house and kissed her on the mouth just inside the doorway, pressing his body against hers and coiling her hair around his fingers.

Then he took her hand and led her slowly upstairs. Isabel had followed willingly, desire alive in her body, each step on the staircase charged with the anticipation of what was to come.

Each step between bedroom and bathroom was painful for the High Sheriff, who liked to shave and make his ablutions while his wife was still in bed. He had been using the same safety razor for forty years, and the same sandalwood soap, which he bought from a shop in Jermyn Street on his occasional trips to London. Afterwards he put on his hearing aid and dressed. When he made his way downstairs it was a slow descent, drawing complaints from his ankles, knees and lower back. A few days ago his wife had suggested that soon they might be more comfortable in a bedroom downstairs. The sheriff had said nothing in reply, but the imputation enraged him. He had been born in this house, in the bedroom where he slept now. His younger version had bounded down these same stairs, feet barely grazing the steps. As a child he bypassed the steps entirely – the bannister was a faster route, though he was often reproved at the bottom of it by his nanny. Sometimes he fancied he could see this dear woman's ghost waiting for him at the foot of the stairs, or he seemed to catch a glimpse of her starched apron disappearing through a door. One could never be sure what happened out of sight, in other rooms. He liked to imagine that, while he sat in the dining room, the family he had known as a boy was gathered in the drawing room next door, entirely unchanged. His father, in plus fours, would be standing near the fireplace.

His mother might be playing the baby grand piano they still owned – though it was rarely played now. Sometimes he could make this reverie so real that he almost seemed to hear the voices and smell the smoke from his father's pipe. After his wife had cleared away the plates he lingered at the table, delaying the moment when he would have to go next door and find the room empty and voices emanating only from the television. How quickly things pass. His grandchildren were a great source of joy, to be sure, but the older he got, the more he dwelt nostalgically on his own childhood. It was seventy years since he had last slid down the bannister and now he must keep a sure grip on both bannister and stair when he went up and down. As if this were not a great enough humiliation, perhaps soon he would be making the journey in a stair-lift. It was unbearable, this great care that must be taken over everything. He would give anything to be reckless again.

Isabel had felt a kind of recklessness as she climbed the stairs in the cottage, but also a passion of surety. Her body longed for Jack's; it seemed fair recompense for the years of loneliness she had endured on the farm and for her sorrow about the baby. As she dressed that morning she had remembered Miss Prince's words: 'You cannot take a step towards something and then walk away from it again.' When they had reached the top of the stairs and moved into the bedroom, Jack had bade her sit down on the bed and she watched as he took off his shirt. He had made her raise her arms above her head, like a child, and pulled off her woollen jumper, creating static that stood her hair on end.

In her bedroom, still sitting on her bed, Miss Smith took off her hairnet, picked up a mirror and contemplated, with dismay, her hair standing on end. They say that every face tells a story: if so, then hers told one of unremitting bitterness. Lines puckered her mouth, riddled her forehead and cheeks and ran in rivulets down her chin. Who would have thought it was possible even to have lined ear-lobes! Then again, she had done nothing to mitigate the ravages of time. The day was not long enough, the facial muscles insufficient to convey all the disapproval and disgust Miss Smith would like to express. Whether she was squinting at a newspaper or peering at her neighbour in the next-door garden, it took quite a muscular workforce to achieve the full degree of sneering contempt she felt for all things. At least she had a face to show to the world, unlike her sister-in-law who could show hers only to the ground. If people did not like what they saw, that was their problem – she felt no obligation to make herself lovable or to put on a cheerful smile.

Miss Smith removed her false teeth from the glass on her bedside table, squeezed a little gel on them and fitted them onto her gums. In the mornings her shoulders were very stiff, and it was an effort to raise her arms and pull off the nightgown, which would be crackling with static after a night between nylon sheets. Now came the rigmarole of underclothes, a clean shirt and a pressed skirt. She always tried to look her best. She did not want to give

anyone, least of all Mrs Smith, cause to think that she had
stopped making an effort, that she had slid into a comfortable decline. She would never forgive her family for ruining
her life. She could have been a nurse – her school quali-
fications were good enough – but her parents had denied
her that opportunity, saying they could not afford the
uniform. Why did they not sell some land, then? But no,
they passed the farm, intact, to their precious son and
advised Miss Smith to 'make a good marriage'. Well, there
were not very many men to choose from after the First
World War and, anyway, she would have preferred to
work. Her brother had been a weak man, who never tried
to make amends for their parents' oversight by sharing the
land as he ought, and she had detected her sister-in-law's
influence in that omission. She would never forgive either
of them – had never even visited her brother's grave. Old
age was supposed to be a time for reckoning and reconciliation. Miss Smith would not yield to such softening
sentiments. She would keep pushing her resentment before
her, as the old yeoman pushed the plough, tirelessly, across
acres of hard land.

After taking off her jumper, Jack had rolled Isabel's tights
down her legs and over her feet. He had unbuttoned her
skirt and her shirt.

'So many buttons,' he had remarked, kissing her breasts,
and then the new patch of skin that was revealed with each
unbuttoning.

'I'm English,' she said, laughing. 'We're supposed to be
buttoned up, aren't we?'

'Not you. Not any more.' And after that she had felt such a flame of desire that her body seemed to catch light, and to melt into his.

Miss Prince, in her bathroom, felt that to grow old was to melt away. As the years went by, one's flesh sloped away from the body's high ground to sit in pools at the base of the neck, the abdomen, or in sagging folds at the point of elbows and knees. One became a tapering candle, with all the drips collecting in the wrong places. Over the years she had done her best to make her flesh obedient. She had dieted. She had tussled with exercise bikes, with dumb-bells and various toning devices. She had owned something called an 'instant facelift', a tool for honing facial muscles. What was the use of it all? One still had to grow old and die. Miss Prince had given up on exercises now, substituting the old regime with an armoury of elas-ticated garments designed to separate one fleshy area from the next; thus she hoped to achieve a more or less convincing silhouette. Now she sat on the edge of her bath and rolled her support stockings up over her legs. It hurt her hip quite a bit to stand up. She put on a shirt from a London department store and carefully did up each mother-of-pearl button.

'Not so bad. It'll have to do.' She was in the habit of speaking to herself ever since her little dog had died, three years ago. Of the many bereavements in her life, his loss had affected her the most. She had not felt lonely in life, until she lost him.

Now there was the make-up. With a kohl crayon Miss

Prince drew on the two bemused arches that served as eyebrows. She powdered her nose and put on lipstick.

To her jacket Miss Prince attached a little cameo brooch. At the front door she eased on a comfortable pair of walking shoes, elasticated on the upper. These days she used a long shoehorn, so that there was no need to bend down and fiddle with laces or buckles. With age, one learned ways and tricks to avoid all those tasks that had once seemed so easy. Elastic was a boon to the elderly, for sure: she had it in her undergarments, in the waistband of her trousers, in her support stockings and shoes. 'Ready to face the world!' said Miss Prince, and off she went to take the morning air.

As she walked along the road that led through Hill Farm, she wondered what had become of her friend, and why Isabel no longer visited.

May had brought forth an explosion of flowers. The verges offered buttercups and orchids, forget-me-nots and stichwort. The dell where the badgers lived had been transformed into a dreamworld where bluebells appeared electric-indigo against electric-green grass. Tom and Mattie went there to eat biscuits they had stolen from the kitchen – a Pre-Raphaelite prince and his consort – lying together in the long grass.

'One day, if you like, we can get married, and then we won't ever have to leave Hill Farm,' said Tom. 'We could run it together.'

'You're not allowed to marry your own sister, silly,' said Mattie.

'Not allowed?' Tom had assumed the adult world to be entirely unregulated, with rules applying only to children. 'That's unfair. I think you should be able to marry whoever you want.'

A light frown crumpled the smooth skin of Mattie's forehead. 'I don't want to get married anyway. I'm either going to be a vet or an aromatherapist when I grow up, and I'm going to live in a cottage by myself, with hundreds of cushions in it.'

'I wish we had more cushions,' Tom agreed. He was thinking that they would be useful for fights, and for jumping on. 'Do you fancy anyone at school?'

Mattie rolled her eyes. 'No. Of course not.'

'But I heard someone say that you liked—'

'That's just a stupid, *stupid* joke. All right?'

'No offence,' said Tom and when he saw that she seemed upset, he added, 'Have one of my biscuits, if you like. Or you can just lick off the chocolate and I'll have the rest. I don't mind.'

'OK, thanks.' She turned to face him, squinting at him through the long grass. 'Don't tell anyone, but Jennifer fancies Jack.'

'How do you know?'

'I read it in her diary.'

'Her secret diary, with the key?'

'Yes. I can open it with the key from my secret diary. Granny gave us both the same one. Don't tell anyone, though.'

'Actually,' ventured Tom. 'I sort of thought you fancied Jack, too.'

'I've gone off him,' she said, rolling back and looking

resolutely up into the sky. 'He used to be more fun when he gave us tractor rides but now he's always busy. If you want to know the truth,' she said, 'I don't even think Jack's that handsome. I think Daddy's a million times more handsome.'

'Well, you can't marry Daddy,' murmured Tom, 'unless he gets divorced from Mummy first. And that's never going to happen.'

The Hayes children were born naturalists. They could while away an afternoon watching water voles emerging from their holes in the mud on the river bank to paddle in the water, or the perch jumping up to snare skaters and water boatmen. Lying on their stomachs, they became an audience of giants for a circus of insects teetering on tightropes. They cheered to watch a harvest spider perform acrobatics on its silken high-wire or ants, the strongmen of the insect world, struggling under record-breaking weights. Hayes, as a child, had collected eggs and blown out the yolks. He had caught butterflies, etherised them and displayed them in boxes, but these children belonged to a more cautious generation. They walked carefully around the long grass where the partridges nested, peering in at the eggs without disturbing them. Even Tom knew that, if an egg had been touched, it might be rejected by a nesting bird. They collected different kinds of catkin for 'caterpillar farms' or made hidden houses behind the fronds of the weeping willow. The gnarled branches of the apple trees behind the farmhouse served as an unofficial gymnasium. Like all children, they spent much of their free time upside down, lithely swinging from branches until their knees ached and their faces went purple.

Although their imaginary games depended on what they found in nature, the children's inspiration more often drew on city life. They had been to London only once, to see a musical with their grandparents, but they knew about cities from watching television. Sometimes they pretended to be chefs in a busy kitchen, concocting exquisite dishes from blades of wild garlic or a few grains of oats and barley. These were served up in the 'sky restaurant', halfway along the branch of a favourite climbing tree. Drinks would be a little drop of nectar from the flower of a white dead-nettle. At other times they pretended that an old, hollow yew was a time-transporting device taking them to other centuries and other planets. Even Jennifer occasionally enjoyed such games, although it was getting harder to lure her away from her bedroom and her calorie charts.

In her absence, Tom and Mattie spent hours outside, trailing across newly sown fields, chewing sorrel leaves, or across the stubble, chewing grains of wheat that had been spilled by the combine harvester. In the summer the wheat came up as high as your shoulder and you could walk carefully across a field if you stuck to the tramlines; flattened heads of corn were too difficult for the combine to pick up. They made daisy-chain necklaces to give to their mother. They decorated themselves with sticky strips of bindweed and pretended to be camouflaged, or monsters, or criminals. Roughly half their exchanges began, 'Pretend that . . .'

'Pretend that I am Mrs Smith,' said Mattie, 'and I am walking along staring at the ground and, because I can't look up, I don't see that a UFO is hovering in the sky above me and next thing—'

'I have to be Mrs Smith,' protested Tom.

'Why? You always get to be Mrs Smith! You don't bloody own Mrs Smith!'

'Anyway, you can't make Mrs Smith be abducted by aliens – it's not fair.'

'Because?'

'She's very old and she could die of shock. If we're playing aliens, I am going to be Jack and you can be the alien.'

'Because you think Jack is a superhero, I suppose?'

'Well, do you want to play or don't you?'

The earth on Hill Farm was heavy and unyielding. In a dry summer such great cracks opened up in it that the surface resembled a parched African plain. The children liked to identify a crack to serve as the Grand Canyon, then send ants – masquerading as Mexicans – on death-defying journeys from one side to the other, under a baking sun. In winter the earth set so hard Hayes complained that you could barely break the surface of it with a ploughshare. Mattie loved to walk across ploughed fields in the winter, when frost hardened the furrows, then you could jump across the field from one frozen ridge to the next and the soil never crumbled underfoot. It made her think of the Christmas hymn they sang in church about earth standing 'hard as iron' and that lovely line, 'snow had fallen, snow on snow, snow on snow'. On such mornings the frames of the children's leaking bedroom windows bore thin strips of ice and the milk-bottle tops were full of holes, where birds had pecked through to get at the frozen cream inside.

'Frost does some important work for us,' Mattie's father told her. 'It helps make the holes which aerate the soil. In nature, everything needs oxygen. Everything needs to breathe.'

Snow was a distant memory now, as the land ripened and the crops threw out green shoots. The hills swelled, the sheep swelled; Hayes, sleeping softly in his armchair, swelled, his belly rising and falling softly. Isabel's heart swelled with love for Jack and his swelled in the same measure. That is the miracle of requited love – all the proportions seem to match.

Falling in love with Isabel had revealed the countryside in a new light to Jack. When he had first arrived in England from Australia he found all the views far too pretty and cultivated, dismissing them in a letter to a friend as 'munchkinland'. This had been unexciting territory, and he was looking forward to leaving it – for Spain, perhaps. Now, for this season at least, he was enchanted by Isabel, by her delicate beauty, her shyness and vulnerability. He felt the swell of her breast under his hand, or her smooth forehead beneath his lips, and wanted to tell her a hundred tender things. No one had ever provoked such a response in him, and he wondered if she seemed more lovely to him because she was different from the women he had met before, or because she was unavailable. Jack did not much respect the institution of marriage, but that did not mean he was unmindful of the potential injury to Hayes: he liked his employer and felt uneasy about abusing his trust. He absolved himself – to the extent that he believed absolution to be necessary – by telling himself that Hayes had been neglectful of his wife and had failed to make her happy. At any rate their affair must be short-lived, because soon he would be leaving England and, eventually, would return home and not see Isabel again. In the meantime, this English summer beguiled him and Jack went about his work with a song in his heart. He found an echo of his feelings in the landscape, in its heaving hills and verdant gorges. Some perfect conspiracy of rain and sun produced these ravishing greens and he understood that such a connivance could take place only in England. You could have talked to him about Keats and he would have heard what you were saying. You could have played him Vaughan Williams and he would have seen where you were coming from.

Isabel was enjoying her own epiphany. Love was her invention and the world had been made festive in order to celebrate it. The unravelling clouds strewed bunting across the sky. The telephone lines were decorated with pigeons and the fences with woolly baubles, where the sheep had collided with barbed wire. The sheep themselves curled around their softening lambs in such a manifestation of love as made her eyes prick with tears. The Charolais, out now in the field behind the house, struck her as magnificent and beautiful. Their expressions, which once had been merely bovine, now conveyed a poetic disappointment that was attractive and intriguing. Their big translucent ears, so tender and vulnerable, caused her a pang, because they reminded her of her son's, at bathtime. She had once hated the glistening nostrils and the great pink lolling tongues. They made her think of a time at school, when an entire tongue had been produced on a plate for lunch. Now she looked at the Charolais in a new light, because they had brought Jack to her.

'You've broken my heart,' she told him, with a half-smile, as they were leaning on a fence one morning, distant from the farmhouse. She could see Hayes travelling across a field a mile away, his red tractor bright against the vivid grass. She prodded Jack in the ribs. 'What are you going to do about my broken heart?'

'Well, I think there is a staple-gun in the workshop. Would that fix it?' He prodded her back.

Tears sprang into Isabel's eyes. Just because she had made the observation as a joke, it did not mean that he should take it as one. She wanted to force him to find solutions, to conjure something possible out of this impossible situation.

'Everything would have been all right if you hadn't come.' She looked down and saw a tear crash against the lichen-covered fence.

'That's not really fair . . .'

'I don't think you understand,' she said. 'I think about you all the time. Sometimes I dream of you.' It was true that she dreamed of him. She had even worried she might speak his name in her sleep.

He put his hand on her face, making her look up at him. 'You know that I feel the same way.'

'Well, stay here, then. Don't go to bloody Barcelona! Don't go back to Australia! If you cared, you would stay.'

'And be a sidekick to your family?' He looped a strand of her hair behind her ear. 'You know that wouldn't be much fun, after a while.'

'Perhaps things would be different, if I had met you

. . .' She did not finish the sentence, but both of them knew that she meant 'first' – before Hayes.

He sighed and pulled her towards him, tucking her head under his chin.

'Let's make the most of things while we can, here and now, without worrying about the past or the future, or what might have been.'

So they made the most of things, meeting whenever it was possible, in the early afternoon, when Jack checked on the lambs and the Charolais in the barn. At half-past two Isabel left the kitchen and walked up the hill to the barn, colour high in her cheeks and a mug of tea on her tray. Twice she crossed paths with Mikey, coming the other way, and each time she held her nerve; the mug alone jittered. Once inside the barn, she slid closed the heavy metal door – which had a tendency to stick and must be wrestled back and forth several times – before advancing, trembling, towards Jack, who would be waiting by the nursery pens. Under the woolly gaze of many upturned faces, he held and kissed her. The mug was abandoned by the door. Later he would throw its contents down the sink: he had given up pretending to like tea. In a corner of the barn, behind the towering bales, they lay down together on an old rug, making quick work of zips and fastenings (she wore fewer buttons now) and listening out for any suspicious sound above the bleating of newborn lambs. They knew that no one could come into the barn without sliding open the metal door and running into the impediment of its sticky runner, which would detain them for a few, vital seconds. Lovers make fetishes of such things: the mug, the rug, the sticking door. Their mutual obsessions bind them, providing a quick stand-in for the shared interests of a longer partnership.

Over the course of a fortnight they made love five times (Isabel kept count, like a schoolgirl tallying up kisses). By the time the children came back from school their mother would be at home, busy with chores. They had never seen so much industry in the kitchen: with baffled expressions they watched her turn out cupboards, scrub the floor and clean the fridge. At four o'clock, when Hayes came to the kitchen to put the kettle on for his own tea, Isabel tried to make sure that she was needed elsewhere. Then she could call blithely to him from the utility room or the laundry cupboard without having to see him and meet his eye.

Her time alone, though, was dedicated to re-enactments of the moments with Jack. Just as a coin in a slot-machine animates a puppet scene, so she could choose to put in motion the memory of their encounters. She had each one mapped out in her mind like a military event: the positioning of hands and limbs, the skirmish of lips, the advance, the withdrawal. Whether she was washing pans or tightening the vice of the meat-grinder on the countertop, cleaning the lavatory or peeling potatoes, her mind was on him, an inventory of him: his hands, his hips, his eyes, his shoulders. She sat on the floor beside the laundry cupboard pairing socks, and shivered to remember how his fingers had found a gap between her shirt and her trousers and eased open the button on her waistband. She thought of him unzipping the back of her dress and planting kisses on her spine. She said his name aloud, to feel it in her mouth, to conjure his presence.

Although she continued to attend to the demands of her home and her family, Isabel tried not to notice them very much, treating the children with a superficial cheer that did not risk disturbing her own deeper feelings. Concentration on this dreamworld with Jack meant banishing outside distractions. To this end, she found reasons not to visit Miss Prince any more, for she no longer wanted to talk to anyone about Jack. She wanted to keep the thought, the smell and the feel of him to herself. On waking every morning her aim now was merely to see him. Her focus was half-past two in the afternoon.

So long as she was carrying a teacup, she thought that she was safe.

As bells pealed out across the valley one evening later that week Mr Payne trotted down the grassy lane that led to the church. He had telephoned the vicarage earlier, and had been informed that Reverend Hollings would be here, in the vestry, 'doing some admin'. He paused in the portico to read the brass-polishing rota, feeling some shame that this was the first time he had visited the church since Debbie and he had moved to the village. Before lifting the handle to the heavy oak door he paused and, wondering if he ought to offer up some perfunctory prayer, murmured a few words about God and hedgerows.

Inside the church the sound of bells was suddenly very much louder and Mr Payne felt overwhelmed for a few seconds. Anne and Jean, the lesbian couple, had invited some campanologist friends down from London to try out the bells. Six middle-aged men and women in jumpers were hanging on the bell ropes. St Cuthbert's was a small twelfth-century church, but the bells had been donated in the 1930s by a large brewery that had owned several hop farms in the village and wanted to make a display of largesse. For decades the brewery had supplied all that the village might need: the cricket pavilion, the village hall, money for fêtes and repairs. They provided social opportunities, too: in the autumn there was an influx of hop-pickers from east London, who slept in shared huts on the farms and cooked over fires outside. In the evenings the village pub rang with laughter. Machines had taken over their work by the late 1960s and, soon afterwards, the brewery withdrew from the village, although it still owned the pub. The memory of its presence lingered on, though, and some villagers, accustomed now to the brewers' largesse, resented the new landlords who could not afford to be so generous. At least they could still count on a set of bells as fine as one might expect of a much larger church. Their sound rang out across the valley. Miss Prince, resting with her feet up, heard it in her cream-coloured sitting room. She was wondering why Isabel had not come to visit for nearly two weeks. Miss Smith heard it two miles away, and tutted about the racket.

Reverend Hollings, who had been pinning up news-letters from an African orphanage, looked over when he heard Mr Payne enter the church and came forward, extending both arms. Unsure of the correct protocol, Mr Payne met him in an awkward embrace. Perhaps Reverend Hollings also expected a kiss? He had limited experience of the clergy, although Debbie sometimes went to church.

Instead the vicar withdrew from the embrace and gripped Mr Payne firmly at the elbows. 'Isn't this splendid?' he shouted, gesturing towards the campanologists. He still could not help saying that things were splendid, and still hated himself for it.

'It's very impressive,' agreed Mr Payne, pinioned, like a bird whose wings are about to be clipped.

'Wonderful!' cried the vicar. He grinned wolfishly at the small creature within his grasp, as though wondering whether or not to eat him. Then he released Mr Payne and said, 'Come along into the vestry.'

Mr Payne followed him towards the altar and then through a little side door into a small room on the left, where there was an ironing board, a kettle and an open chest in which folded surplices awaited Sunday's communion. There was a small safe, too, where the chalice and communion dish were kept. In the centre of the room was a table, and an old, sunken armchair into which Mr Payne was invited to lower himself while Reverend Hollings perched on the edge of the chest and seemed almost to cling to it, from the way his knuckles whitened under their skin. He crossed his legs and began to jiggle one of them.

'Now, please do tell me about the project you wished to discuss.'

Being slung uncomfortably low in the chair, and with his face only inches from the vicar's restless knee, Mr Payne felt himself to be at a disadvantage; this was not how he had envisaged their meeting. Nevertheless he began to explain to the vicar about hedgerows, how they gave essential protection to wildlife, providing nesting sites and corridors between areas of woodland. Having got into his stride, he talked about how they held a key to understanding England's rural past and how they were under threat from modern intensive farming.

As he listened, Reverend Hollings' fingers slackened their grip on the edge of the chest and his leg ceased its jiggling. Soon he was quite swept up in Mr Payne's passion for hedges, and began to feel a fervour he had not known since working in the inner city and campaigning against drug misuse.

'In the county of Cambridgeshire alone, half of the hedges have gone.'

'Whatever for?' cried Reverend Hollings (it was almost a howl). 'To what end?'

'Partly to make it easier to operate the machinery, which is getting bigger all the time. Partly so that more land can be cultivated. It's vanishing very fast, Reverend Hollings.'

'Geoff, please,' said the vicar earnestly. 'And I will call you Robin, if I may?'

He removed some clutter from a chair, which he brought over to Mr Payne so that they could sit together at the table. 'I do have some experience of leading campaigns, at my previous parish in London.' He remembered now the banner they had strung up in front of the church, reading 'Gun Amnesty Now'. What a palaver it had been just to find two volunteers with long enough ladders and a head for heights.

'Oh, which part of London?' enquired Mr Payne.

'Hackney, it's in the—'

Mr Payne glowed with happiness. 'I know Hackney, I used to live there, too.'

For twenty minutes or so they chatted animatedly about cinemas and cafés, pollution and crime. By the end of it Reverend Hollings and Mr Payne were experiencing, in a smaller way, the sort of euphoria that had Jack and Isabel in its grip – that feeling of matching proportions and equal sympathies. The vicar had wanted for years to get his teeth into a campaign. The Third World was all very well, and of course it would always be central to the Church's mission to represent the world's disadvantaged, but here was something on home ground with which to galvanise local opinion and bring people together. The small, shining spot on Reverend Hollings' pate paid beaming tribute to Mr Payne's glowing nose.

'What kind of campaign did you have in mind?'

'I thought we might start with a booklet, to explain the history of hedgerows in this village. There is one on the farm where I live – it's extraordinary. There's a way of dating hedges that I take to be fairly accurate and, by that criterion, well, I think it may be over five hundred years old. That means it was first planted *before* Henry VIII came to the throne. The Americas had yet to be discovered.'

'Extraordinary!'

Mr Payne beamed, and his new friend beamed back.

'So a booklet, with a time-line, perhaps? With some botanical descriptions of the plants, as it were?'

'Yes, and perhaps of the wildlife that lives in hedgerows.'

'We might be able to sell it at the village fête and raise funds for a campaign of preservation.'

There was a knock just then at the door, and Jean appeared.

'Just to let you know that we have finished ringing – if Sue can tear herself away from that massive clanger! Thank you very much, Geoff. Everyone's had a great time.'

'Splendid!' said Reverend Hollings, administering himself a mental kicking. 'Great! How did it go?'

'Oh, it was really quite something,' said Jean. She looked overheated from her exertions and the constraints of her jumper. 'Did you hear our treble-bob?'

'I would certainly like to hear it again!' cried Reverend Hollings, without acknowledging that he had missed it the first time. 'And, Jean, may I introduce you to Robin Payne? He is spearheading a new campaign to protect our countryside – such important work.'

'It's a pleasure to meet you,' said Jean, stoutly extending an arm, and with it a firm handshake. 'Please let me know if there is anything I can do to help.'

'Actually,' Reverend Hollings thoughtfully tapped a long index finger against his upper lip, then directed it at Jean, 'you make woodblock prints, do you not, Jean?' Before she could answer he sprang forward on his bouncy soles, a lupine smile flickering over his lips. 'I hope I'm not misrepresenting you?'

'Not at all. I've been interested in woodblocking for a long time, though recently campanology has rather taken up my energy.'

'I'm just wondering if Jean might be able to produce some illustrations for our booklet?'

'That would be a marvellous addition,' agreed Mr Payne.

'Splendid,' said Reverend Hollings. 'Shall we have a cup of tea?'

And the three of them all smiled at one another, content to be in the company of fellow minds and kindred spirits.

EIGHT

The life of the Hayes children would have struck many an outside eye as idyllic. They lived the country life, idling their holidays away in fields and haylofts, or making occasional excursions in cars that were untidy and smelt of dogs, even when there was no dog to explain the smell. At Hill Farm they could come and go as they pleased because the back door was rarely locked. Someone was invariably assumed to be at home: Isabel, in other words, although she was not at home as much as her family supposed.

People driving past the farm on the top village road must sometimes have seen the young Hayeses in the fields – cavorting with the lambs, or swinging on branches – and smiled at the sight. Perhaps some of those passers-by wished they could have given their own children such a carefree start in life. The weekenders may even have felt a pang, as they travelled back to London, that they had made the wrong choices. 'Look how idyllic it is,' they may have said to one another, 'this Area of Outstanding Natural Beauty. How lucky those children are.'

Social scientists have told us that there are as many wife-batterers, self-harmers and drug-abusers in the country as in cities. There is an equal or greater loneliness. Yet still we prefer to believe otherwise, vouching that there is more happiness among the rose-entwined cottages of England's ancient villages than in the bustling streets of its cities.

Mattie knew the word 'idyllic' and had also heard of 'bucolic', though she was not sure how close it was to 'bubonic' (she was similarly confused about 'peasants' and 'pheasants'). At any rate, neither qualification made room for the reality of life in a twentieth-century village. There were fields of golden corn, to be sure, and even spring days when gentlemen tipped their caps at ladies on bicycles, on their way to arrange the flowers in church. But what about the farmhand who read magazines about sadomasochism, or the boy at the post office who used to flash at children getting off the school bus? They must be bucolic too, for they were as much a part of rural life as tractors and the tupping ram.

Despite appearances, the young Hayeses were not entirely carefree. Like all children, they had worries that they kept to themselves and of which their parents were mostly unaware. Tom secretly feared that a tree was growing inside his stomach, because he had swallowed several cherry stones. Jennifer fretted that she was too fat. Of the three of them, Mattie had the most to worry about. For a long time she had been miserable at school.

From the outside, the school where Mattie and Tom were pupils looked like a delightful place to learn. It was a converted oast-house, ivy-clad and boasting a weeping willow in the front garden and trees for climbing in the back. Three of the classrooms, the old oasts, were round; 'So you can never be sent to stand in the corner!' quipped Hayes. There were about eighty children at the school, which had a staff of five female teachers and just one man, a feeble specimen called Mr Evans. Inspectors remarked on the atmosphere of calm and contentedness, but Mattie was very far from contented: a bucolic bully had been making her life a misery for several months. Relationships forged at school can damage you in lasting ways. Mikey had known this for years, and Mattie was just discovering it.

Her tormentor, Sandra, was one of the most popular girls at the school. Both her parents worked, and she wore the key to her front door on a string around her neck, so that she could let herself in when she got home in the afternoons. Since no one else was allowed to wear any sort of jewellery, Sandra's latch-key gave her a certain status. She was, besides, very pretty and clever, with dark hair, long legs and thick eyelashes. She had been both captain of the school netball team and winner of the previous summer's tennis trophy. She was the sort of girl one could imagine turning cartwheels on the High Sheriff's lawn.

Given her popularity, it was a mystery why Sandra needed to bolster her ego by picking on anyone, or why she had selected Mattie for that purpose. Mattie's career at the school had thus far been fairly uneventful. She was not particularly clever, or funny, but neither was she irritating; she was no swot or snitch. But those who exercise power need continually to find new ways of consolidating it, and perhaps this was the case with Sandra: she may have feared that her legs and lashes, her many trophies, would not indefinitely guarantee her popularity.

It had started one afternoon at the end of January. Mattie's mother had agreed to bring home Peter Bourne, son of Harry – the gentleman farmer – whose wife was going to spend two nights at a health farm. Peter was a year younger than Mattie, and was one of the very few boys remaining in the school at that level. For a reason no one understood very well, most boys left the school by the time they were eight. The problem fed itself. Parents, fearing the school's creeping feminisation – fears that the presence of Mr Evans did nothing to allay – tried to move their sons at the age of seven or eight to a larger school in the nearest town, so the boys at this one petered out in the final years. But not yet Peter. Peter had not petered out.

He was a dismally unattractive child who had trouble with his sinuses. Mucus bulged permanently at one or other of his nostrils, and sometimes both of them. It seemed beyond Peter's powers to shift it, though he could sometimes hoik it out of view with a deep sniff: but that was only ever a temporary measure. The nasal obstruction meant that Peter had to breathe through his mouth, and his breath smelled of sour milk.

That afternoon Isabel had walked back from school with her three children and Peter. She had given them tea and then the three siblings went upstairs to play. Peter would not join them, though, even when Isabel ordered her children to return downstairs and invite him to choose a game. He refused even to remove his coat. Instead he had sat glumly at one end of the table waiting for his father to arrive, whereupon he had been taken home, to the great relief of the children upstairs.

Next day at school, when they were in the cloakroom changing after swimming, Sandra announced to the other girls, 'Hey, everybody. Mattie went home with Peter yesterday. She's in love with him.'

Sandra's jokes were meant to be smiled at, and Mattie obliged, albeit ruefully, and the joke looked unlikely to go any further. Every day at school, especially at break time, there were remarks about people falling in love and kissing, prompting laughter amid unanimous expressions of disgust and horror.

A few days later the girls were in the cloakroom again when Sandra renewed her attack. This time some girls had been talking about their plans for the weekend when Sandra glanced slyly at Mattie. 'I know what Mattie's going to do this weekend. She's going to be having sex with Peter.'

This time Mattie did not laugh, but blushed with deep embarrassment. Sandra's daring provoked a ripple of admiration among the other girls, most of whom laughed, though a handful seemed to have qualms about making light of this. Sex had been mentioned among them before, but only in the context of adults, or of impossibly ludicrous figures, like Mr Evans. No one had ever dared to attach this dangerous word to someone in their own class. None of them really knew, anyway, what it meant to 'have sex', except that it involved private parts and the removal of clothes. The mere thought of Peter without his coat on was outlandish. To dwell on his private parts was awful.

Having caused such a satisfying sensation, Sandra might have relented then. Instead, after her display of bravado in the cloakroom, her bullying became more sustained, as if she needed to keep herself dosed up on regular jibes. It got to the point where she made some kind of taunting remark most days.

'I'm on your side,' whispered Venetia, a quiet, pale girl who was regarded as an oddity at school, because her father had a handlebar moustache and collected vintage cars. Most of the other girls, however, wanted to impress Sandra, and joined in the persecution. The girls' cloakroom was the locus for nearly all of this activity and Mattie began to dread getting changed. This room, at one end of the school building, seemed to collect all its institutional smells. Dank odours of mashed potato stole here from the dining room and mingled with the sulphuric tang of the lavatories coming the other way. The smell of the cloakroom became intimately associated with the torment Mattie came to expect there, triggering a lifelong hatred of mashed potato.

Soon Sandra showed that she was not unwilling to extend the scope of her torment. Hitherto, the classroom had been safe territory – the girls would not dare tackle Mattie there – but now she began to find notes in her desk bearing lovehearts, with her initials and Peter's entwined. His initials, inside a heart, were penned onto the cover of one of her exercise books and, when she had scratched them out, she had had to endure an upbraiding in front of the class about defacing school property. Every so often she saw Peter around the school and marvelled at the injustice of their association. He was a small and scrawny boy, a good five inches shorter than her and permanently bubbling at the nose. She could not fathom why Sandra and her friends should have linked her with someone so repellent.

There were weeks at a time when no one said anything to her about Peter and, greatly relieved, Mattie would assume that the bullying jag had run its course. Then someone would make a joke, or write a note, and give the campaign fresh impetus. She hated going to school, but Mattie would not have dreamed of telling her parents about the ordeal she was facing there: the last thing she wanted was to worry her mother; and, as for her father, he simply would not have understood what the fuss was about. She did not want to tell Jennifer, either, because she feared her sister might think it was funny. Instead she resolved to face the torment alone, with stoicism – and to win back Sandra's approval, if possible.

She saw her chance one morning at the beginning of June, in a maths lesson. Mr Evans had invited the class to gather around his desk to look at some geometry problems. Mattie found herself standing right behind Mr Evans' chair, while Sandra was opposite, on the other side of the desk. Mr Evans was very young – perhaps younger than twenty-five – although he did not seem so to the girls. To them he was a freak of nature, not only because he was the sole male teacher in the school, but because he looked very foolish: he had acne, lank hair and thick-lensed glasses.

A vase of roses stood on the window ledge to Mattie's right. The flowers were drooping now and shedding their petals. As Mattie's attention drifted from the geometry to Mr Evans' pink scalp, so vulnerable under the lank strands of hair, she became mesmerised by the idea of sprinkling petals onto it. The idea began as a fantasy, until it occurred to her that this would be precisely the kind of gesture to impress Sandra and her other tormentors. The petals were temptingly to hand and – without giving herself a chance to think twice – she reached for them and sprinkled them onto Mr Evans. It took a second or two, and afterwards she could not remember the action of pulling off the petals, just the maths teacher's bespectacled eyes goggling up at her over his shoulder. It was hardly surprising that he was angry and affronted, but much worse than his reaction was Sandra's: Mattie had expected to elicit, at the very least, her grudging admiration. Instead Sandra's expression was one of disdain, as if she found Mattie ridiculous.

Being sent to see the headmistress won her no favours either, and that afternoon, when they were changing in the cloakroom, dejection got the better of her. At Sandra's prompting, one of the other girls had pulled away Mattie's towel as she was changing. Everyone laughed raucously at this (the ones who used to have qualms about bullying had learned to overcome them) and a chant got going: 'Mattie loves Peter! Mattie loves Peter!' Venetia remonstrated with the girls, but they ignored her. Now, for the first time, Mattie allowed herself to cry. In her underwear, she curled up behind the coats, waiting for the girls to realise that they had gone too far and to stop. But in spite of her sobbing the chanting continued, and at the back of her mind Mattie registered that enormity in very precise terms: she had cried, but they had not stopped, and among the group were girls she had once considered friends. It was unbearable to stay in their presence any longer. So quickly she put on her clothes and shoes and, instead of returning to the classroom, Mattie walked purposefully to the door and right out of it. She was not planning to go home, however. She wanted to go to Miss Prince's, to drink fizzy orange.

When Miss Prince opened the door to find Mattie outside, her expression was one of dismay rather than the cheerful conspiracy that was usually on offer. Mattie did not realise how stricken her appearance was. Having pulled on her clothes very quickly, she was dishevelled; it was raining, and she had left school without a coat or jumper.

'Mattie, is your mother with you?' asked Miss Prince. Mattie shook her head.

'What has happened? You'd better come in.'

Mattie followed her into the hall and made for the sitting room, hopefully anticipating an offer of biscuits and a drink.

'Shoes, Mattie.'

She was dripping everywhere and, before Mattie could be allowed into the sitting room, Miss Prince fetched her a towelling robe and took her wet clothes to put them in the dryer.

'What is it, Mattie? Tell me what's happened. Is it something awful?'

Miss Prince's voice was gentle, yet it suppressed a detectable impatience. Mattie could not make sense of the anomaly and that was because, on the occasions she had come here before, she had misinterpreted Miss Prince's habitual pleasure on seeing her and her mother as being something destined for them both – she had not realised that it was really only her mother's company Miss Prince wished for. Now she wondered why the fizzy orange was not forthcoming. Something seemed wrong about this scene: it was not how she had imagined it as she ran up the road from school in the rain. Miss Prince's stolid presence beside her on the sofa was not as reassuring as it should have been. It had not occurred to her that she would have to explain herself to Miss Prince. The prospect of going over the events of the last few weeks filled her with weariness.

'Your mother will be worried, dear. Now tell me what's the matter.'

'It's nothing,' Mattie mumbled. 'It's just the girls at school.'

'What about the girls? Stop chewing your nails, dear.'

'The things they've been saying.'

Miss Prince bristled barely perceptibly. 'What have they been saying? Mattie, you must tell me.'

This exchange was more inquisitorial than Mattie had bargained for. What was she to say? How was she to broach the subject? Her eyes wandered around the walls of the sitting room and she spotted a new macramé addition to Miss Prince's collection: an owl with beads for eyes and a beak. It did not look much like the owl that was living in their tractor shed.

'Well?' asked Miss Prince.

'They keep talking about ... about ...' Mattie could not bring herself to utter the contaminating word in the context of Miss Prince's cream upholstery. She feared introducing Miss Prince to something new and terrible. The thought filled her with self-disgust. She said in a whisper, 'I don't want my mother to know ...'

'Is this about your mother?' asked Miss Prince, with a frown. Then she repeated, impatiently, 'Come on, Mattie, you must tell me. And then we'll have a drink and some biscuits before you go home. I promise not to tell your mother. Now, what is it that the girls keep talking about?'

'About sex,' said Mattie, as quietly as she could. Even so, the word filled her mouth with filth.

The effect on Miss Prince was galvanising. Never mind her sore hips, she sprang to her feet and moved towards the kitchen, holding a quivering hand to the side of her face, as if she had hurt it, as if someone had slapped it hard and she wanted to shield the mark from Mattie.

'I *see*,' she said, with her back to Mattie as she reached

the door. 'Allow me to put on the kettle. I'll be back in a minute.'

Mattie waited on the sofa. She could hear the whirr of the tumble-dryer in a room next door and the ticking of a carriage clock on the mantelpiece. Adults do not realise how lucky they are to spend their days in such peaceful surroundings, she thought. They do not know how horrible it can be at school.

Miss Prince was evidently too impatient to wait for the boiling kettle. Only a minute after leaving the room she came back into it.

'Mattie, it is very, very wrong of those girls to be talking about – what you said. It's something they know nothing about. It's wicked of them to speculate. Do you understand?'

'Yes, Miss Prince,' said Mattie, who felt finally vindicated by this pronouncement, even if she did not understand it entirely. They were wicked indeed.

Miss Prince disappeared for longer now, returning a few minutes later with the familiar patterned tray bearing a cup of tea, a glass of fizzy orange and a plate of biscuits. But she continued to seem distracted. She had barely sat down before she voiced concern about the clothes drying in the other room and said she would go to see if they were ready. As Mattie watched the large, comforting figure rise again and prepare to leave, she was so dismayed to think that their tea might soon be over that she blurted, 'Miss Prince, who is the boy in the photo?'

Miss Prince turned to her with an expression of bafflement. 'I'm lost, Mattie dear, which boy do you mean? Is this something else to do with the girls at school?'

'No, I mean the boy in the rummage box. There's a

photo of you with him. I think you were dressing up, for a party or something—'

Miss Prince cut her short. 'Yes. I know now who you mean.'

Then she returned to sit on the upholstered armchair that was usually hers when Mattie visited with her mother. Miss Prince had said she preferred it to the sofa because it was higher, and put less strain on her hips and knees. She lifted one of her legs onto a footstool that showed a pattern embroidered by her mother, one of the very few items she had kept from her childhood home. It gave Miss Prince pleasure to put her feet on something pretty that her mother had made.

'He was someone I knew when he was a boy and also when he was a young man, and we loved each other very much. But then he was killed in the war.' It was the version she had told over the years, when required – so much easier than the truth, that her mother had forbidden the courtship because Sebastian was her cousin.

'It is possible to lose everything you know, Mattie. One would think that to lose so much might kill a person, but it does not always. The person is left behind, and has no choice but to go on, day after day, year upon year. So when life gives us a chance of happiness, we must take it with both hands. It would be a crime to do otherwise. Now let's sort out your dry clothes, and then you can go back to school.'

'It's nearly home time, so I can go there. Please don't tell Mummy about any of the other things.'

Miss Prince had moved again, this time to the desk, where she was scribbling a note, which she then put into an envelope. 'Your secret's safe with me, dear,' she said, patting Mattie on the back. It was more like a prod than a pat, speeding her young guest towards the door. 'Now, Mattie,' said Miss Prince, brandishing the envelope, 'please give this to your mother when you get home. Don't forget, or I'll be angry! Some new aromatherapy products have arrived that your mother might be interested to see. More of my potions and lotions! This is an invitation to come and try them.'

'Would I be able to come?' Mattie asked hopefully.

'No,' replied Miss Prince, firmly. 'Perhaps next time.'

In the kitchen at Hill Farm Isabel opened the envelope with a trembling hand. A note inside said: 'COME AND SEE ME TOMORROW MORNING AFTER YOU DROP THE CHILDREN OFF.'

As an afterthought, in case her missive should fall into the wrong hands, Miss Prince had added another line:

'I HAVE RECEIVED A NEW CONSIGNMENT OF LAVENDER OIL!'

When Isabel rang the doorbell the next morning Miss Prince opened the door with an alacrity that suggested she had been hovering very nearby. Ushering her visitor in, she pressed the door closed behind her, an audible click of the latch signalling the start of an imprisonment that Isabel prayed would not last longer than twenty minutes. After reading the previous evening's note she had thought it unlikely that her friend would demand her presence so urgently for the sake of some Lavender oil. On the other hand, Isabel realised that Miss Prince was offended by her absence, and that it might be unwise to let her nurse that resentment – and for these reasons she had made her way reluctantly to the Old School House. This house was not a refuge any more, Isabel thought, as she approached the grey façade; its lack of windows denoted not intimacy, but conspiracy and shame. She no longer looked forward to the sofa's soft embrace. In fact, she cringed to remember her revelations on that sofa.

So, twenty minutes would be enough. Isabel was resigned to having coffee and some inconsequential chit-chat, but then she wanted to be free to think of Jack without distractions, back in her house, perhaps in her bed. By the front door she removed her shoes and walked into the sitting room, taking in the wall-hangings and flower arrangements – the chintzy ornaments that had once seemed so appealing. It amazed her now to think how she had loved this room. Miss Prince's style, which had recently seemed so sophisticated, now struck her as affected and overdone; the *objets* were merely objects. It was absurd, in point of fact, to polish the leaves of a rubber plant. She noted, with curiosity rather than unease, this sudden change in her own taste. It is hardly surprising that we should so readily betray other people, she thought, when we show so little loyalty even to our own once-cherished convictions. All the elements in this room were the same. She alone had changed and, in this sense, Miss Prince's counsel offered all those months ago had been right: it was possible, easy even, to change. You could change so much that you were barely recognisable to yourself. She glanced over her shoulder then, and saw that Miss Prince had not followed her into the sitting room, but was still standing with her back against the front door, watching Isabel with an expression that seemed to broadcast some awful event.

'Are you going to show me the Lavender oil?' asked Isabel, raising half a smile.

'Mattie knows,' said Miss Prince, without moving from the door.

'No!' This was Isabel's instinctive reaction, but then she felt a flash of annoyance about Miss Prince's theatrical stance against the door, like some overblown soprano ready to tackle a cadenza. 'Mattie knows? Knows what, exactly?'

'She knows about you and Jack. The girls at school have been laughing at her and goading her.'

Isabel felt horror bloom in her face and a sharp ache in her throat. She stared at Miss Prince in bewilderment for a few seconds. Then she said, willing it to be true, 'There is nothing to know.'

Miss Prince abandoned her stance and broke away from the door. 'Oh, come on!' she said, her voice betraying the anger she had felt about Isabel's abandonment. 'Mattie came here yesterday, in the pouring rain, because the girls had made her so upset. I sent her home to you and – I agreed to keep her secret. On thinking it over, I decided it was my duty to—'

'But she told me that it was because she was feeling sick, that she didn't like the mashed potato.'

'In that case she was protecting you, my dear. She didn't want you to be upset.'

Then Isabel felt anguish wash over her like a wave. She stumbled to the sofa, sat on it and buried her face in her hands, gasping. The air in the room was like a syrup filling her mouth. She could not breathe.

Miss Prince had evidently been waiting for such a reaction. In a trice the older woman came to the younger one's side, and held her head against her shoulder. Underneath them, the sofa springs sighed and stretched to accommodate this new load. For a moment she said nothing, simply patting Isabel's head and rocking her gently in her arms. It was such a recognisably maternal gesture that Isabel was persuaded to cry like a child. The tears were for Mattie, and for Hayes, but above all they were for herself and the injustice of her situation – because Isabel had wanted to pursue the secret of her love for Jack for longer and because it was Miss Prince who was speaking softly into her hair, drawing strands of it between her fingers, when so recently it had been him. No one had ever treated her with such tenderness as him. To think now that no one ever would again made her feel wretched and unloved.

'There, there,' said Miss Prince, patting Isabel's head as though she was a lost lamb returned to the fold. Her hand's pressure nudged Isabel's head towards her cleavage, which was slick with the residue of some floral scent or cream. 'Don't be so upset.'

'I knew that I was doing the wrong thing,' Isabel sobbed. 'I should have stopped before, or never started. I've hurt so many people.'

'There, there,' repeated Miss Prince. 'It's natural to feel some guilt, but life is complicated. There is a ying and a yang to all things, is there not?'

Isabel made some muffled agreement, while not being at all sure what ying and yang were; they sounded like children's television characters.

'You're very upset,' Miss Prince murmured into her hair. 'But it doesn't need to be so bad. Let us find some solutions.'

'But what can I do? I can't take back what's happened to Mattie. I can't start again.' Weeping was making her nose run, and Isabel pulled from her pocket the little handkerchief that she had once intended to give to Tom.

While Isabel blew her nose Miss Prince drew back from her, reaching absent-mindedly for a cushion on which there was an embroidered axiom about life being too short to deny oneself chocolate. She placed the cushion behind her, in the small of her back, then repositioned herself on the sofa.

'Mattie is a child,' said Miss Prince softly. 'She will forget all about this. She can be thrown off the scent. It wouldn't be hard. You and Jack just need to find somewhere else to go.'

Her eyes levelled with Isabel, who marked their cool intent on her own hot face.

'Perhaps you could come here,' said Miss Prince.

The older woman's gaze was so compelling that Isabel was, for a few seconds, unable to look away from those green eyes, unblinking under their shimmering silver lids. When she lowered her own eyes, it was perhaps a token of the abasement she felt, hearing Miss Prince's suggestion and noting her own failure to reject it with force. She examined her red, nail-bitten fingers lying in the clasp of Miss Prince's French-polished nails and let herself explore the new landscape offered by Miss Prince, in which it would be possible to spend more time with Jack, to have sex with him without fear of interruption. A greediness sprang up in her that frightened her. The manicured fingers held hers tight. Then Isabel thought of Mattie – saw her child's face before her eyes – and felt such a wave of nauseous claustrophobia that she knew she must get out of the cream-coloured room. She pulled away, stumbled to her feet and, without looking at Miss Prince, she said, 'That isn't possible. I've got to go now.'

In the hallway she struggled to put on her shoes, fumbling with the buckles. Miss Prince had followed her there and stood watching, using the thumb and finger of one hand to rotate a ring on the other.

'I've upset you, my dear. I'm so sorry. Why don't you come back and sit down for a while until you feel better? You haven't had your coffee yet.'

Isabel worked up an appearance of temporary composure, forcing herself to smile at Miss Prince for what she hoped was the last time.

'I'll talk to you again very soon.'

Outside she drew in deep breaths of air and tried to calm herself, but the thought of Mattie having suffered at school on her account caused Isabel such a biting pain that she could not help crying aloud as she walked up the road towards the gateway to Hill Farm. At that point she leaned on the gatepost and looked out across the fields. In the distance she could see a tractor pulling the sprayer across a field of wheat. Isabel wished that it was Jack driving the tractor, but even from this distance she recognised Mikey's boiler suit and the slack profile of his jaw. She hated Mikey for being himself and not Jack. The desire to see Jack was so strong that it made her body hurt.

She waited for a few minutes beside the gate, then turned into the farm and began to walk down the hill towards the farmhouse, so absorbed in her thoughts that she did not notice Mr Payne coming in the opposite direction until it was too late to avoid him by taking a different route.

'Are you another sufferer?' asked Mr Payne cheerfully, as their paths crossed.

Her heart jumped, and she cast about for an excuse to explain her distress, just as she had the first time that Miss Prince had come to the farmhouse, when she had lied about cutting up onions. If only she had never got involved with Miss Prince! Before Isabel could formulate a convincing theory for the benefit of Mr Payne, he provided one for her. 'I get hay fever too. This time of year, it's miserable for us, isn't it?'

At twenty minutes past two o'clock Isabel stood in the kitchen, beside the range and the boiling kettle. Anyone who had seen her, standing so still, might have thought there was a reason for this young woman to listen so attentively to the roiling water, as if she was waiting to discern some message there, or in the tumult of steam.

Hayes caught sight of her on his way to the back door and was surprised to see his wife so subdued. Lately she had been busy and cheerful, tackling jobs around the house with unaccustomed enthusiasm.

From the doorway he said, 'Everything all right, love? Off on your tea rounds?'

Isabel raised pale eyes to meet her husband's. 'I don't know,' she said. 'I'm not feeling awfully well.'

His own eyes filled with concern.

'You've been very busy recently, with all that spring-cleaning. Perhaps you need a rest. Jack's got the cottage close at hand. I should think he can get his own tea. No need to go spoiling him!'

'Yes, perhaps you're right,' she said quietly, lowering her eyes. 'I think I might go and have a rest, before the children come home.' She moved the kettle off the heat and put down the lid on the hob.

Mr Payne was now deeply involved in his work on *The History of a Hedge*. The day after his conversation with Geoff Hollings he had spent a profitable hour at an art shop in the nearest town choosing calligraphy pens, inks and paper. Back at the cottage he had moved a table in the second bedroom, which was at the front of the house, over to the window, and organised on it all the things he would need for his project, as well as an electric kettle, a biscuit tin and a small basket of instant-milk sachets.

His usual habit was to spend three or four hours of the morning at his desk. He worked very slowly. Simply penning the title of the booklet had been a job of several days, with an entire morning spent applying flourishes and curlicues to the initial 'H'. There was an ancient feel to the scratch of the calligraphy nib on paper and he perceived a monastic element in his work, even if his surroundings were at odds with such an idea: a monk's cell would not be likely to contain so many pictures of kittens. All the same, Mr Payne felt a religious devotion to the task. To make a beautiful record of a natural phenomenon was a labour of love and, he soon realised, the perfect curative: this was exactly what he had been needing.

When he had finished the title Mr Payne began to make meticulous drawings of the plant species he had discovered in the hedge. Jean's woodblock prints had been rather foisted on him, but Mr Payne, a talented watercolourist, was not to be denied his own illustrative contribution. First he tackled the hawthorn with its tiny cream flowers. Beside the picture he wrote in a flowing hand about the mythic and religious attributes of the tree. It made the tip of his nose glow to write of the plant's associations with carnal love. Had the crown of thorns worn by Christ been made from it? What was the source of the superstitions that said one should never have it in the house, 'or a death will follow'? Mr Payne had it in the house regardless; he was neither a religious nor a superstitious man, and it was more convenient to sketch the flowers at the table in his room than outside.

He worked to a constant background noise of agricultural activity. Tractor engines thrummed and throbbed outside his window. Trailers were opened and closed with a clank. Sometimes cattle were driven past the house on the way to fresh pasture. The Herefords were out in the field all the time now, while the Charolais spent most of the day in the barn. Jack was charged with taking them out each day, then rounding them up again to return them to the cattle shed. Mr Payne liked all these sounds. They were certainly an improvement on the disputatious noises of an office. Whether it was a clank, a throb or a thrum, the sounds became elements in the background soundtrack to his work – a mechanical symphony to accompany his research into the Middle Ages.

He had planned a time-line that would meander across

the pages, with botanical illustrations of plants and their associated lore displayed on either side of it. Now he began writing about the events of the late fifteenth century, which was when he supposed this hedgerow to have started its life. What a wealth of history was here: the reign of Richard III, Henry Tudor's victory at Bosworth, Caxton's printing press. In medieval times the scent of hawthorn was said to evoke the Great Plague of London. He allowed his nostrils to quiver above the creamy blossoms and take surreptitious sniffs. The scent was unpleasant, certainly, but anyone who thought it noxious had never worked in Bulky Refuse.

Mikey, walking up through the farm at about three o'clock on Wednesday afternoon, crossed paths with Jack, who was walking down the hill, looking unusually preoccupied.

'All right?' muttered Mikey.

'All right?' Jack returned. Nowadays that was often the extent of their exchanges. On this occasion, though, Jack raised a hand to his forehead as though just remembering something he wanted to tell Mikey.

'Oh, by the way,' he said, frowning, 'I saw you spraying Cooper field this morning.'

'Yeah?'

'You were going way too fast, man. On a gradient like that. All it takes is a rut or something and you could have turned her over. That tractor's got no safety frame – you could have killed yourself.'

Mikey felt himself redden and his pulse quicken. 'No, I was not.'

'Well, I saw one of the wheels actually come up off the ground.'

'The wheel did not fucking come up. I think I do know how to drive a tractor by now.' Mikey was spitting out the words, conscious of the saliva gathering in the corners of his mouth. And he felt uncomfortably hot in his boiler suit, while Jack, by contrast, looked cool and calm in jeans and T-shirt, as though he never broke a sweat.

'Nothing to get overheated about, mate. I just thought I'd mention it.'

'Yeah, well, why don't you mind your own beeswax next time?'

'Sure,' said Jack, with a shrug. 'I'll remember to do that. Whatever you say.' He turned and continued on his way, absently clicking his fingers, demonstrably unruffled by this encounter.

Smug bastard, thought Mikey, as he walked on up the hill, burning with anger. Who was Jack to waltz into their lives and start ordering people about, as if he owned the place? Hayes was their boss. And why could he never think of anything clever to say to Jack? 'Mind your own beeswax' was something his mother would say. He clenched his fist and struck his own thigh as he walked, making the matches rattle in his pocket. Then Mikey itched to burn something. He thought of the hay stacked up in the barn and dry as tinder. He thought of the tractor shed and the fertiliser store and he felt a hot rush of adrenaline. *Kaboom!*

*   *   *

At the suggestion of his new friends, Mr Payne met Jean and Geoff to have a drink and talk about the project. They made for an awkward-looking trio, advancing cautiously across the green towards the pub – the vicar tall and lanky, Mr Payne very slight and Jean short and sturdy. At the entrance to the pub all three of them got caught in a swing door behind some buffoon who appeared to be impersonating a zombie, arms outstretched and tongue lolling out of his mouth, in a shameless attempt to impress the bar girl. That was enough to persuade them to take their drinks into the saloon, which was quieter, and decorated with pretty garlands of dried hops and old photographs of hop-pickers on twelve-foot stilts, grinning down into the camera. The men had each ordered dry white wine, while Jean had a pint of stout. Jean talked about her last job, as a conservator at the Ashmolean Museum and, before that, as an archaelogist. She told them about some of the strange and rare artefacts she had found while working on digs, principally in Jordan. Following suit, Mr Payne talked about the strange and rare artefacts that were sometimes disposed of as Bulky Refuse.

'Even a prosthetic arm, once!'

Reverend Hollings flung back his head and, baring his canines, howled with laughter. Jean said, somewhat surprising the others, 'People can be very wasteful.'

Next door, in the public bar, Dave was on a mission to disrobe the peanuts girl; only three or four strategically placed bags covered her now. Dave was eating his fifth packet while describing the work of a chicken-processing plant to a captive audience. He used his thumb and forefinger to extract a single peanut and convey it to his mouth, each time wiping these fingers delicately on his trousers – an uneconomical procedure for such a small reward, and one that left a salty trail across his hip.

'You've got your stunning, you've got your killing, you've got your scalding, you've got your defeathering, you've got your drawing, you've got your—'

'Feet, Dave,' interrupted Tone.

'Eh?'

'Foot-removal.'

'Beg pardon: your defeathering, your *foot-removal*, your drawing, your cleaning, your washing and cooling, your packing, your weighing, your freezing, and *voilà*, off to the supermarket.'

'Bloody hell.' Jack, who was standing at the bar with the others, shook his head. 'I never would have known it was so complicated.'

'No one does,' said Dave, with the air of one who has shone light onto a mystery and revealed something of his own genius in the process.

'Most people still think their eggs get hatched by actual hens,' said Tone.

'What, and how do they get hatched, then?' asked Hazel, who was drying tumblers.

'You can hatch them a thousand at a time, in a hatchery, using lights.'

'Man, that sounds too high-tech,' said Jack. 'I think I'll stick to cattle.'

'Is that what you did, when you were back in Australia?' asked Hazel, her eyes shining with admiration.

'Yeah, I've worked with cattle for years, but not this kind. The Charolais have only recently started being exported and there still aren't too many outside France. They're really special and really expensive.'

'Why, what's so special about them?'

'You just can't beat them for strength, and the quality of the meat. And they put on weight fast.'

'Sounds like Dave's last girlfriend,' said Hazel, smirking into her tumbler.

'Shut up,' growled Dave, administering himself another peanut.

'They're beautiful, too, and they're very good-natured.'

'OK. So not like Dave's girlfriend, then . . .'

'Shut up and give us another bag of peanuts.'

'What about you, mate?' Jack turned to Tone. 'What do you do at the chicken-packer's?'

Tone took a deep drag on his cigarette and puffed out thoughtful smoke rings. Sitting at the bar in a black polo neck and faded jeans, he looked like a French philosopher interrupted mid-reverie. He laid the cigarette down carefully in the groove of an ashtray. 'Their hearts, their kidneys and livers – right?' He spoke quietly and his long, elegant fingers enumerated the organs, appearing to hold them delicately in front of him, as if he meant to lay them down on the bar with great tenderness: a sacrificial offering to Hazel. Tone's fingers were so expressive they drew attention away from the inscrutability of his face, as if the key to his motivation lay here, in the fingertips, and not, as is conventionally supposed, in the eyes.

He paused, as though to be sure that everyone had the measure of these three vital organs. Then he said, 'The hearts, the livers, the kidneys. I take them and I put them in a little bag. The bag goes in the cavity.'

'You put their hearts in a bag, Tone?' Hazel broke off drying glasses for a moment.

'Yeah,' said Tone, drawing on his cigarette. 'Why?'

'I don't know, Tone. It's just, I didn't know that. There's something sad about it.'

There is a ying and yang to all things. While a thoughtful sadness descended for a moment on the drinkers in the public bar, gaiety ruled the saloon bar, where Mr Payne and his new friends were on a roll. Reverend Hollings was keeping them entertained with anecdotes relating to his own clumsiness, about his tendency to trip over his surplice and the awful moment, during his ordination, when he had dropped his new Bible on the bishop's toe. Even Jean's tales of textile restoration at the Ashmolean met with gales of laughter. They were a happy threesome, to be sure.

Walking home that night, along the farm's bottom road, Mr Payne felt exhilarated by the evening's bonhomie. The night was alive and crowding in on him. There was a full moon overhead and a tang of cold in the night air that made his cheeks prick. He felt manly and unafraid. Not only had he spent an evening in a pub, but he was walking home alone and in the dark, and neither of these facts alarmed him, as they might once have done. Moreover – and it was a small point, but worth remembering – he was not a virgin and had not been one for several years now. Here he was, a sexual being, among other sexual beings (he could hear them rustling in the hedges), walking alone at night. No one could dispute that he was manful, *puissant*. Perhaps Debbie would be waiting for him at home in provocative underwear (though not, he hoped, burning unattended candles). He took the opportunity of this solitary walk to experiment with a saunter, a sort of sexy saunter, and then – why not? – a swagger. The twitching and rustling in the hedgerows was disconcerting, all the same. He thought it might embolden him to whistle and then, giving that up as a lost cause, settled on what he hoped was a virile kind of humming.

Suddenly, a figure lurched out of the dark. 'Help!' shrieked Mr Payne, jumping two feet in the air. He thought it must be a fox. It was Mikey, who tried to calm Mr Payne by touching his shoulder, which only made him scream louder.

'I'm sorry,' said Mikey. 'I'm just on my way home. Forgot my torch.'

'That's all right,' said Mr Payne, his small, smooth hand nursing his pounding heart. He walked on, up the hill towards his house, thinking how extraordinary it was that a farm labourer would still be working at eleven o'clock at night. Surely there was some regulation to prevent such practice?

The truth, though, was that Mikey had not been working, but drinking in the tractor shed. He had been sitting in the dark. He was damned if he would go to the pub while Jack was there.

NINE

Isabel lay half-asleep in her bed at Hill Farm imagining Jack was in it with her, re-creating in her mind the pressure of his hand on her thigh, his head on her shoulder. Under closed lids, her eyes moved in secret re-enactments as she tried to prolong her dream, fending off wakefulness. Then, with a jolt, she remembered Miss Prince's revelation of the previous day and her eyes sprang open. It was very early on a Thursday morning and the village was stirring. At the manor house, a mile away, the High Sheriff was also beginning to waken, the silken canopy on his four-poster bed coming into hazy view. He had been dreaming about the Queen, and the summer fête, which was fast approaching.

Celebrations were to be centred on the village green, a small and self-conscious area of grass demanding festivities and expressions of community, if only to justify the exigencies of the mowing rota. Five years ago the High Sheriff had donated to the village a lawnmower, which was kept in a locked shed behind the hall, and every few weeks one or other member of the parish council came to mow the green, leaving it in tidy stripes. That was about the limit of their communal effort; they did not hope to do more than keep the village looking neat. There was no urge among them to win prizes for the Best Kept Village, with all the associated pressures and anxiety such a trophy brings.

All the same, the village green aroused strong feelings. 'It must be *used*,' people exclaimed, as though not using it meant ushering in some fearful era of decline, with villagers abandoning community life for the easier entertainment of their televisions. In this respect their fears were justified, for it is not always easy to enjoy, say, the lumbering gyrations of morris dancers. Although she pretended otherwise, Isabel disliked the spectacle of large men hopping about in beards and bells and waving handkerchiefs.

'If it weren't for the hard work and enthusiasm of a small group of us, there would probably be no fête at all,' grumbled the High Sheriff to his wife, who was trying to ignore him because she wanted to keep on sleeping. 'People nowadays have very little gumption.' Although this was something he truly felt, he said it also because he liked the feel of that word in his mouth, with its flavour of wartime grit, of unwavering good humour. 'If it were left to the young people,' he went on, 'nothing would ever get done.'

'That's only because there aren't any young people,' muttered his wife into her pillow. She opened one eye and looked at the clock, resigning herself to an early rise. 'They seem to have run out, or run off, or something.' Just as her husband took his lead from the Duke of Edinburgh, so she liked to take hers from the Queen, pronouncing 'off' as '*orf*'.

By now the High Sheriff was not listening to her, but there was truth in what his wife said. Twenty years ago, when there had been ten farms in the area with perhaps a dozen labourers on each of them, it had been easy to muster six teams for the tug-o'-war. Since then the number of farms had fast diminished. As old farmers died, or found themselves unable to meet the new requirements of government agencies, their land was swallowed up by larger concerns. Mechanisation had usurped the working man. Hay-making, once a job for five or six men, could now be done by two using a baling machine. A threshing gang of eight men would have taken a day to harvest a field of corn in the 1930s. Now the same work could be done in less than half the time by just three: one on the combine harvester, one driving trailer-loads of wheat to the grain store and one supervising the dryer.

'Times change. Our challenge is to change with the times,' said the High Sheriff's wife, throwing back her blankets and jumping out of bed, ready for the day.

At Hill Farm the grandfather clock struck seven o'clock. Isabel gazed up at the ravaged beams overhead. She could not stop her mind racing with hypothetical conversations. Some of these were with Jack and others with Mattie. It hurt her brain to think so much and not arrive at any conclusions. She had not managed to see Jack yesterday, but today she must.

Hayes had just taken today's *Times* into the bathroom, and a gentle rustling of pages suggested that he would be occupied there for another twenty minutes. She knew that Jack would be getting ready to leave the cottage on his way to check on the livestock. Meanwhile the children were just beginning to wake up; it usually took them at least ten minutes to find their clothes and get dressed. She jumped out of bed, threw on some clothes and left the house. In two minutes she had run down the overgrown path to the farm cottage and disappeared behind the privet hedge that enclosed it.

At the door of his cottage Jack broke into a smile at the sight of her. His smile filled her heart with a sensation of pure oxygen and she could not help but smile back, for all her anxiety and worries.

'I'm sorry I couldn't come yesterday.'

'I missed you! I had to go drown my sorrows at the pub. Is everything all right?' He raised a hand to her cheek, but she drew away from it, fearing that it would be unbearable to let him touch her and then to walk away. Instead she caught his hand and held it fast with both of hers.

'I need to talk to you, but not now. Will you be in the barn this afternoon?'

'After two o'clock I can be there.'

'I'll come up then. I've got to go now.'

'Kiss me first.' He tugged her hand, pulling her towards him.

'I can't now,' she said, but he was kissing her anyway, catching the side of her mouth with his as she tried to turn away. 'I'll explain everything this afternoon.'

She returned to the house, glancing around her as she ran back down the path, as if there would be anyone to see her at that early hour. The farmhouse was a long way from any neighbours, and yet Isabel had a sense of the village as a watchful place – and this was not merely a symptom of her guilt. She remembered people's sidelong glances in church, the eyes peeping over bifocals and prayer books. It was one of the reasons she had stopped attending services. People always seemed to know more about Isabel's life than she had told them.

By the time the lavatory flushed upstairs Isabel was already back indoors, busy in the kitchen, making toast for her children's breakfast.

And so the working day began. Jack moved among the cattle and lambs; Hayes moved among his stacks of papers, his stapler and guillotine; Mikey moved amid the ripening corn. Each was moving towards his fate. At the chicken factory Tone was safeguarding hearts by putting them into bags. Hazel was at the pub, drying off tumblers. At Hill Farm, Isabel paced up and down the back corridor wondering what she was going to do, what she would say to Jack, how she would find a way to speak to Mattie. There were hours to go until two o'clock. The clock ticked on and time seemed not to keep pace.

At the Rectory, Reverend Hollings had ironed his surplice and was setting off to visit Mrs Smith, who had recently been too ill to attend church. Home visits were a part of Reverend Hollings' routine. So many of his parishioners were elderly that sometimes it seemed more of them languished in bed than filled the pews. Two or three times each week he went to visit them in his old Simca, which was itself ailing and unreliable in the mornings. He left it parked with its nose pointing downhill, then in the morning he climbed in, let off the brake and sat waiting for the old lady to cruise down the hill for a few yards before he started the engine. She coughed, shuddered into gear just as he made the road, then off they would go, down into the village and past the war memorial, before crossing the bridge and turning right. Mrs Smith lived at the end of a long straight lane, which had once been a railway line. Her home, the old station house, still had a plat-form outside it, servicing ghost trains. There was a sign bearing the faded letters 'Trains to London,' and a finger that pointed into a thicket of brambles.

Reverend Hollings carried his portable communion set in a black case that made him look like a doctor. Sometimes he made a joke of that – 'Now where *is* my stethoscope?' – but it would not have been appropriate with Mrs Smith, who found any thought of medical interventions alarming. Standing on the old station platform, he knocked on the door and then let himself in, calling softly before entering the sitting room. In a corner of the small room there was a makeshift bed on which Mrs Smith lay propped up on pillows, tiny and shrunken, like a grandmother who has been looking forward to seeing Red Riding Hood and now finds herself entertaining a wolf. Reverend Hollings crept towards the bed and made gentle enquiries after his parishioner's health. Now that she was prostrate, he could get a much better look at Mrs Smith than was ever possible when she was standing. Her face had grown very gaunt and her pale-blue eyes, sinking into cradles of bone, looked ready to be soothed to sleep. Reverend Hollings was surprised to see what big ears she had. An electric fire was positioned dangerously close to the blankets that were draped over Mrs Smith's bed and he nudged it away with one of his rubber-soled shoes. Then he stood to read the catechism, rocking back and forth rhythmically as he did so, letting his toes investigate the comfort of his modulated insoles. As Mrs Smith sipped the communion wine, he murmured a blessing and raised his eyes to heaven, noticing thick cobwebs in the corners of the rooms.

'I hope you will be back in church soon, Mrs Smith,'

he said to her, when the ritual was over and he was packing away his things. 'We need you in the choir.'

'I don't think I will be here much longer, God willing,' Mrs Smith replied. 'Please let Miss Smith know that I forgive her.'

Down at the post office Mrs Lyall pinned her hair-piece into position and prepared herself for another day of minimal activity. Once there had been three shops in the village. Mrs Lyall's was the last surviving of them, and she took pride in her role at the community's hub. One way or another, she got to hear of everything. Secrets swirled around her like a vortex, with Mrs Lyall at its centre, giddily hanging on to her hair-piece. It was in her power to choose what was hidden and what revealed. She was not ashamed to have spread rumours about the baritone's naughty wife, about Mrs Hayes' miscarriage, about Jean Temple's lesbian ménage. On the other hand, she would not hear a word against the High Sheriff – whom she had secretly loved for fifty years – and would never be drawn on gossip in the morning, for she was the postmistress then and exuded a corresponding air of stern efficiency. In the afternoons, when the post window was closed, Mrs Lyall's business was mostly in sweets and biscuits, with a matching sweetening of her disposition and a readiness to talk. That was when her hair-piece began to slip, her attention drifted, and sometimes her expression glazed over and she dozed off in her chair behind the counter. The Hayes children had found her in this semi-conscious state before, when they came in to spend their pocket money on Fruit Salads, which cost half a penny.

They had twenty pence each and spent all of it, every week, on Fruit Salads, infuriating Mrs Lyall as she tried to count out one hundred and twenty sweets into three paper bags.

Between the customers, who came only rarely, Mrs Lyall gazed blankly towards the memorial, or the pub, where she had misspent her youthful summers, drawing admiring glances with her backcombed beehive from the hop-pickers who travelled down from east London. It made her smile to remember the 'hop boys'. She missed the hubbub, the hustle-bustle, the hurly-burly of those days. The things they had got up to! Not far from that pub, in some long grass down by the river, her son had been conceived. After that she had been hurried away from the village by her mother and sent to live with an aunt while she had her baby. Then a story had been concocted about a marriage, and a husband who was a ne'er-do-well and had left her in the lurch. The truth was that she could not say for sure who the baby's father was; there had been several possibilities. Her married name was improvised from a sugar packet.

'They was good times, though,' she said aloud, in the empty shop. She adjusted her hair-piece and traced the line of her cleavage with a manicured nail.

It was at an upstairs window at the post office that Mrs Lyall's son – a teenager by then – had spent a summer month flashing at school children as they got off the bus. That was more than twenty years ago, though, and now the boy was grown up and gone away to Newcastle; Mrs Lyall believed her reputation to be quite restored. She hoped that her son was not flashing at people in Newcastle, but if he was – well, at least it was far away, and Geordies were not easily shocked.

All day long Mrs Lyall stared out at the green and seemed

to see all time pass before her, as though she had been staring at this same scene for hundreds of years and could glimpse, between the passing cars – the light glinting on their windows making bright, moving squares like television screens – the villagers of yore, the ancestors of the villagers she knew today. She could picture an earlier Miss Smith, lip curling in disdain at the antics of a travelling apothecarist, or an ancestor of the High Sheriff, carrying a nosegay to ward off the plague.

She may have looked as though she was staring into nothing, but Mrs Lyall saw and watched everything. She knew all the villagers, and a peculiar lot they were, but they did not seem so to her because she had always lived among people like this. The one who struck her as odd was Mr Payne, the day he came in looking for fine-tipped pens.

'Hi,' he had said, swinging through the door.

Mrs Lyall acknowledged the inappropriate greeting with a nod. It was before lunch, and she was all the sterner for it.

She watched him clucking among the shelves, picking out a pen and studying it with a frown. He held it up and waved it at her.

'Have you anything with a finer tip than this?' he asked, without bothering to enquire how she was, without even remarking on the weather.

'The tips that we have are the tips that you see,' enunciated Mrs Lyall. It was her habit to speak of 'we' partly as a psychological trick to make her feel less vulnerable (although Mr Payne appeared an unlikely thief or rapist). 'We' also reminded her of her son, who had worked with her in his school holidays, and made her think of the Queen, whom she admired very much. She was even now awaiting the arrival of some Royal Family merchandise.

Mr Payne clicked his tongue then, rather rudely, it seemed to her, and replaced the pen. 'I think I shall have to look for something else.'

And, after the door's little bell had announced his departure, Mrs Lyall rolled her eyes and muttered, 'Suit yourself, Mr Townie.'

Mr Payne had now finished driving his elegant line through history. With a calligraphy pen he had ascribed finely illuminated labels to Galileo, the Act of Union, the moon landing and other historical events and figures. Now he wished to write a series of descriptions about some of the ordinary people who traditionally worked in the countryside and may have taken their lunch in the shade of the ancient hedgerow. He began with the yeoman farmer, ploughman, shepherd and cattle-drover, making little watercolour sketches of each.

On that Thursday morning he was working, as usual, at his desk in the front bedroom, listening as the rural symphony to which he had grown so accustomed played on. Absorbed in his task, Mr Payne barely noticed the sounds. After an hour or so, however, he half-registered the introduction of a new element into the cacophony. This was a kind of frenetic buzz that climbed in pitch, then fell away for a few seconds' rest; he rather liked it, and subconsciously found himself matching that pattern with his brush: swISH-sh. He was not familiar enough with farm life to be able to identify most of the mechanical noises he heard, but he knew that this one sounded different, like something he had heard before. For a moment he paused, brush in the air, head cocked to one side. He looped some of his ringlets behind his ear, as if that might help to identify the noise. Then, drawn back to the flowing line of his brush, he bent once more over the page. The noise must have continued for quite a while longer before Mr Payne's bladder alerted to him to the fact that it was time to get up, shake out his stiffening limbs and go to the bathroom, where he stood before the avocado-coloured lavatory musing on all the work he had done and what there was still to do.

The window in the bathroom was made of frosted glass, but its upper section was usually left open, and so it was today, affording Mr Payne an inch or two of the view outside as he stood at the lavatory. Glancing out of it, Mr Payne saw Hayes in the back field standing in his usual pose, hands dangling slightly apart from his body as though he did not know what to do with them. He looked as if he were watching someone. Hayes raised a hand to smooth down some errant hairs and then, with the same hand, made a series of gestures, apparently to a person who was working just out of sight, using the equipment that was making the noise. Curious, Mr Payne stooped and ducked his head a little, adjusting his gaze so that he could follow Hayes' indications, and now saw a man holding a power-saw cutting back branches from a hedge. So that explained the noise! His bladder had been very full and it was a great pleasure to empty it. In this moment of urinary release he found the sight of men doing manly things, using power-tools, pleasing: this was substantial work with substantial machines. But that was not yet the complete scene, because now the mottled glass in the lower pane showed some colourful movement. When he had finished urinating Mr Payne adjusted himself and his trousers and leaned over the bath so that he could peer through the little window – sticking his nose right out of it – and give his full attention to the scene outside. The colourful object revealed itself as a digger, which now trundled into view, with Mikey at its wheel. Mikey drove it towards the hedge, lowered the claw, sank its teeth into the ground beneath the hedge and upearthed a great chunk of soil and bush. Mr Payne watched all this placidly, enjoying the sharp tang of uncovered soil in this crisp air. He thought for a moment how immensely lucky he was to be doing work that he enjoyed in a place that he liked. He would much rather stay here than ever return to Hackney and the horrors of Bulky Refuse. And so it was that the truth of the scene outside his bathroom window dawned on Mr Payne only very gradually, as though it had come swimming through the frosted glass and become crystallised, one atom at a time, in the cool air of the bathroom. Finally, in a dreadful moment of clarity, he deciphered the meaning of what was happening outside: he was witnessing the destruction of a hedge, of *his* hedge.

His heart began to palpitate and Mr Payne straightened up suddenly, scraping his nose on the window frame, then he ran from the bathroom and down the stairs to the back door, yelping with the injury to his nose, and to his heart.

Hayes did not see Mr Payne until he appeared in the field, and then he marvelled at the sight of this fellow bounding towards him, his hair springing in all directions, his white legs pumping up and down like pistons.

'Are you "jogging"?' he called out amiably. There was a lot in the newspapers currently about the potential dangers of this new form of exercise, imported from America.

'Stop! Stop!' called Mr Payne, gesticulating extravagantly, but neither man heard the other, because of the noise of the digger and the power-saw. Finally, though, Hayes realised that his tenant was exercised, not exercising. He motioned to Mikey and the contractor with the power-saw to halt their work.

All three waited then, as Mr Payne arrived panting at Hayes' side. He had to stoop, with his hands on knees, while he got his breath back. He was still trying to mouth words.

'Stop, stop. Please. You can't do this.'

'Are you all right?' asked Hayes. 'Have you hurt your nose?'

'No, I mean you mustn't – you can't take out this hedge.'

'What do you mean we "can't" take it out?' said Hayes. 'Of course we can. We practically have taken it out now, anyway.' He gestured towards the strip of land where once the hedge had stood. Only a few sorry sticks of hawthorn remained. The wild flowers that Mr Payne had photographed and sketched were stripped away; a few ravaged specimens clung to the edge of the cleared land. His precious dogwort was dangling from one of the digger's teeth.

Tears streamed, then, from Mr Payne's eyes. 'You can't take it out. It's hundreds of years old. It's part of our history.' He sank to his knees and sobbed with all his heart. 'I've been studying it.'

Hayes turned towards the ragged branches and contemplated them for a few seconds, as though trying to establish what there was to study. Mikey watched from the seat of the digger, but the man with the power-saw put it down and came to stand beside Hayes. Once they had switched off and set down their power-tools, the men seemed deprived of male expression. Quietened, they reached for a less muscular vernacular, appropriate to this unusual circumstance. The contractor, who had often seen his wife cry for no apparent reason, mumbled something about taking deep breaths.

'You don't understand,' sobbed Mr Payne. 'You've killed a part of me.'

Now Mikey stepped down from the digger and stood beside Hayes, scratching at that place on the top of his head with all his fingers. They watched as Mr Payne scrabbled at the grass and soil by his feet. The sight was so pathetic that Hayes felt a stirring of compassion for his erstwhile foe. He reached down, awkwardly, and placed his hand on one of Mr Payne's tiny shoulders, giving it a squeeze, as he would one of his son's. The weeping showed no sign of abating, however. After a moment Hayes said, 'I doubt that it was hundreds of years old, but, even if it was, look around you. Everything is hundreds of years old. The hills you can see were made by glaciers, millions of years ago. But does that mean we can never change anything? Come on! If that were the case we would never have progressed beyond the Stone Age.'

'Plus,' said Mikey, unexpectedly, 'it's only a hedge.'

That observation and the continued presence of Hayes' hand on his shoulder were enough to rouse Mr Payne from his despair. Angrily he shook himself free. Then he jumped to his feet.

'You can't make a change like this, not without asking for consent. This is in an Area of Outstanding Natural Beauty!'

'Oh, for God's sake. Not that again.' Hayes turned away towards the horizon, gathering stray hairs and shepherding them home, across his pate or behind his ears.

'There is a reason for rules and regulations,' continued Mr Payne. He felt as though he were back in Hackney confronting not Hayes, but Ron, the truculent union leader. This time he would not be cowed. 'This is an AONB, and I'm going to report you to the relevant authorities.'

'Really? Are you?' said Hayes, feeling his blood pressure begin to rise in a more familiar response to Mr Payne's presence.

'Too right I am!'

'Come on. There's no need for that,' remonstrated the contractor.

'Well, frankly,' Mr Payne gasped like a goldfish, and spread his arms, 'I'm left with no choice.'

'In that case,' said Hayes, 'I suggest you take your AONB and stick it up your ARSE.'

Mr Payne fixed Hayes with a glowering scowl. The tip of his nose glowed with menace, and the scrape on its bridge turned a livid red. 'You haven't heard the last of this,' he said. Then he turned and stalked away.

When they had finished tearing out the old hedgerow and broken for lunch, Mikey had instructions to get on with clearing ditches at the bottom of the farm. Instead he went down to the tractor shed. Being distant from the farmhouse and other buildings, it was a good place to hide from Hayes and while away some time. In spite of the fact that one side of it was open to the elements, he found the shed a comforting place to be. Over the years it had become a repository for pieces of equipment that were no longer used on the farm. There was an old weighing scale in one corner and some hop-pickers' stilts leaned against a wall among bags of fertiliser. In the other corner, spare tractor tyres were stacked in a rubbery cascade. Everything was woven together by ancient spiders' webs, mantled in dust. Mikey came here whenever he thought he could get away with it. He reckoned that he could settle down on the tyres with a newspaper for half an hour, or longer, without being missed on the farm. If he was doing cultivations in a field near the tractor shed it was all the more tempting to take a few unofficial breaks. In the past he had brought tea with him, but now he had got into the habit of putting cider in the flask instead. From this corner he could see anyone approaching the shed before they saw him; that advantage gave him time to hide his reading matter and pretend that he was doing maintenance work on one of the machines. Fortunately for him, he knew much more about tractors than Hayes did, so he could claim, for instance, to be checking the cooling system with plausible authority. If neither of the tractors was in the shed, he could pretend to be looking up something in a manual.

That afternoon, the day when everything changed, Mikey was sitting at the back of the shed doing a crossword. He was meant to be getting the ditches cleared while they still had the loan of a digger, but he did not feel much like it. He thought he would have a little rest and a drink first. Later he wondered if the alcohol had dulled his reactions: he did not notice when someone not only approached the shed, but came right into it. It gave him a start to look up and see Jack standing in front of him.

'Hey, Mikey,' said Jack. 'Sorry to interrupt your break. I need to ask you something.'

Jack's casual remark threw Mikey on the back foot,

because both of them knew he was not supposed to be having a break. It had been a long time since they had eaten their sandwiches here together at lunchtime.

Mikey thought for a few seconds, then made the decision not to move from the tyres. He decided not to do Jack the honour of standing up.

'What?' he said.

'It's just that . . .' Jack scratched the back of his head and looked at the ground, as though trying to make sense of a scenario in his mind's eye. 'You attached the fore-end loader on the Massey, right?'

Mikey said nothing, but let his gaze caress the space above Jack's left shoulder, presenting a dreamy countenance that was calculated to infuriate.

'You had the sprayer on yesterday, didn't you? Then you must have put the fore-end loader back on – correct?'

Mikey sniffed, took a swig of cider and belched. 'Yeah, that sounds about right.'

'Jesus, is it right or not?' Jack stared at Mikey, whose eyes met his briefly, then slid away over his shoulder.

'It's right. So?'

Jack's eyes flickered over the objects in the tractor shed, as if Mikey's shiftiness obliged him to fix his bearings.

'I don't know where you learned how to farm, mate. You put the thing on wrong. I'm in the shed this morning moving bales and the whole fucking arm comes right off. You must have left out the lynchpins. The vibrating made the bolts work loose.'

Mikey said nothing, but stared at Jack's shoulder, his mouth gaping open, his cheeks reddening as though they had been pinched or slapped.

'Now, what I'm thinking is: say I had been standing in front of the tractor loading it up when that had happened? The whole attachment could have fallen on my head.'

He noticed that Jack's voice was shaking a bit. He must be very angry, or shocked. He was pleased to have provoked this change in Jack's composure.

'It didn't, though, did it?' Mikey said with a snarl, for this was his repertoire – sneers, jeers and mockery – one learned in the playground and never relinquished. All Mikey's defence mechanisms were childish ones: he had never progressed to more sophisticated techniques. He still liked to stick his tongue behind his lower lip and call someone a 'spaz'. He would still repeat back to his mother exactly what she had said to him, in a silly voice, to make her sound stupid. He was not above retorting, 'Same to you with brass knobs on.' He cut a lank and puerile figure beside Jack, and Mikey was not oblivious to the fact. All the prettiest women liked Jack best. Mrs Hayes had never offered to bring *him* tea while he worked! Now he watched Jack, standing in front of him, handsome and self-assured, with all his travels and his experience, while Mikey had lived his whole life in a semi with his mother. His days were numbered, Mikey thought to himself. It was pretty obvious Hayes was having second thoughts about him, now that Mr Ozzie-Bollocks had come on the scene. Any day now he would be joining Dave and Tone at the chicken-packing factory.

'I don't think you get what I'm saying, mate,' said Jack.

'No, as a matter of fact I don't get it, *mate*. I don't *get* what you're saying,' said Mikey. Outright denial was another playground tactic he had never seen any need to improve upon. It was great though, denying all knowledge of the lynchpins, when in fact he could feel them, right now in his pocket, where he held them between the fingers and thumb of his left hand. The cider he had been drinking before Jack came in was having an effect now, warming up his chest cavity, filling him with defiance.

Jack stood with his hands on his hips, appraising the man in front of him. If he smelled the cider on Mikey's breath, he did not mention it. For a time he nodded slowly, without saying anything, as though making some secret assessment of the situation. Finally he said, 'Then you must be one fucking stupid idiot. You're a liability, Mikey. It's bad enough that you almost killed yourself going so fast on the tractor. I warned you about it, but you don't bloody listen. Now you go trying to kill me, and I'm telling you – that's too fucking far, man. I'm going to have to tell Hayes about this.'

He turned to walk out of the tractor shed. Mikey watched him take a few steps before he felt a roar of blood in his ears. 'Hang on a minute,' he said, and Jack turned back towards him. There was a second in which he registered Jack's expression – questioning, almost courteous – before he punched him hard. And Mikey, who was never lucky in anything, got badly lucky this time: his blow caught Jack square on the chin and made him stagger backwards, causing him to trip over a coiled hose that was lying on the ground. Jack crashed his head on the concrete with enough force to send a spurt of saliva flying out of his mouth. He uttered some sort of groan, then lay completely still.

'That's for calling me an "idiot", *mate*,' said Mikey. He

took another swig of cider while he waited for Jack to stand up.

Jack did not move. His eyes were fixed on a point high up among the rafters. He seemed to be looking up at the barn owl, the 'screech owl', which was blinking down on him with a level gaze. But Jack could no more see it than could Mrs Smith.

Isabel was waiting for Jack too – up at the barn. It was a quarter-past two and she had brought the tea, jostled the door, stepped gingerly across the straw-strewn floor. Now all she had to do was wait. A few sheep being kept in the barn fixed baleful eyes on her, but she tried to avoid their gaze, not wanting to provoke a round of bleating. For thirty minutes she waited, her heart banging in her ribcage as she thought over the things she was going to say. She wanted to tell Jack that she loved him, that she had never felt for anyone else what she felt for him, but that things had changed and she could not see him any more. When forty minutes passed, and then fifty, and he still did not come, she took the tray and cup and walked back home.

She had a drink – a glass of Hayes' whisky – before the children arrived home from school. This was to steel herself before speaking to Mattie. What sort of woman needs a drink before she can talk to her own daughter? For half an hour she waited, silent in the kitchen before the children came clattering home: first Mattie and Tom, then Jennifer. When they sat down to tea Isabel joined them, placing herself at the end of the table, to make a surreptitious study of her younger daughter's reactions. Tea was generally a cheerful occasion at Hill Farm, perhaps because it barely required Isabel to cook anything. Today she had anticipated that Mattie might be subdued or anxious, but if anything, she appeared more ebullient than usual. Jennifer's anecdote about an embarrassing tennis lesson, in which someone's pants had nearly fallen down, prompted as much raucous laughter in Mattie as it did in Tom. Isabel wondered what was going on behind the hazel eyes, the childish brow. Was this the face of a girl whose innocence has been destroyed by her own mother's behaviour? What was she thinking? She felt she ought to know her daughter's mind, but found this effort of interpretation exhausting. Isabel's own subterfuge was beginning to feel like a full-time job. She was having to get up in the morning and make cold arrangements of lies and alibis, as other women of her age laid out arrangements of meats and salads.

Isabel had already resolved that, no matter what the girls at school had told Mattie, she was going to deny all wrongdoing. All other courses were too painful to contemplate. It was hardly likely that any of the girls had actually seen her in the barn with Jack (she shuddered to think such a thing was possible). More likely, they had concocted a story from bits and pieces of gossip and a generous dose of fantasy. That brand of childish innuendo should be easy to gainsay. But the thought of having to establish exactly what Mattie knew, and of the denials and lies that would follow, overwhelmed her and made her feel nauseous. After the children had finished tea and gone outside, Isabel went upstairs to the bathroom and splashed cold water onto her face. When she came out of the bathroom, it was to find Tom waiting by the door.

'What is it, darling?'

'Well, the thing is, I don't know if I'm allowed to tell you.'

'What? Tell me what?'

He started hopping from one foot to the other. 'Well, the thing is, in assembly Mrs Wright said Mattie was a *foolish girl*, in front of the whole school. Because on Tuesday she ran out of school in the rain without telling anyone where she was going. Mrs Wright said it was dangerous and she could have made herself ill.'

'I had better speak to her about it, then, hadn't I?' she said briskly. There could be no shirking the issue now. 'Where is Mattie?'

'Outside, playing on the apple tree.'

Isabel harnessed Tom's indignation as the impetus necessary to carry her downstairs and into the orchard, where she sent him away with an admonition about needing to speak privately to his sister. Then she picked a path through the goose-droppings to the apple tree where Mattie was sitting on a low branch, tunelessly humming a pop song. She seemed not to see her mother until Isabel was standing in front of her.

'Mattie, darling.' Isabel laid a hand on one of Mattie's grubby knees. 'Please tell me what's wrong. Whatever it is, we can sort it out, I'm sure of it. Just tell me what's happened.'

'I don't know what you mean,' said Mattie, looking guiltily away.

'Leaving school yesterday, in the rain, and then getting reprimanded in school . . .'

'Miss Prince promised she wouldn't tell you!'

'She didn't, but Tom told me about assembly. Look, I hate to think of you being in trouble' – and she thought, although she did not say it, 'all because of me'.

Sequestered on a branch, Mattie had no choice then but to tell her mother about Peter and the bullying. And as Isabel listened to the story unfold, she felt an amazing lightening of her spirit because, however bad this was, it was not half as bad as what she had been imagining.

'So you were upset yesterday because of these girls? Because of what they had been saying about you and Peter? And that's why you went to Miss Prince?'

'Yes.'

'There wasn't anything else?'

Mattie shrugged and looked puzzled. 'What else would there be?'

'No, nothing,' Isabel pressed on hurriedly. 'And what about Mrs Wright? Does she want to speak to us: to Daddy and me? Is she going to punish you, or anything?'

'I don't know. I think she might write you a letter.'

Isabel rested her forehead on the branch in front of her and breathed a sigh of relief, which Mattie mistook for despondency.

'It won't be anything serious. There's nothing to worry about, I promise.'

That should have been her line, but Mattie seemed altogether the more authoritative party here. Isabel saw that her daughter had taken one of those mysterious leaps in maturity that children spring on their parents. They seem to grow up in fits and starts, Isabel thought, rather than along the smooth curves described in child-development books.

'You don't have to worry,' Mattie insisted. 'The girls in my class think it's cool that I didn't tell on them. I went to Mrs Wright's office and I took all the blame myself.'

'But it isn't all right, Mattie. They *should* be punished. Especially this Sandra. Her behaviour is unforgivable. Perhaps I ought to go in and speak to Mrs Wright.'

'No! I really don't want you to. Also, Mum, Venetia's asked me round. Her dad keeps vintage cars, and you're allowed to play in them, and dress up in old-fashioned clothes. So, can I go? Please.'

'Of course you can,' Isabel smiled and squeezed Mattie's knee. 'I'm very proud of you, you know.'

How easy it was, to let things go, to pretend everything was fine.

Evening descended on the farmhouse. The Hayes family was in the dark – and not just about that afternoon's altercation in the tractor shed. Power-cuts occurred in the county from time to time and Hayes had learned to be prepared for them, with candles and matches on the mantelpieces or side tables of every downstairs room. Most of their candlesticks were improvised out of old wine bottles. Isabel and Hayes rarely drank wine, but, when they did, she kept the bottles with their pretty labels evoking continental vineyards. One of her favourites had a wicker covering, on which the dripping wax had formed bright-red stalactites that Tom liked to pick off and stick up his nose. Candles were not strictly necessary, this June evening. But the children insisted on having them: they were not to be deprived of the drama of a power-cut, even if it was still light outside.

The lack of electricity had curtailed Isabel's culinary efforts and so, to the children's delight, supper had been tinned macaroni cheese, which they had eaten cold, before carrying their candles through to the sitting room where a log fire was burning. Their house had central heating, but it was used very little and any benefit the system could have brought was lost in a greater regime of draughts. The range kept the kitchen warm, and the sitting-room fire heated, powerfully, a semicircle inside which the family arranged itself in the winter or on days such as these, when clear skies were a prelude to chilly evenings. The rest of the house remained immutably cold, most of the year round.

Hayes was a perfectionist when laying the fire each day, making a complex puzzle of the logs, pieces of coal, twists of newspaper and finally twigs and scraps of kindling. *The Times* was useful on two counts because, once Hayes had lit the fire, he took a double-page spread and held it across the mouth of the chimney, creating a suction effect that caused the flames to roar and blaze behind the newsprint. *The Times* turned translucent for a few seconds – as though with the fervid indignation of its columnists – before Hayes surrendered it to the flames and watched it go whooshing into the chimney. The day's murders and scandals, ingested that morning in the lavatory, were sent up in the evening smoke.

For a few minutes the family was transfixed by fire.

They watched as the flames construed a thousand different combinations of red and yellow, sending some sparks up onto the sooty flue to twinkle briefly, while others leaped out into the room and smouldered on the hearthrug. If a missile looked big enough to cause damage and was accompanied by a smell of singeing, Hayes leaped up, with surprising agility, from his chair to extinguish it before it made a hole in the rug, which was anyway pockmarked from previous attacks. Mattie and Jennifer, watching the flames from the sofa, fell into a kind of trance. Tom preferred to sit right beside the fire, until his cheeks and his ears burned pleasurably. Imagining himself as a kind of surgeon, he kept the bellows, the poker and tongs all to hand, using one implement or another to make minor alterations to the fire, forever adjusting the blaze until his father ordered him to leave it alone.

'This may be our last fire,' said Hayes, 'now that the weather is getting warmer.' There was something sad about the assertion. It signalled an end to the homely season, to the family gathered around the hearth, and a new imperative to go outside and seize whatever opportunities summer would bring. But summer was so often not what one had hoped for, thought Hayes. There was sure to be rain or machinery breakdowns or some other obstruction to the harvest. Picking up his newspaper, he wondered what nasty surprises lay in store for him this year. He was grateful, though, that this summer he would be able to count on the good sense and hard work of a man like Jack.

The children, who were drinking hot chocolate before they went to bed, sat around in thoughtful contemplation.

'Who is your worst, most deadly enemy, Daddy?' asked Tom.

'Pigeons,' said Hayes.

'What would your super-power be?'

'Eradication of pigeons and aphids.'

Hayes rustled his newspaper, indicating that he would rather read than talk. Tom, impervious to hints, stared thoughtfully into the flickering fire. 'You could have a kind of laser gun, or some sort of gungy thing to squirt at them.'

'Well, we do try squirting gungy stuff at aphids. It doesn't always work.' He rustled the paper again. 'Shouldn't you lot be in bed?' It was after nine o'clock, and Isabel ought to have overseen bedtime by now, but she could find no enthusiasm for the task.

'Just five minutes, Daddy,' implored Mattie. 'We are *allowed* to stay up late for special treats.'

'Power-cuts count,' added Tom, in case this had not been understood.

'Remember the day when we all had to stay indoors while that plane sprayed the crops?' asked Jennifer.

'That was cool!' said Tom. 'Did that work?'

'Mr Payne didn't think it was cool,' said Jennifer. 'When he came round to complain, he looked really cross.'

'My super-power would be invisibility. What would yours be, Mummy?'

She did not hear him. Isabel was grateful for the fading light: it meant that she need not arrange her features into a benign mask for the sake of her children. Sitting in the shadows, apart from the others, she was wishing that life were kinder. It would have been wonderful to pursue her relationship with Jack a little longer. If only there could be more ying in life and less yang – or should that be the other way around? If only joy were not always corrected by retribution.

'Mummy!' shouted Tom, causing Isabel to jump in her seat. 'I *said*, what would your super-power be!'

'Oh! I think – well, probably housework that did itself.'

'What about a magic Hoover permanently attached to your arm?'

'That sounds lovely.'

Her first thought after hearing about the saga of the bullies had been: if Mattie does not know about Jack, why not let things continue as before? Since their conversation she had had time to reflect on events with more composure. She took the fact that Mattie did not, after all, know about her affair as a kind of reprieve – but it would be reckless to rely on something of the sort happening again. For one thing, Miss Prince's prurient curiosity was too dangerous to her and to the family. Now, as she sat in the gloomy half-light, her body was alive with a tension that made it impossible to keep still. She kept crossing and recrossing her legs, while her fingers fiddled with the loose braiding on her chair's seat. She wanted to see Jack and he was so *close* – only yards away. Why had he not come to the barn after lunch? Perhaps some business on the farm had kept him away, or was it because of something she had done? She had turned away when he tried to kiss her that morning; she had not let him touch her cheek. It caused her anguish to think about this now. But surely Jack had known how much she had wanted to kiss him! Perhaps it would do no harm to see him now, for a few minutes, as a kind of leave-taking. She wanted him to know that, in spite of everything, she loved him. The afternoon that they had frightened off the swans, he had joked that she was ungrateful. She wanted to tell him how grateful she was for all that he had brought her.

'You know, I don't think Jack has any candles in the cottage,' she announced. 'I should probably take him some over.' She made her voice weary, as though this were a necessary chore, but as soon as she said it aloud, Isabel was struck by the genius of her idea.

'Surely he can make do?' said Hayes, frowning slightly. He was squinting at the paper, a candle throwing shifting shapes onto the wall beyond him. 'And what about the children? Are they ever going upstairs? Has bedtime been abolished or something?'

'They're perfectly capable of going up on their own!' she retorted. 'I don't have to do everything, do I?'

'Precisely my point. Jack's a resourceful young man, after all. He doesn't need mollycoddling. I don't think a power-cut will be the end of the world for him.'

It enraged her that anyone should try to stand in the way of her plan. She felt like shooting back with something hurtful, but instead she waited, and after a minute she said, 'But soon it will be dark and he may not know what's going on. I think I should at least go over and explain the situation.'

Hayes shrugged, causing a shadowy commotion on the wall. 'Well, if you think it's absolutely necessary.'

'I do really, all things considered.'

She went as quickly as possible to the back door, grabbed a coat and was about to rush out when she remembered that she should also take a torch and some candles from the drawer in the kitchen. Outside, the sky was a darkening indigo. On the approach to the cottage she could see that there was no light showing anywhere, so Jack must be sitting in the dark. As she arrived at the gate that led into the little front garden, Isabel felt such immense joy at the thought of seeing him that she seemed to be floating. It was extraordinary that the prospect merely of seeing someone could cause such euphoria. She sketched some romantic vignette around their meeting in the dusk, how they would fumble for each other's faces and lips. So certain was she that Jack was close that, when a figure stepped out from behind the hedge, she cried out in delighted alarm.

It was Mikey, though. He was getting good at scaring people in the dark.

'God, you gave me a shock!' Isabel had to keep up the display of delight, animating her features, so as not to give herself away – it would not do to let her face record any sign of disappointment.

Blinking, Mikey said, 'Sorry, Mrs Hayes, I was just looking for Jack.'

'Well, so was I,' said Isabel cheerfully. 'I thought he might need some candles.' She held the box up and rattled it, to prove the substance of her alibi.

'Yeah? Yeah, right, that's a good idea.' Mikey nodded hard, then appeared to remember something. 'But he's not at home, though.'

'I see. Were you looking for him, too? Of course – you just said you were!'

'Me? Oh, yeah, I just thought he might like to go down the pub. But he's probably already down there.'

'Oh. That's a nice idea. Yes, that's probably where he

is.' An evening at the pub sounded appealing and for a moment Isabel felt crestfallen, to think of Jack having a life beyond this farm – and her. She had been so absorbed by their romance that it had not occurred to her to think that he would have other friends and other things to do, but of course he must: he was younger than her and did not have a family here – he was bound to need friends. It surprised her, all the same, that Mikey was one of them. The figure standing before her was more like a boy than a man, with such a gloomy and woebegone manner and so little of interest to say. Isabel supposed that he must have hidden depths. The pub was the place where such depths might be fathomed – she saw that now. In fact, had Jack not mentioned that he was there last night? She and Hayes went to the pub occasionally, but her husband never wanted to sit in the public bar where there was often a throng of people and an inviting fug of smoke. Hayes preferred the chilly solitude of the saloon, with its framed pictures and table service. They had sometimes been the only people there and, when Hazel brought their ploughman's lunches through, snatches of shouted conversations and laughter billowed in with her through the swinging doors. Hazel's throat and cleavage, glistening with sweat, seemed to bear the imprint of next door's warmth and jollity.

She could imagine Jack in the centre of such a throng now, for Isabel, like Mikey, was so preoccupied by ulterior thoughts that it did not occur to her that the pub might be closed because of the power-cut. Hoping to hide her disappointment, she made herself sound deliberately brisk.

'Well, if you do see Jack, and if it turns out that he needs candles, just tell him to come and ask me tomorrow. God knows how long these strikes are going to continue.' She began to walk away, then turned back to him: 'It's getting dark – are you sure you'll be all right walking down to the pub? I can lend you my torch if you like.'

'Oh no, that's all right, Mrs Hayes,' said Mikey. 'I'm used to the dark.'

The following morning Hayes was driving back from a meeting with the bank manager and brooding on Mr Payne. It was not so much a fear of the AONB inspectors that worried him. He thought it was unlikely they would come; if they did, they might impose a fine, but it would be nothing when set against the advantage of having that big new field. It was more a feeling that he was being wilfully misunderstood by a tireless antagonist. Ever since Mr Payne had arrived on the farm he had felt himself under siege, pursued with questions about steroids, sulphates and intensive farming. No matter what he did, he was cast as the pantomime villain. He wanted to tell Mr Payne that the countryside was not the rural paradise so often imagined by city-dwellers. It had always harboured horrors as well as beauty. This part of Sussex, for instance, had once been notorious for hoodlums and armed gangs hiding out in the woods. You would be lucky to travel on a road like this one without running into a highwayman: who would have wanted the 'right to roam' then? Then there were famine and disease, harvests so bad that the corpses of starved men and women were left lying by the road. In these days of antibiotics and easy remedies, people simply forgot how dangerous life had once been. If they needed reminding, they should visit the graveyard at St Cuthbert's and look at the graves of sixteen children who had died in the 1920s, after an outbreak of diptheria caused by unclean water.

Hayes pulled off the village road into the farm, turned off the engine and let the car rumble down the hill. As he drew in front of the farmhouse he saw that another car was there. It was Bourne's swanky Land Rover – not a speck of mud anywhere on it – and there was Bourne, standing waiting for him, grinning like a simpleton.

'Ah! I have two words for you,' said Bourne as Hayes swung his heavy frame out of the car. 'The Charolais.'

'And I have one for you,' said Hayes, straightening up. 'Ditches.'

'Oh, Gawd.' Bourne groaned and clapped one hand to his brow theatrically. 'You're really not going to let me forget about them, are you?'

'Certainly not. I've told you: find out which ditches are yours, or we agree to split the cost of servicing all the ditches between my land and yours.'

'All right, all right. Now can we go and look at the Charolais?'

'By all means.'

Bourne's heifers were in a field beside the barn at the top of the farm, standing like monuments on the brow of the hill. Jack had been bringing them out here every day to exercise before herding them back indoors, because it was only two months now until the shows and it was important to keep them clean and free from parasites.

The two farmers leaned together on a fence. Neither

man knew that the Charolais had been out all night, because Jack had not come to take them inside the day before.

'White cattle do look terrific on green grass, don't you think?' said Bourne cheerfully.

'Is that why you wanted them, Harry?'

'You know me: I can't resist a pretty girl,' said Bourne.

Two or three of the heifers turned to look at him with docile expressions. One urinated, lifting her tail in a dainty curlicue to keep it clear of the yellow jet.

'Look at those backs – straight as rods! Look at the strong forelegs, the muscling. Lovely animals. Butchers love them too, you know, because the carcass produces the right cuts for today's market.' Bourne turned his ruddy features towards Hayes. 'You don't see their attraction?'

'Yes,' said Hayes.

'But?'

'Sometimes it seems as though we think everything foreign is better. We used to want to keep Europe at arm's length. Now we're all for cosying up to them: digging tunnels under the sea so that we can get even closer. We're no longer proud to be an island.'

'They'll probably never get round to the tunnel. As for Europe, it can only be a good thing, Hayes. We British farmers have never known how to stand up for ourselves, but the French are much bolshier. They'll do our fighting for us.' He slapped a meaty hand on Hayes' shoulder. 'Why don't you join me in this Charolais business? We'll make our fortunes.'

'It would be a new departure, for sure,' said Hayes. 'Anyway, tell me how you are going to prepare them for this show? Are you going to teach them tricks? Song-and-dance routines?'

'Ha-ha, very good! Jack's going to spend some time with them in the halter, so that they get used to the feel of it. They'll need to wear it for half an hour each day. Then on the day itself we need to shampoo them and brush them all over to make their hair nice and fluffy. Jack's been looking over all the requirements – I'm sure he has it in hand. Where is Jack, by the way?'

'I had to go to an early meeting at the bank, so I haven't seen him this morning, but he was supposed to be doing some spraying for me. He should be up in the top field. Shall we walk up there and see?'

'Come on, then.'

As they walked further up the hill together, two sturdy men planting sturdy feet on the ground, it dawned on Hayes that he actually rather liked the company of Bourne. He brought up the incident with Mr Payne and the hedgerow – telling the story with some trepidation, because Bourne himself was a city type and he could not be sure where his allegiance would lie. To his relief and satisfaction, Bourne agreed entirely with him, lambasting Mr Payne as a 'coward' and a 'little shit' for daring to threaten Hayes on his own land. It was very pleasurable to hear Mr Payne described in such terms. Speaking as a lawyer, Bourne went on, he could not see that Hayes had any case to answer. They were still talking about this as they reached the field where Jack was supposed to be working. Here they found another fence to lean on and continue their discussion about farming and the environmental lobby.

'People want cheap food, and plenty of it,' said Hayes.

'But they also want the corn fields to be full of poppies and cornflowers, and aphids for the ladybirds to eat. They want us to look after the countryside, but only if we do it their way and without making any mess or smells. We can't win.'

'The British only ever like farmers when there's a war on,' agreed Bourne. 'What we need is another war, Hayes. That would shake things up!'

So they stood talking for quite some time before there was a lull in the conversation and they remembered the reason for coming to the field.

'Now where is he? Where's he got to?' asked Hayes, scanning the field with his hand shading his eyes. 'Shall we go in?'

There was a kissing gate to be negotiated before the men could gain access to the field, then they strode to the middle of it and looked in all directions. There was no sign of anyone working anywhere.

'Where the hell is Jack?' asked Bourne.

TEN

When Hayes had set off to see the bank manager first thing that Friday morning he had left Isabel and the children at home, preparing for school. Isabel, entirely preoccupied by the previous day's events and her failure to see Jack, made breakfast without a word, laying out the things mechanically, paying no heed to her children's hullabaloo. Afterwards, in her room, she sat on her bed gazing out of the window at a cloud bank bulging with rain. A mile away across the valley it was raining already and the distant hills appeared sheathed in a fine gauze, while the nearer fields were glossy with the anticipation of rain. Living at the juncture of several different weather systems, the inhabitants of the British Isles rarely know which climatic phenomena may assail them next. So often their best-laid plans are wrecked by unexpected rain or wind. And now the quality of the wind blowing through Isabel's open window changed suddenly, becoming both sharper and colder, as though riding the same Siberian front that had once brought the swans south. It felt ominous, Isabel thought with a shudder: a wind of change.

'There is a terrible tangle here,' she said quietly, as much to herself as to Mattie, who was sitting on the bed beside her. 'I hope you won't hate me.'

Mattie braced herself. She had discerned a darkening in her mother's mood that morning. Of all the children, she was the most alive to alterations in Isabel's tone and manner. Over the last few weeks she had not been unmindful of the changes in her mother's posture and dress, along with a lighter disposition, a greater readiness to smile and laugh, even while cooking. The source of that transforming happiness was as much a mystery to Mattie as was today's despondency, but then adult behaviour struck her as mysterious generally. Her fear was that her own problems at school were to blame for the unhappy atmosphere and Mattie hated to think that she could have upset her mother, when usually she tried so hard to please. Jennifer was often caustic at home, but Mattie took pride in being her opposite – she was the kind-hearted daughter, the one who collected posies of wild flowers for birthdays or made haphazard cupcakes on Mother's Day. It did cross her mind, though, that there was another possible reason for her mother to be upset: she had heard her speaking on the telephone to Miss Prince, postponing a social arrangement, and her voice had sounded oddly clipped. Perhaps they had argued and were not friends any more; Mattie knew that having a best friend was complicated. So, although she usually protested about the pain caused by her mother's combing, this time she said nothing, fixing her eyes on the rose-patterned wallpaper as Isabel tackled a particularly intractable knot.

Insufficient hair-brushing was an acknowledged failing in the Hayes family. The girls both had thick hair that was prone to tangles, while Tom's hair was often found to be harbouring lice. Yet when they were little their hair had been so soft, Isabel thought. She remembered how, when they were first old enough to sit up, she used to place them on a tartan rug in the orchard outside the kitchen window, facing away from her so that they would not see their mother standing at the sink and immediately demand her company. For a few minutes they were contented, freed from that urgent love of babyhood as they listened to birdsong and looked at the patterns made by sunlit leaves. She could get on with the washing up, meanwhile gazing on the soft folds of their infant necks and their woolly curls unobserved. Isabel still found it immeasurably poignant to look down on her children's heads, as she must often do, when delousing or sorting out tangles, and think how much she loved them.

Now she bent and kissed the top of Mattie's head. 'I think that's got it all out. Thank you for being patient.' Then, still bending over the child, she added, 'I am so sorry that I didn't know about the bullying at school. I wish that you had told me.'

Mattie had resisted the pain inflicted by the comb, but could not resist this sorrowful tone of her mother's and immediately started to cry. Interpreting these tears as a delayed reaction to the events at school, Isabel put down her comb and took Mattie in her arms.

'Darling, why didn't you tell me about all this business with Peter? It would have been easy to put right. It makes me angry to think—'

'But I know you have lots of worries, and I was trying not to upset you!' Mattie burst out. 'Anyway, it's all over now, I told you that. I *did* explain. Is the tangle gone?' Her mother's cheek felt to have been resting against her head for a long time. 'No offence, but you seem to be in a bit of a daze.'

'Yes, I'm sorry!' said Isabel, coming to her senses with a start. 'We'd better get off to school.'

At the manor house the High Sheriff was eating a late breakfast in preparation for a morning he planned to spend rounding up new blood for the parish council. Breakfast at the manor house was a formal affair: the sheriff's boiled egg came accompanied by a silver spoon that bore the family crest. A toast-rack, cruets, salvers, salt cellars – all of them similarly embellished – adorned the table. His wife grumbled that it meant their cleaning lady had to spend too much time polishing silver. He was well aware that she thought him a snob, not understanding that this was a way to honour a connection with his youth and his long-deceased parents.

'I'm off, dear.' It was by now about ten o'clock. The High Sheriff dabbed his mouth with a napkin and rose carefully from the table.

'Do be careful,' said his wife. 'Remember your knees.'

Remember them? He could scarcely forget the buggers! Both his knee joints were arthritic and hurt, particularly in the morning. He picked out a walking stick from the collection by the door and set off through the village, greeting passers-by with a smile and a shake of his silver-topped cane, as though they were loyal subjects and he a benign autocrat. The road through Hill Farm leading down to Hayes' house was steep and he had to descend it with the care of a mountaineer, for fear his knees would buckle underneath him. As he walked, he rehearsed in his mind the lines he meant to say to Hayes about the importance of having farmers on the parish council: at the moment there were none, and there was a danger of village affairs becoming dominated by people who seemed not to have much sympathy with rural ways. The vicar was very friendly, but he had lived in London until recently and spoke a kind of urban language the High Sheriff did not fully understand. Jean Temple, who usually seemed so reasonable, had complained about the insensitivity of farmers in matters of conservation. There were a couple of newcomers – he forgot their names – who had been heard to grumble about the messiness of trailers carrying bales of straw down the farm lanes. What did they expect? This was a farming community, not a park.

As he rounded the corner towards the farmhouse the High Sheriff saw not one, but two farmers – Hayes and Bourne – standing together with Isabel Hayes.

'Ah, good morning!' he cried, waving his stick at them. 'Isn't it a splendid day?' As he drew nearer the group he said to Hayes, 'I haven't seen you for a long time. Now tell me: what did you make of the pheasants?'

'They were excellent,' said Hayes, 'very . . .' But he could not think of any suitable adjective, and his mouth moved around as though he was still chewing on that tough old bird. He was confounded for the moment; all three of them were covered in awkwardness.

Wanting to explain, Isabel said, 'I'm sorry, you've come at a difficult time. We've lost a labourer.' She had learned of Jack's absence less than an hour ago. Hearing herself voice it aloud set her heart banging in her chest and, to compose herself, she had to look away, over the fields, at some light glinting across the valley.

'Sorry, bad ear,' shouted the High Sheriff, swivelling his head to present her with a better alternative. 'Say again?'

'We're missing a labourer,' shouted Bourne. 'A stockman, nice fellow, an Australian. He was expected for work this morning and never arrived, according to the fellow he works with. Name's Jack. Do you know him?'

The High Sheriff thought hard for a moment, and a memory came to him of the jumble sale, of Isabel laughing admiringly at the antics of a dynamic young man in a checked shirt. He could not be sure, though, that this was a genuine memory and not a dream – he often confused the two – so he thought it safer to shake his head and say, 'No.'

'Actually, we were just going over to his cottage now,' said Hayes, 'but if you need to speak—'

'No, don't let me stop you,' said the sheriff, who was pleased to have stumbled on a drama in what might otherwise have been an uneventful morning. Looking towards the cottage, he added hopefully, 'Is that the crime scene?'

'Well, I sincerely hope not!' said Bourne.

'I mean, one hears cases of people fainting and knocking themselves out,' said the High Sheriff. 'It can easily happen, if you're working hard, on insufficient calories.'

That seemed an unlikely scenario but, all the same, the presence of the High Sheriff, with his silver-topped cane, lent the group authority, warranting their further investigation.

The four of them made their way down the short path that led to the cottage, past the hedges and under a confusion of briar roses that caught in Bourne's hair and required some dextrous disentanglement on Isabel's part. The front door was unlocked. Hayes opened it a crack, then called tentatively: 'Jack?'

They waited. Hayes looked questioningly at Bourne, who passed the look, unaltered, on to the High Sheriff, who said, 'Well, I think you should go on in.'

Isabel, struggling to maintain composure, looked away again, up at the scudding clouds.

Hayes pushed the door open wide then, and called again, 'Jack? Are you all right? We're coming in.'

Inside, the cottage was much as Isabel had last seen it. In the kitchen, spread out on the table, were the components of what appeared to have been a hurried lunch. The other downstairs room, a small sitting room, showed no sign of disturbance. Jack rarely used this room, preferring to sit in the kitchen and listen to the radio in the evenings.

'I'll look in the bedroom and the bathroom,' said Hayes. They let him go first, fearing some grisly scene awaited.

The High Sheriff turned back to Isabel and said, confidingly, 'You know, it's also possible to faint in the bathroom, perhaps, and knock your head on the tiles. Or to slip after getting out of the bath. All too easy. Happens very, very often.'

The observation was made so close to Isabel's face that she could smell marmalade on his breath. She sensed that the sheriff would like to list other sorts of fatal domestic accidents, but she could not bear to hear about them. She cut him short by nodding, tight-lipped, and looking away.

When Hayes called down that there was no one upstairs, Isabel and the others followed, in creaking procession, up the steep staircase. The last time she had climbed these stairs it had been to have sex with Jack. In his room the bed was unmade and the quilt Isabel had lent him lay crumpled and pushed to one side. She could imagine him throwing it off and rising naked from the bed. He always got up early.

Now all of them filed into the room.

'Well, he isn't here,' said Hayes, hands on his hips. 'I'm stumped. I think we must assume that he's done a bunk.'

'Surely not!' cried Isabel.

'Well, you have to wonder,' said Bourne, stroking his upper lip.

It was a small room with few objects in it other than the unmade bed, and it was upon this centrepiece that the three men became balefully fixated. For a horrified moment Isabel imagined that a ghostly hologram of her love-making with Jack could somehow have become printed in the air. The High Sheriff used his stick to prod at the bedclothes and then to lift them up, revealing the secret territory of the sheets underneath. That struck Isabel as such an incursion that she wanted to protest. When she opened her mouth, though, she could find no convenient sound to force through it.

'It's very unfair on Isabel,' said Hayes, finally.

Isabel felt herself flush. 'Why? No, not at all – it's—'

'Well, because you went to so much effort to make the place nice for him. All the furnishings and the pictures – you fitted him out royally. Even last night you were out in the cold and dark to bring him candles. You went out of your way, Isabel, it has to be said.'

'And he's thrown it in your face,' said Bourne, with sympathy.

'I'm sure that he didn't mean to,' Isabel stammered. 'There must be a misunderstanding. I think something must have happened that we don't know about.' She heard her own voice growing suspiciously shrill. More calmly she said, 'There's bound to be an explanation.'

She fixed her eyes on the quilt, which showed a pattern of Dutch milkmaids carrying buckets on a yoke, and which had for years been folded at the top of the airing cupboard in the farmhouse. She thought of the countless times she had seen it there, when retrieving blankets and towels from the cupboard or returning them there, never guessing that one day she would lie naked on it as a handsome young man kissed her throat and breasts. She saw now that objects have secret histories, and secret futures, too. All those years of journeying back and forth from the airing cupboard had been leading to one luminous moment of ecstasy with Jack, and now they would stretch away from it again, into a fathomless future.

Bourne cleared his throat. 'I think I must shoulder the blame for this. I confess . . .' he began to say, but then his face went suddenly red, as though someone had grabbed his tie and yanked it. He cleared his throat again and rearranged his feet, planting them more squarely on the floor, rooting himself in preparation for the confession that was coming. 'You see, I had my doubts about Jack. I knew that his papers weren't entirely in order.' Bourne folded his arms, and the fleshiness of his arms and chest made this a somewhat bulbous arrangement.

'Oh, well,' said the High Sheriff. 'We need look no further.'

'Quite,' said Bourne, looking at his feet. 'He came here

on a student visa, and I admit that I knew that when I took him on. He wasn't officially entitled to work, but he was just such a bloody nice chap and bloody good at what he did, so I didn't think it really mattered. I thought it was very unlikely to be a problem – we've had chaps in that kind of situation before, cash in hand, no National Insurance number, sort of thing . . . Well, I hold my hands up. Guilty as charged.' Then he actually did hold his hands up, drawing the attention of the others to the red, meaty fingers and the gold signet ring jammed onto the smallest of them.

The sheriff surveyed the surrendering man with curiosity. He was wondering how to use this admission of guilt as a bargaining tool when it came to recruitment for the parish council. The men were always harder to noose, but once you had them rounded up, their women-folk often followed. The men could mow and the women do the cleaning and flowers – that was the ideal arrange-ment. Bourne would be a fine addition, but the sheriff's back was beginning to ache now and he very much wanted to sit down. 'Well, I think we have our solution.' He looked hopefully at Isabel. 'Shall we all have a cup of tea?'

'Hang on a minute,' said Hayes. 'Do you mean to say that Jack's done a runner because of some mix-up over his papers?'

'It's entirely plausible,' said the High Sheriff. 'Plenty of young men come into the country looking for casual work of this kind. I take it there was no contract?'

'No.' Bourne rubbed his lower lip with his finger, then bit the corner of it.

'Well, you see it means there's nothing at all to hold

him here. Perhaps he got into some sort of unpleasant-ness, some kind of disagreement, and decided to cut his losses. He had nothing to stay for. There was absolutely nothing to keep him here. It's a lack of gumption, a lack of backbone – that's the problem with—'

'It just seems out of character,' interrupted Hayes. 'He was a very hard worker and always a charming person to deal with – didn't you think, Isabel?'

'Yes, charming,' said Isabel, with some considerable effort. She found the presence of these three in Jack's bedroom, standing around the bed where they had lain together, almost impossible to bear.

'Ah, well – if you'll forgive me – charmers are usually the worst!' The High Sheriff directed the comment, accom-panied by hearty laughter, at Isabel.

'I'll go back to the farmhouse and put the kettle on,' said Isabel, her voice almost a whisper. She walked back down the stairs towards the front door, then paused at the entrance to the kitchen and, glancing inside, caught sight of Jack's corduroy jacket on the back of a chair. There is nothing more forlorn than the sight of objects whose owners are missing, for even a mundane possession seems imbued with the character of the person who chose it. When events are mysterious, one feels that objects may hold a solution, some locked-in knowledge about what has happened. Isabel picked up the jacket and held it to her face, inhaling Jack's smell, laying her cheek against the fabric. A thought struck her and, gingerly, she looked in his pockets; nothing was there. Then she cast around the room for clues. Most of the objects here were, of course, not his, but hers: there was a pretty china set that had belonged to her mother and used to accompany the family on day-trips to the seaside. The big brown teapot was one they had used for years at home; the electric kettle she and Hayes had bought as an experiment, before deciding that they preferred the ritual associated with a kettle boiling on the hob. On the table were a plate, half a loaf of bread, cheese and a jar of pickle – the detritus of the last meal Jack had eaten here in the cottage. That must have been yesterday's lunch, thrown together not long before the time he was due to meet her in the barn. It made no sense: if he was suddenly going to leave, would he not at least have cleared these things away? But now her terrible fear was that she had driven him away. He had been going to see her, as planned, then decided against it at the last minute, opting to 'cut his losses' as the High Sheriff had said, and go. *There was absolutely nothing to keep him here.*' Perhaps he had felt, in a stronger measure than her, guilt about betraying Hayes, fear of causing him harm. Then again, what sort of guilt or fear allowed you to eat a cheese sandwich before your getaway, but not to clear it up? If you had the presence of mind to prepare a sandwich, why would you forget your jacket?

'Ah, you're still here.' Bourne appeared then, in the kitchen door. 'Find anything?' He gestured at the jacket.

'No,' she said. 'He left his lunch things.'

'Yes, well, we're going to have a good sort through everything now and see if we can find anything useful – you know, phone numbers and so on.'

'You didn't have anything?'

'No, I never asked for it. Don't ask me why. Madness, to employ someone on a farm and not take details of next of kin. I don't know what I was thinking of.' Bourne screwed his hand into a fist and used it to deliver little hammer blows on his ruddy forehead. With a sigh he said, 'It would be good for me to know at least that he is OK, you know?' He chewed the corner of his lip again.

The words 'next of kin' brought vividly before her the possibility of Jack's death, one that she dismissed with force. Surely the room around her belonged to a living man! A dead man does not leave an open jar of pickle on the table, or a load in the washing machine. A dead man's room, she thought, would be suffused with some kind of vapour, like the icy mist that moved through their valley on winter mornings, above which the farmhouse seemed to float. There would be a stasis about everything inside it, each object so tender with meaning that one handled it with the same hesitation due a ripe peach. There was too much life in here. But, looking at Bourne, she could see that he really was worried and she remembered then how his little boy, Peter, sitting at the kitchen table in a duffel coat, had chewed his lip with the same expression of anxiety. Isabel could not allow herself to join him in that concern; she refused to countenance such a dreadful fear, so she smiled at Bourne and said, 'I think there is nothing to worry about. There must be an explanation for all of this.'

'I hope you're right,' he said.

As she went past him to the front door, she smiled again and patted his arm, then walked back to the farmhouse without bothering to look across the valley. The panorama had entirely changed its meaning since the previous day. Its 'outstanding beauty' was dead to her now.

* * *

In the kitchen she heaved the great kettle onto one of the hobs. So long as a kettle was boiling nothing could be wrong: there was no more reassuring sound than water quickening. In the past, on particularly miserable days, Isabel had sometimes boiled the kettle just to obtain that reassurance, with no firm thought of wanting any tea. It was thanks to Jack that that time of desperate sorrow seemed so long ago: he had rescued her from it. But now he, too, seemed to be travelling away from her, back in time, leaving her stranded in an uncertain present. If it was really true that he had gone, then Isabel would have to fight not to succumb once more to melancholy. She pictured, with dread, a future ordained by routine: new coats, new shoes, geometry sets, colds and stomach bugs, sports days, Sunday roasts, lasagne for special occasions and sometimes a ploughman's at the pub. Hers would be a life measured in socks, and shopping lists, sweetened by regular cups of tea, as she surrendered to the passing days and years. In the future, when she looked back, she would come to see her love for Jack as one glorious interruption in the cycle, and all too brief.

She began, in a desultory fashion, to prepare a salad for lunch but, all too soon, Bourne and Hayes returned to the house. The High Sheriff was not with them, having continued down to the village, where preparations were underway for the next day's fête. The men stood together at the doorway. Bourne leaned his forearm against the top of the frame and allowed his torso to bulge into the room.

'Well?' said Isabel.

'We've been through everything,' said Hayes. 'He's left behind some clothes and a few bits and pieces. But his passport and wallet, money and so on, have definitely gone. So our conclusion is that he's taken off, scarpered.'

'It makes sense,' said Bourne. 'After all, he got his wages yesterday. He waited until payday. There's no money to be found there.'

'I don't understand,' said Isabel. 'Why would he leave his clothes?'

'Well, they're just working clothes, pretty worn through, to be honest. If he's on his way to the continent he won't need them.'

Isabel thought, without saying anything, that that was not the way people behaved. Even on the continent, clothes were needed. Besides, she disliked all this jolly terminology used to describe Jack's departure. He was not the kind to 'scarper', to 'bunk off' or 'do a runner'.

'Are you going to report him missing to the police?'

'When he's taken his money and passport with him? I can't see any reason for it. No crime has been committed, after all. And we don't have his family's address or contact details. He's probably halfway to the next place by now – wherever that is.'

'He said he was interested in going to Barcelona,' Isabel said suddenly. 'He'd been reading about the anarchists in the Civil War.'

'Had he now?' said Bourne. He nodded grimly, as though this information explained everything. 'Well, there you go. I never knew he had those tendencies. You just can't tell what people are like, can you?'

'Perhaps we should telephone – some sort of consulate or . . .' Her throat was tightening around the words as she spoke them.

'I think that's excessive, love,' said Hayes. 'We need to talk to Mikey to see if he knows anything. Perhaps Jack spoke to him before he left, or gave him a message for us.' Then he said to Bourne, 'Is it worth your looking at home to see if you can find any contact details for his relations?'

'Yes, of course, I'll look. But I don't think I . . . but of course I will look.' Bourne was staring at the floor despondently.

'I'm sorry, Harry. This leaves you in a bit of a fix with the Charolais.'

'No, I'm sorry,' said Bourne, looking up. 'I'm the one who foisted Jack on you, after all. As for the cattle, the best thing may be to move them to a show specialist for final preparation. They can get properly groomed there and prepared for the show. I'll sort that out as soon as I can.' He glanced at his watch. 'I should go now.'

Their mutual apologies set the tone for a kind of reconciliation. Bourne shook Hayes' hand, clapping him on the shoulder. Then he walked towards Isabel, as though planning an embrace. But neither of them could overcome their cultural embarrassment, so instead he patted Isabel on the arm, returning the gesture she had made in the cottage.

In the wake of Jack's disappearance a restlessness pervaded the house, which seemed to shift on its very foundations. That was no illusion. Years earlier a surveyor had come to Hill Farm, with moisture meters and a stethoscope, to make a structural report. A disappointed-looking man, neatly mustachioed, he had spent a morning delving in the cellar, before revealing to Hayes that the house was moving down the hill: 'about a quarter of an inch every ten years'. At night they heard it trying to move, groaning and creaking, such a creaking as might make you think of the High Sheriff genuflecting in church.

'All of us are going downhill,' thought Hayes, brooding in his armchair that evening. He had been watching the news and found nothing to console himself in the litany of bombs and murders.

Upstairs, Isabel paced the creaking corridor in a ferment of despair, causing all the furniture to knock against the walls and the windows to judder in their frames. Her first reaction to the news of Jack's disappearance had been muted, for bewilderment had brought its own tranquillising properties. Now her mind was racing with possible explanations and imagined catastrophes. She had kept a mental catalogue of every conversation, every gesture between Jack and herself. Obsessively now she revisited the details of them all, scouring them for meaning, making merciless inventories of all that she had done and said, or failed to do and say. She could find no occupation that would soothe her, even though there were cupboards and drawers that needed her attention. She walked towards the tallboy, thinking she might rearrange the linen and then, hearing Hayes go out of the back door, decided instead to pick up the handpiece to the upstairs telephone and dialled a local number. The telephone rang three times before it was answered by a familiar voice.

'Sheila?' Isabel's voice rose scarcely above a whisper.

'Isabel! My dear, is that you?' said Miss Prince. 'Are you all right?'

'He's gone, Sheila, without saying goodbye – or

anything.' Sobs rose violently in her throat and she choked on the words. 'I don't know if I'll ever see him again . . .'

There was a silence on the other end of the line.

'Are you still there?' Isabel heard herself sound like a frightened child. 'I don't know what to do. Tell me what to do!'

'My dear, I'm sure that he will come back. Something unforeseen must have happened. Perhaps he has left a note, to explain everything?'

'A note?' She seized on this word, as though it actually signified hard currency. With the back of her hand Isabel wiped her nose and eyes. She had never even thought to look! 'I didn't ever – perhaps I should go now and see if . . .'

'And you know that you are always welcome to come here and—'

Isabel set down the receiver, extinguishing Miss Prince's voice. She hurried downstairs and over to the cottage. The door had been left unlocked and everything was as it had been that morning, but in the evening's half-light the scene inside the kitchen was already acquiring the sombre quality of an aftermath. The room's contents looked like ghosts of themselves. With a lurching feeling she thought of all the things she had been so eager to bring over to the cottage – box upon box of crockery and household items – that would have to be packed up and taken away again. Never mind that now: time was short and, much as she would have liked to linger here (lying where he had lain, touching the things he had touched) her plan was to make a quick survey of every room, ransacking drawers, cupboards and boxes, anything that might contain a clue to Jack's where-abouts and intentions.

When she had worked through every room and found nothing, Isabel returned to the kitchen doorway and stood contemplating the clutter on the table once more. As she stood there, looking into the kitchen, words drifted back to her from their first conversation in this room, that evening she had come to the cottage bringing him things for the house. What was it Jack had said? *'I've probably been guilty of trying to escape things. I was afraid of getting bored. I didn't want to be trapped.'*

As the words played over in her mind, the scene before her began to make a ghastly sense. Isabel saw that there was no great mystery here: Jack had got bored, that was all. He had waited to collect his wages, then moved on. The escapee had even left his dirty dishes for someone else to wash. Smart move! She picked up a plate from the table and let it drop, taking satisfaction in the way it smashed onto the tiles. 'That one won't need washing!' she said. Then she sank, wretched, onto the floor, her face in her hands.

It was long after midnight, and a full moon lit up the sky, casting a storybook glimmer on the valley below. Moonlight glinted through a chink in the curtain, on the fragment of mirror affixed to Tom's half-made periscope. Mattie and Jennifer were asleep, but Tom lay awake and thought of all the creatures that were active at night: the owl on the prowl for rodents, the fox sniffing around their goose shed, the bats and rats, the badgers ambling and snuffling around their sett. By daylight he was not afraid of these creatures – he even liked most of them. It was their furtive activity while humans slept that chilled him. He would prefer all living creatures to keep the same hours; it was not right that some were awake while others slept.

His bed, in the room he shared with Mattie, was tucked under the eaves and sometimes Tom could hear the scampering of clawed feet very close to his face. His mother attributed the noise to birds, but he thought it sounded more like four-footed creatures. What if there were mice, or even rats, living in the rafters, patiently nibbling a hole through from their world to his? There certainly were rats living in the barn next to the farmhouse. They had gnawed a sizeable hole in one of the doors, and fed on spillages of grain on the floor inside. Once he had seen a really fat specimen sitting on a step outside the barn, holding a grain in its claws while its belly flopped over its back feet. It looked like a fairytale villain, with all those rolls of fat and an expression of wickedness. Then there was the time that he and he and Mattie had seen a dead rat, stretched out on the road. Its lips were pulled across snarling teeth as though it had been killed mid-leap. They had raced back to the farmhouse to deliver the news, but then spoiled the impact of their story by arguing over the size of the animal. Mattie said it was as big as a rabbit, while Tom thought it was as big as a cat. Mattie had once told him that rats jump at your throat when they are scared. It made Tom shudder to imagine such a thing. He pulled his blankets over his head and tried to tuck them around his ears.

Everything seemed more intense in this dark, under-blanket world. Tom practised some belching, which reminded him of church. He wondered if God could still see him, underneath the blanket. It used to be that, when they went to church, they had to confirm their belief in God as the maker of things that were 'visible and invisible'. Since the new vicar had arrived, the words had been changed to 'seen and unseen'. No explanation was given for the change, and it was one that troubled Tom. He was happy to acknowledge the presence of invisible forces. After all, there were superheroes who could make themselves invisible in order to frustrate the plans of criminals. Things that were 'unseen' were altogether more menacing. The word put him in mind of the strange noises that gurgled from pipes or emanated from the attic. Their father had urged the children to look beneath the surface of things, but Tom was daunted by this instruction.

Fear drove him further under his bedclothes and into a tented world smelling of lavender. It concerned him, however, to think that the very top of his head was still exposed. A solution might be to move right to the bottom of the bed, but he dreaded to think what terrors lurked down there. He felt his exhaled breath settling like a warm mist on his cheeks, and it occurred to him that it might be possible to run out of oxygen should he remain under the bedclothes, but he also felt too frightened to venture out from them. He thought how sad his mother would be, if she were to find him here dead in the morning when she came to wake him up for school, but he could think of no way to avoid it, so he faced this eventuality with a helpless resignation. The picture of her sadness affected him more than the thought of his own death, and he began to cry.

Tom delivered himself a rebuking kick; he often kicked himself as a punishment for dwelling on fearful scenarios.

It was hard to do if you were standing up (and hurt if you were wearing shoes) but was easier in bed, albeit somewhat scratchy. When that did not stop the thoughts, he tried making a list of all the things to which he was looking forward – this was what his mother had instructed him to do whenever he could not sleep. The next day he planned to finish the periscope, following instructions he had found in 101 *Things to Make and Do*, and deliver it to Mrs Smith. His mother had said they could get a book about stars out from the library. That was two things, but it was no good: his mind kept returning to the rats and bats, to the things that were 'seen and unseen,' and he felt more frightened than ever. He climbed out of bed and ran blindly down the corridor towards his parents' room, hopping over the noisiest floorboards and letting his toes make minimal contact with the floor, which he now imagined to be writhing in creatures.

Isabel felt her child get into bed beside her and folded him into her embrace. It always amazed her how delicious he smelled, considering how dirty he got during the day and how rarely he washed. He was like a hedgerow creature, collecting burrs and bracken in his hair. 'Where's Daddy?' asked Tom, then promptly fell asleep, conferring his burden of anxiety to his mother. Where *was* Hayes? Without committing herself to full wakefulness, Isabel extended one leg into his half of the bed and found that the sheets were still smooth and cold. Sometimes her husband sat up late at night playing Patience, but never this late – it was nearly two o'clock in the morning. She decided not to worry and resolved to go back to sleep; then, having made the resolution, felt more fully awake than ever. For a while she lay in bed looking at the ceiling and then, carefully, she extracted herself from the bed without moving Tom and went down the creaking corridor. She did not want to think that Hayes had been awake all this time, worrying about Jack, or about Mr Payne.

Downstairs she looked for him in the kitchen, but found the room empty, abandoned to the mutterings of the fridge-freezer and the heavy sighs of the range. She passed through the dining room and beneath the sleepless gaze of her husband's ancestors. Hayes was not in the sitting room, so she went on to the farm office, and there, in the half-light, she saw him sitting at his desk. The room was dark, except for an anglepoise lamp casting a pool of light in which Hayes had spread his papers. He seemed to be working on his accounts. Monstrous shadows grew from the objects at the periphery of the light: his stapler, his guillotine and the coffee-flask. Hayes was sitting completely still, and to start with she thought that he must have dozed off in his chair. Then Isabel saw that he was tapping with one fingernail on the desk top. This was not mere finger-drumming, no meditative tic. He was tapping with deliberation, and appeared to be watching the spot as he tapped it. Isabel coughed softly and Hayes turned and saw her with a start. Then he smiled with unusual benignity and she wondered, for a moment, if perhaps he was drunk.

'What are you doing?' she asked.

'I'm talking to a death-watch beetle. Listen – can you hear? You have to be *absolutely* quiet.'

She smiled, because she had heard him impose this absolute quiet before. Hayes had always been someone who knew about nature, about how to watch and wait. She thought of the times, before the children were born, when they had gone for long walks through the fields and woods, and how he had delighted in pointing out to her the signs and traces of animals, or the animals themselves: the barn owl, nesting partridges, a hare or a fox. Once they had waited almost until midnight before walking down to the bottom of the farm to watch the badgers in their sett. The experience of waiting quietly together was as much a part of the pleasure as the uncertain reward of seeing an animal in the wild. Not to be heard, smelled or sensed, to wait silent and undetected, was the closest a human came to being an invisible element in the landscape. If Hayes had brought binoculars on the walk and she wanted a closer look at something, she would need to bring them up to her eyes without removing them from his neck, or he would draw her close to his chest so that she could look through them, and there was a quiet eroticism about the contact. Now, as she stood in the doorway to the office, she thought how kind he was, how he had taught her to enjoy nature, to watch and to listen. And she remembered, with a stab of regret, that night when she was nineteen and they had gone swimming in their underwear and seen the sea lit up by phosphorescence. Being very young, she had interpreted the phenomenon as symbolic of life's romantic potential. Now it suggested something more potent to her: the magic property of light in times of darkness.

Both of them waited in silence and after a few seconds she picked out the beetle's distinctive ticking noise. 'Yes, I hear it.' She smiled.

'It's the male's mating call. He thinks that he's about to seduce a gorgeous female death-watch beetle, poor thing. He'd get a hell of a shock if he could see me, big lump that I am.'

'You're not a lump,' she protested quietly, but the words caught in her throat and he seemed not to hear them. Louder, she said, 'It sounds rather romantic.'

'I don't know about that. Death-watch beetles are meant to be a very bad omen, you know. A sign of impending death.'

'Please don't say that.'

'Don't worry, in this case the beetles are the ones who are going to cop it. We'll have to get the blighters fumigated. It's going to cost a fortune.' He sighed, and smoothed some errant hairs over the top of his head. 'Do you think I've gone raving mad, talking to beetles in the middle of the night?'

'No,' she said and hesitated, leaning her forehead against the frame of the door. Hayes looked smaller to her than usual, as though he was being consumed not only by his worries, but literally, by his own green jumper. Isabel saw her husband as needing a reassurance that she felt unable to supply.

'Tell me what this paperwork is that you're doing,' she said. 'What's so urgent it has to be done in the middle of the night?'

He smiled ruefully. 'You really want to know? I'm going over some figures, for the bank.'

'Again? What do they need to know now?'

Hayes heaved a sigh. 'It boils down to this: we need a new combine harvester. Last year we lost several days of perfect weather because of the old one breaking down. We can't afford to buy a new one, but I've found out there's a local finance company that's selling one for fourteen thousand, with only three hundred and seventy hours on the clock. The farmer who had it's gone bankrupt – couldn't keep up his hire payments – so they want to move it. I need to be able to act fast, but I *can't'* – she could hear his voice strain against the pressure of his frustration – 'I can't actually *do* that until I've secured the loan, which means jumping through a whole new set of hoops for the bank. Do you understand?' He looked up at her, as if, for a moment, hoping that she really might understand, that together they might marshal these columns of figures into a fighting force, to stand against all manner of foes, including Mr Payne and his ludicrous dreams of country living, his ignorance about the reality of farming.

Isabel nodded, but blankly. 'Surely they understand that we need to have the right equipment?'

'The situation is this,' Hayes pressed on. 'We owe the bank a fortune. We can't afford to buy a combine. We also can't afford not to buy a combine.'

'Catch-25,' said Isabel, softly sympathetic.

'Twenty-two,' said Hayes, rubbing his eyes with the balls of his hands. 'It's Catch-22.'

'Yes, of course it is – see how useless I am at numbers!'

Hayes grimaced and returned his attention to his papers.

'But I can learn. I can try to improve,' she said, coaxing from him a more conciliatory smile. 'Why don't you get some sleep now, then perhaps tomorrow, with a fresh mind and, you know . . .' Her voice trailed away.

'Yes, all right. I will come soon.'

Isabel knew that this was the moment to step into the room, to sit down beside her husband and offer her support. She wanted so much to reach out to Hayes, yet she could not take that step. Instead, she stood for a few more seconds in the doorway, then walked quietly away. Isabel still yearned for Jack, and she did not know how long it would take for that yearning to ebb away.

ELEVEN

After witnessing the destruction of his beloved hedge Mr Payne had taken, weeping, to his bed, his flowered duvet pulled over his head. Fearing the worst, Debbie had called the priest. She had explained that her husband was fragile, 'a sensitive soul', and that he had been ill before. She told him about the hedge. Reverend Hollings had said that he would come over straight away.

Reverend Hollings had always been comfortable perched on the ends of beds, and therefore had felt no awkwardness at the end of Mr Payne's. While his friend had sobbed into the pillow, ringlets tumbling all around him, he uttered soothing platitudes and patted a lump under the covers that he supposed must be Mr Payne's foot. Remembering the attention Christ had shown to feet, he felt moved to give it a kind of compassionate squeeze.

After a while he said, 'I'm afraid, Robin, that the inheritors of the land are not always its best protectors.'

'And to think that I am living so close to the oppressor, Geoff,' said Mr Payne into his pillow. 'Cheek by jowl.'

With this sentiment Mr Payne emerged from under the duvet, red-tipped nose first. The sobbing subsided then and, sniffing, he said in a frail voice, 'What is there for me to do now?'

'Well, let's think,' said Reverend Hollings, gripping one of his own knees with both his hands and rocking back on the bed – even when he was thinking, he was dynamic. It was in this attitude, mid-rock, that he had come up with the idea of writing to the newspapers, a solution that so neatly met Mr Payne's craving for revenge and self-expression that he immediately sat up in bed and wiped his eyes. Together they had composed a letter initially intended for the *Guardian*, until Reverend Hollings had proposed *The Times* as an organ more likely to reach those in power. Mr Payne's spirits improved significantly once the letter was drafted and, after the vicar had left, he hopped out of bed and returned for the first time to his desk, where his determination to punish Hayes was redoubled by the sight of his special calligraphy pens, his paintbrushes and watercolour drawings, all tools in a project that had come to naught. Reverend Hollings had said he should not take such a dismal view. The book must still be made, but now it would not be *The History of a Hedge*, but *Elegy for a Hedge*.

'It has a ring about it,' said Reverend Hollings, 'a pleasing assonance. *Elegy for a Hedge* or perhaps, simply, *Hedge Elegy.*'

Mr Payne had sat down and copied out the letter in a flourishing hand, full of rage and purpose. Then he had taken his letter down to the post office, where he had demanded to know if Mrs Lyall thought his letter would arrive in London the next day; and, equally imperious, she had told him that it was sure to do so – what else would one expect of the Royal Mail?

* * *

It was Farmers versus the Rest of the World, thought Hayes grimly as he stood in the office early on Saturday morning. By chance he had looked in his diary on his way to pick up the morning paper, otherwise he would have forgotten about today's fête and the annual tug-o'-war that was its centrepiece. Hayes was in no mood for festivities – and Jack's absence from the team would be a significant blow – but he was damned if he was going to let his side down. They must not let themselves be defeated by events.

For as long as anyone could remember, the Farmers had won the tug-o'-war, leaving their assorted opponents – 'the Rest of the World' – in a defeated tangle on the ground. It was the same every year, and that was the point: the farmers were supposed to win. Their annual victory served as a reminder on one part, and a corresponding acknowledgement on the other, of the farmers' vigorous role at the heart of rural communities. In that sense, the solicitors, shopkeepers and teachers arrayed against them were literally fall guys, but the farmers were magnanimous in victory: the prize was a crate of beer donated by the High Sheriff and they always shared it with the losers.

Hayes picked up *The Times* from the front doormat and went back upstairs to the bathroom without trepidation, for he did not know what dangerous places bathrooms had already proved to be that week. Mr Payne's hedge revelation had struck in the context of an avocado suite; Hayes' would have an aubergine setting. The slow manner of their ghastly enlightenment would be very similar. Once he was settled comfortably, Hayes leafed through the home and international news, before turning to the Editorial and Letters. He read several before his eyes travelled down the column headed 'Hedgerow Protection Vital'. Even the phrases that letter contained – 'farmers' greed', 'rape of the countryside', 'action urgently needed' – seemed at first of no specific relevance to Hayes; the clichés stirred a familiar indignation in him, that was all. But when his eye alighted on the words 'Area of Outstanding Natural Beauty', that phrase made sudden, despicable sense of all that had gone before and he felt the pages of the newspaper quiver in his tightening grip. Beneath the letter was the signatory's name: *Robin Payne, BA*.

Alone in his bathroom, Hayes snarled.

The lavatory flushed, the bathroom door slammed and Hayes, trembling, marched into the bedroom brandishing the newspaper. Without saying anything, he threw it onto the bed for Isabel to look at.

'What is it? What's happened?' cried Isabel. She looked frightened and pale. Some alteration had come over her, and Hayes realised for the first time that this alteration was bound up with Jack. She thought there was something about him in the newspaper.

'It's – no,' he shook his head, 'it's nothing to do with Jack. It's that bastard Payne. He's written to *The Times* about us.'

The scene was set. The village green had been mown and left in stripes ready for the fête. That morning the High Sheriff had supervised the erection of a tea tent and stalls for cakes and jams, knick-knacks and geegaws, a tombola and a Lucky Dip. The same second-hand books that had been circulating for years, round every fête and jumble sale, made another hopeful appearance. Jean and Anne were selling chutneys, with all proceeds going to the restoration of the church roof. Mrs Lyall, dressed as a Romany gypsy, was reading palms for fifty pence a go.

'You are going to meet a tall, handsome stranger,' she told Mattie.

'You are about to make a discovery that will change your life,' she said to Tom.

By the time Jennifer entered the tent, Mrs Lyall was growing bored with easy ambiguity, the fortune teller's stock-in-trade. 'When you are twenty-three you shall marry a man called Kenneth and have five children,' she told Jennifer, who was immediately filled with a sense of mysterious self-importance and rushed out of the tent to share the revelation with her sister.

'This is rubbish,' said Tom, once the children had made several tours of all that was on offer. 'I'm going back to the farm to play at the tank.'

Inside the tea tent the air was hot and smelled of canvas and mown grass. The sheriff's wife was on duty at the urn, waving away the wasps and complaints about the heat with disapproval: England had suffered much worse during the war. People entering the tent with a purpose seemed to suffer an immediate loss of energy, then let themselves be borne along on a current of warm air towards the trays of scones and curling ham sandwiches, and finally delivered to the sheriff's wife – who sent them impatiently away again with cups of tea. Hayes, finding himself jostled towards a cluster of people he did not recognise, realised with a start that one of them was Mr Payne, ridiculously attired in shorts and a collar-neck shirt. No man over the age of eighteen should wear shorts, thought Hayes, feeling rage descend on him once more. As the crowd bore him towards his antagonist's circle, Hayes quickly rehearsed some strategies of humiliation. He had to say something about the letter, surely? How he longed to punish the little runt! He noticed that Mr Payne was talking animatedly to a young woman, who was nodding with enthusiasm. Soon Hayes was close enough to eavesdrop. 'A diet based principally on vegetables and nuts would free up all the land we currently use to feed cattle,' Mr Payne was saying. 'If the political will were there, we could feed the world organically.'

As he spoke Mr Payne held his hand in front of him, squeezing two fingers and a thumb together in a neat little gesture that suggested he held the solution, some grain of truth, within their grasp. The woman cast admiring glances at this invisible axiom.

'And you know nuts really are an *excellent* source of protein,' Mr Payne added.

Looking at that tiny, self-important hand, Hayes felt a bead of violence, like an electric pulse, zip through his body. Nuts? He would give the bastard nuts! He'd nut the bastard, right here, in the tea tent, in front of the vicar!

Feeling himself begin to tremble, Hayes made a gigantic effort of self-restraint. This was not the moment to tackle Payne – his hands were occupied with the teacup for one thing. As he drew level with the group, though, he could not resist a minor act of sabotage.

'Why not share your theory with the farmers of China and India,' he interjected, keeping a level tone and with a pleasant nod to the young woman. 'Ask them: would you like to have crops that are resistant to aphids, that hold up better in strong winds and produce nearly four times as much grain? Would you like to feed millions more people, or would you rather break your backs pulling out weeds so that a few of us can eat organic porridge?'

Mr Payne, who had not known that Hayes was standing behind him, grew pale and then very red, and opened his mouth in preparation for a retort.

'Just a thought,' Hayes said, and went pushing on through the crowd.

At half-past two the High Sheriff ceremoniously tied his spotted handkerchief to the rope for the tug-o'-war. The men took up their positions. Bourne was joining the Farmers in Jack's absence, and there were two other men on their team – but Mikey was also missing. The Rest of the World comprised five men, including a couple of estate agents who had started marketing cottages in the area to Londoners as holiday homes.

'Hang on. We're a man down,' called Hayes, as the High Sheriff was about to blow his whistle.

'Say again?' returned the sheriff. Then he walked over to him and said, 'Your young man, the Australian – is he still AWOL?'

'Both my young men,' said Hayes ruefully.

'I see.' The sheriff cast a glance at the Rest of the World, then confided, 'I would say the vicar doesn't really count. Or the little fellow.' Geoff Hollings, who had been reluctant to take a side, had gamely insisted on wearing his cassock as a handicap. Mr Payne, with legs like spindles, was certainly no asset.

But the other team had ballast in the form of Sergei, a

huge Ukrainian dissident, recently arrived in the village. Sergei ran a restaurant on the other side of the river and could be found there on Saturday nights, singing tearful folk songs about Soviet tyranny to a captive audience. Meanwhile the two estate agents, who had looked effete in their jackets, removed them to reveal powerful biceps and gluteal muscles. The High Sheriff raised his whistle to his lips. The men on both sides braced themselves.

At Hill Farm all was quiet. Tom, having run back along the bottom road, had reached the tank and was gazing down into its dark water, clotted with algae, on the hunt for newts. Sun glinted on the upstairs windows of the farmhouse. Behind one of them was Isabel, lying on her bed. She had not moved from it since that morning, feeling that to remain still might be a way to prevent any further unfurling of events. It was impossible for her to go to the fête, to show enthusiasm for toffee apples and the tombola – however much the children had wanted her company. Much safer to remain here, unmoving, *absolutely quiet*, as Hayes might put it. Perhaps she could be so completely still and silent as to be absorbed into her surroundings. It had been wonderful to be the object of Jack's attention, but now all she wanted was to be unnoticed, undetected.

The air had hung heavy over this corner of the Weald, but a sudden breeze rippled across the valley. For a moment its corn fields appeared like the coat of a giant animal, being stroked by a giant's hand. In her bedroom

Isabel felt cool air wash over her hot face and breathed deeply.

The same breeze enlivened the spectators on the green, and when the sheriff blew his whistle shouting broke out straight away, as though this were a test of noise rather than strength. Those onlookers who were not shouting watched, with amusement and alarm, as the participants' faces grew redder, the veins began to stand out on their necks and their eyes to bulge. Like recalcitrant bulls they strained against the rope, digging their heels into the cosseted grass of the village green. There was snorting and blowing on both sides. Nostrils flared. Mr Payne tossed his ringlets, his soft hands sliding on the rope. Bourne, in his mustard-coloured corduroy trousers, was the Farmers' anchorman – but his thighs were no match for the opposition's. Mighty Sergei, his eyes wide and his teeth bared, had thighs that could topple an empire and, leading the Rest of the World, the estate agents were a purposeful duo. They were used to hauling in fat commissions together and this was just a different kind of rope-work. 'Heave!' shouted Hayes desperately. He could see Payne's scarlet face, on the other side, contorted with effort. The estate agents were wearing sports footwear with superior traction while, in their leather shoes, Bourne and Hayes struggled to maintain a grip. 'Heave!' shouted Hayes, but the Farmers heaved in vain. Eventually the unthinkable happened: the Rest of the World won.

'Never mind, old man!' said Bourne. 'There is always next year. We'll be better prepared next time.'

'If Jack had been here we would have won,' said Hayes, rearranging his tousled hair. 'And Mikey. They've let us down, both of them.' He looked up to see Mr Payne laughing with his teammates and clenched his jaw. If only he could wipe the smirk off that face! People in television soap operas seemed to hit each other all the time (there had been a letter complaining about it to *The Times*), but more restraint was expected of a man of Hayes' standing. He pulled himself together and took a deep breath, reminding himself that the village fête was no place for a brawl.

Mattie and Jennifer, lying on the grass behind the tea tent, did not witness their father's disgrace. Jennifer was trying to get her legs brown. Mattie had walked round the green a dozen times looking for Miss Prince, who had said she would be selling aromatherapy oils at the fête and that Mattie could help out on the stall. There was no sign of the stall, though, or of Miss Prince.

In fact Mattie, who had so longed to be Miss Prince's friend, who had thrilled to the notions of aromatherapy and macramé, was to meet her idol only once more, two months after the fête, when the summer holidays were well under way.

Mattie was walking home to Hill Farm, with Venetia, her new best friend, when they saw an apparition in white trousers on the road ahead. Mattie knew that it must be Miss Prince. Nobody else in their village wore white trousers, except for visiting morris dancers. Miss Prince was facing away from them, up the road that led out of the village, as though looking out for someone.

'Hello, Miss Prince,' Mattie said, when she and Venetia were a few steps away.

Jumping at the sound of Mattie's voice, Miss Prince

turned and looked the girls nervously up and down. Her hand went up to fiddle with a pearl necklace, creamily iridescent against her bronzed cleavage.

'Well, hello, Mattie – what a nice surprise!' She glanced back up the road. 'I'm just watching out for the removals people. A lot of visitors miss my turning, you know. They think it's only for the church.'

'What is going to be removed?' asked Mattie, brightly, stealing a glance at Miss Prince's bunion. She was conscious of wanting to make a good impression in front of Venetia, whose manners were often praised by adults.

Miss Prince laughed and seemed to relax. 'Everything, Mattie dear. I am moving, you see. To Devon, to the English Riviera.'

'Oh,' said Mattie. She tried not to show how much this revelation shocked her. 'Well, that's good, because you've already got the perfume.'

After some puzzlement, Miss Prince laughed again. 'Yes, you are quite right! You always were a very perceptive child.' She studied Mattie's face for a minute. Lowering her tone, and with a cautious glance at Venetia, she asked, 'How are things at home?'

Mattie shrugged. She could think of no way to convey the atmosphere at home. Some days she barely even recognised her house as a home. But, anxious not to seem gloomy, she tried to look on the bright side, as so often instructed by her mother. 'It means we'll get a dog,' she offered. 'We've wanted one for ages.'

'Does it? Well, my, that *will* be fun,' said Miss Prince overweening, as adults often are when dealing with a child who has suffered some tragedy – they want to scoot the sad event away with a cheery tone. Then she stood up very straight, like someone pretending to be a soldier in a play, looking as if she were about to march off to Devon in her gold-thonged sandals.

'The removals van will be coming any minute, Mattie, and I don't want to keep you and your friend waiting, so we'd better get on and say goodbye.'

Mattie nodded, but tears filled her eyes when Miss Prince leaned to kiss her forehead. Enough bad things had happened recently without Miss Prince leaving, too. It grieved her to think that the contents of the Old School House – which had seemed like heaven to her – were going to be taken away for good. She gave up trying to seem sophisticated and sobbed noisily.

'Mattie, don't take this to heart,' said Miss Prince, with unusual feeling. 'You know, life does not always turn out the way we hope. Sometimes things happen that' – she hesitated, the words seeming to catch in her throat – 'that can't be undone, and it is better to move on. Now, be brave and give me your hand.' Mattie sniffed and did as she was told, expecting Miss Prince to shake her hand. Instead the older woman bent and kissed the palm of Mattie's hand, then closed the fingers over it. 'That's a kiss for your mother. Will you take it back to her for me?'

'Yes.' Mattie nodded vigorously, using her free hand to wipe her tears away and her running nose.

All the way down the hill she kept this hand closed, even though Venetia teased her and said that it would not make any difference, because a kiss was not something real that could be carried around.

* * *

The day after the fête, as he was shaking hands with the departing parishioners after the Sunday-morning service, Reverend Hollings clasped Hayes' hand with particular vigour, laying his left hand upon their joined right ones, as though hoping to initiate a game of 'one potato, two potato'. It would not have surprised Hayes: he found the tenor of services at St Cuthbert's increasingly childish. At the start of his sermon, Reverend Hollings had told them that he would preach on the subject of finding fault with others. He asked them to memorise the reference to the passage about finding a speck of dust in your neighbour's eye: Matthew, Chapter Seven, Verse Five. At the end of the sermon the congregation was invited to shout out that reference together, on a count of three. Hayes had been sitting behind the High Sheriff and noticed the old man's ears redden with indignation. He wondered what gimmick the vicar would think of next. It would not be long, he felt, until a guitar entered the proceedings.

Now, in the portico, Reverend Hollings leaned confidentially towards Hayes' ear. 'If I may,' he said, 'I would like to visit you this afternoon with Robin. I realise that this is a sensitive issue, that there is hurt on all sides, but I do think that Robin has a legitimate point to make, as it were.'

For a moment Hayes struggled to think who 'Robin' might be – he could only ever think of the tenant as a 'Payne'. Then the penny dropped and, with his hand sandwiched between the vicar's, he had little option but to assent.

'This afternoon then. Perhaps at four o'clock? Thank you so much for your understanding.' Reverend Hollings grinned and his lips rose high, revealing oversized canines.

Hayes led his children up the village road and back to Hill Farm, fuming all the way. Trust Mr Payne to get the priest involved! He was one of those types who go bleating to the nearest inspector or authority figure at the first sign of an argument not going his way. Presumably he had been like this as a child, too, forever running to Mummy with shrill protestations, forever pointing the finger at his perceived aggressors.

The Sunday roast sat heavy on his stomach that afternoon, as Hayes watched Mr Payne and Reverend Hollings walk up the garden path to the front door. Clearly they meant business – the front door was so rarely used that Hayes had to think for a few seconds to remember where he kept the key. The men had brought Jean Temple with them, too. So Mr Payne had armed himself with the advocates of God and Reason. If he had known that seconds were required, he would have called on Bourne and the High Sheriff to serve as his own pistol-bearers.

He met the visitors at the door and showed them into the sitting room, where they stood about like awkward emblems.

'How can I help you?' asked Hayes. He did not invite them to sit down; he would not feign a hospitality he did not feel.

Realising that there were to be no comforting preliminaries, Reverend Hollings, the group's appointed spokesman, stuttered into action.

'Well! Ah, the thing is – yes. We're here because, well, as I think you know, Robin feels very aggrieved about the removal of the hedge that used to be close to his house and that formed, as it were, an important part of the vista from his window.'

On cue, Mr Payne shaped his face for grievance. It was a small, angry and rather blotchy face. If it had belonged to a child you might have wanted to give it two kisses and a toffee, and the anger would have melted away. Mr Payne was an adult, though, even if he seemed immensely childish to Hayes. How was one supposed to respond to such a petulant little bully?

'I know how he feels,' said Hayes, 'because I have read his letter in *The Times*.'

'Ah,' said Reverend Hollings. He had not bargained on Hayes being a reader of *The Times*. Still, he would not allow himself to be distracted from the task in hand. His vocation was to unite people, and here was a union begging to be effected. He could picture a scene of mutual apologies and, perhaps, embraces. It might only be minutes away.

'Robin feels no malice,' persisted Reverend Hollings, in spite of all evidence to the contrary, 'but he would like an acknowledgement of his distress.'

Hayes sighed heavily. He felt a saturating weariness pour through his bones. 'I'm sorry,' he said. 'But this is a spectacularly bad time for us, spectacularly bad. We've lost a farmhand who was very useful to us and we need to replace him, which isn't easy at this time of year. And – there are other things . . .' His voice trailed away in another sigh. He was thinking of the death-watch beetle, his new debts and the money that must be spent, hand over fist, every day to keep the farm in business.

'You're just saying that to stop me calling in the inspectors,' said Mr Payne, nastily.

'That isn't fair,' said Isabel, who had come quietly into the room while Reverend Hollings was talking. 'I don't think you quite grasp the difficulties that we face, Mr Payne.' She was surprised to hear herself speak out. So, too, was Hayes, who was looking at her with astonishment. 'Farmers are going out of business every day. It's a real struggle to make ends meet. Besides which, my husband is a great lover of nature. He would never set out to "rape" the countryside in the way you suggested in your letter. That was a disgraceful allegation.'

For a moment Mr Payne appeared wrong-footed. Then he said sulkily, 'Well, obviously you'd say that.'

Now Tom, who was loitering in the doorway, said, 'I suppose Jack could be in the tank.'

'Shut up, Tom, for heaven's sake!' growled Hayes, unleashing the fury that he would really like to direct at Mr Payne.

Tom's mouth turned down at the corners and he prepared to cry.

'It's all right, darling,' said Isabel. 'It's just that this isn't the time for jokes. Please do take a seat, everyone, and I'll make us all some tea.' Tea would make things better, surely. When people were made to sit down, to drink tea and to eat cake, their impetus for violence melted away. It was not possible to hold on to aggression and a bone-china cup simultaneously.

She made to leave the room, and the people within it reorganised themselves accordingly, each of them taking a cautious step one way or the other. There was so much antagonism in the air, no one wanted to make any inadvertent body contact.

That was when Jean suddenly exclaimed, 'Good Lord!' and fell to her knees. She began to pat the floor, as though looking for a contact lens.

'Are you all right?' cried Geoff Hollings, springing forward on cushioned soles.

'Gracious – it's a carpet beetle! *Anthrenus verbasci*, if I'm not mistaken.'

'My word! How do you know, Jean?'

'I'm quite familiar with these chaps. They're a menace in museums. We had some old carpets that were badly damaged by them, and another year they got into a collection of animal hides and caused havoc. You have to keep checking everything. Well, hello again, my friend.'

She picked the beetle up in her hand and carefully stood up. Then Hayes, Reverend Hollings and Mr Payne gathered around to look at it.

'See the markings on its back? Those black-and-yellow splotches are characteristic of this variety. It's a male, by the way.'

'What do they actually live on, Jean?'

'They're living on the carpet!'

Everyone looked down then, at the threadbare Persian rug underfoot, another legacy from Hayes' spinster aunts. 'They have a taste for the good stuff! Then they migrate from room to room spreading the infestation, you see. They can become very hard to get rid of. Regular vacuuming helps a good deal, of course.'

Isabel, who had not left the room, bit her lip. She vacuumed rarely.

'Well, how extraordinary,' murmured Reverend Hollings.

Hayes was also transfixed. His enthusiasm for nature could override even a concern for the fabric of his house. 'If you'll excuse me for a moment, I have a magnifying glass in the office – I'll just go and get it.'

'Oh, do you have an empty matchbox, too, by any chance?' asked Jean.

'Very likely. In fact, come along with me, Jean – I have something else you may be interested to see.'

As they walked down the back corridor to the office, Isabel heard Hayes telling Jean about the death-watch beetle and her response: 'Good Lord, have you got some of those chaps, too? This house is a right old menagerie!'

Isabel was left now with Mr Payne and the vicar and felt the air in the room hang heavier. Wanting to release Reverend Hollings from the obligation of smiling constantly, she invited the men to sit down and reiterated an intention to make tea: this was something to which she would hold firm. In the kitchen she heaved the kettle onto the hob and, hearing the water begin to respond, felt her pulse calm. Tom had followed her into the kitchen and stood at the door, his face mottled and red, his lower lip quivering. She recognised this Vesuvius moment: an eruption could come at any minute.

'Are you all right, darling?'

'Daddy thinks I was being rude, when I wasn't!' He broke into snorting tears. 'He told me to shut up, and now everyone's cross with me!'

Isabel sighed and went over to her son. Crouching in front of him, she placed her hands on his arms. 'They're not cross with you at all. They're just worried – about other things.'

Well, how was I supposed to know that? It was just an idea. He didn't have to get so cross.'

'Yes, I know. I understand that. Why don't you go upstairs and play with the girls?'

'No way! They're doing fashion shows.'

'Oh, I see. Well, perhaps you can help me to put some biscuits on a plate and pass them round.'

'Technically Jack *could* be in the tank. His belt is there.'

'No, I don't think – what do you mean, "his belt"?'

'I was playing with the newts yesterday, and I saw Jack's belt lying at the bottom of the tank. I was making the newts have competitions to race up to it. Like a kind of finishing line. Mummy, you know you can pull the tails off newts and they grow back?'

'Never mind about that now,' Isabel kept her hands on both of Tom's arms, as much to steady herself as him. She had not eaten much since learning of Jack's absence on Friday, and her light-headedness blurred the edges of everything so that she felt she needed to keep a sure grip on objects around her. She made an effort to speak calmly to Tom. 'Tell me about the belt. How do you know that it's Jack's?'

'I recognised the shiny bit, you know the thing that makes it attach.'

'The buckle?'

'Yes. It's sort of square and it's got a pattern on it.'

She knew very well the buckle that he meant. The sun had drawn her eye to it that first afternoon when Jack had driven her in the van down to the flooded field. She had seen it again when he pulled on his jeans after they had made love in the cottage. He had worn it always. It was unlikely, she thought, that he would have left the farm without it. A quick pain struck her in the abdomen and she leaned back, against the fridge, feeling suddenly dizzy.

'Will Jack be OK? I miss him a lot. He said he was going to show me how to make a catapult.'

'I think you must be wrong about the belt, darling. There are lots of buckles that look like that, and lots of metal things that look like buckles. It must be something else that you saw.'

'I'm not bloody wrong!' Tom shouted.

Tom's obstinacy about this made her feel irrationally annoyed. She gripped his arms tighter, willing him to admit that this was a prank or a misunderstanding. 'If you saw Jack's belt, why didn't you mention it before? You should have said something yesterday!'

'I didn't know I was supposed to. You're hurting me!'

The kettle was boiling now and steam surged into the room. Isabel straightened up and walked over to the high cupboard where her best china was kept. It was a tea set in delicate pink, with a gold-leaf pattern that had all but worn away over the years. As a child she had first seen these cups and saucers on her grandmother's 'occasional table', a piece of furniture she supposed to have magical properties (if it was only 'occasionally' a table, what was it the rest of the time?). Few of the magical associations of childhood survive into adulthood, but this tea set retained a mysterious lustre for Isabel, even though her mother had put it to more prosaic use, entertaining local members of the Women's Institute. For a moment she imagined that these tea-drinking stalwarts were assembled before her now, in the farm kitchen. What would they say, she wondered, about the events at Hill Farm? How would they pronounce on her adultery?

Now she heard Hayes and Jean returning from the office, laughing and talking. If Jean had arrived with the enemy party, it sounded as though she was perhaps defecting to the other camp. That was good: Isabel did not like to see her husband the victim of a gang, even one that comprised such eccentric members. It would help Hayes to have an ally who could take a pragmatic view of the decisions he had to make as a farmer. She poured water into the teapot and arranged cups on the tray, keeping her mind deliberately occupied with these levelling thoughts as a way of allaying the panic that was creeping over her. Tom's claim about the belt could not be dismissed out of hand. As she went to the fridge for milk, an image of Jack lying, drowned, in dirty water asserted itself so power-fully that she abandoned the tray and walked back into the sitting room, where the others, awkwardly arrayed, were quiet and expectant, as though they had known all along that she would have an announcement to make and were simply waiting for her to be ready to deliver it.

'Tom says that he has seen Jack's belt, at the bottom of the tank.'

Brows furrowed in the room. The visiting party was perplexed.

'The tank?' said Jean. 'A septic tank?'

'No,' said Hayes. 'There is a water repository at the bottom of the farm, an old fire precaution. But, Isabel, Tom's imagining things. You know that he has an over active mind.'

'He's quite sure it's Jack's belt. He recognises it. It has a—' She stopped herself. 'Apparently it has a distinctive buckle.'

Hayes said nothing, but his eyes stayed on her and she willed herself not to look away. No one spoke and only the ticking of the grandfather clock broke the silence. Then Hayes drew on his arsenal of comforting tics: hair-smoothing, face-rubbing, nose-pinching. When he looked up at her again, it was with an expression of defeat. Isabel moved towards her husband and put her hand on his arm.

'We need to . . .' she said.

'Yes,' said Hayes, rousing himself. 'I'm afraid we'll have to defer this meeting,' he said, looking at each of his visitors. 'I'm sorry, but I hope you understand.'

'Of course – this isn't the moment,' agreed Geoff Hollings, patting the air in front of him with both hands, in a generalised calming motion. He turned towards the front door. Then something (perhaps it was a thought of Martin Luther King) made him turn back again. 'Don't go to this place – this tank or whatever it is – alone. Let us walk with you.'

'That's asking too much . . .' Hayes began.

'Geoff's absolutely right,' said Jean, firmly. 'We'll go with you. You may need some backup!'

Mr Payne was prevailed upon to make a pale assent.

'Well, that's very good of you,' Hayes said. 'In that case, I think we'd better go now. Are you ready, love?'

'Yes,' said Isabel. 'I will just get my cardigan.'

She had meant to do that quickly, but, once upstairs, she felt such relief at being alone that she knelt down on the floor by the chest of drawers and held her head in her hands and then, finding that insufficient reassurance, she lay flat on the floor, stretching out her arms. A terrible pain gnawed at her stomach: a combination of nerves and hunger, she supposed. She tried to persuade herself that there was no need for alarm; the fact that his passport was missing meant that Jack was most likely safe. She closed her eyes and pictured herself lying on Jack's bed with him beside her. He was propped on one elbow, smiling at her, tracing the lines of her ribs with his fingers. She felt herself returning the smile now, when it was too late. *Too late.* Added together, all the time they had spent together amounted to no more than a few hours. It was not enough, she thought with desperation. If he was going to leave, then why could she not have had her fill of him first? She would have had more of everything: more sex, more conversation, more time alone. Now the noise of the group gathering downstairs at the front door reverberated through the floorboards. 'Jack,' she said aloud. 'Please be all right.' She rolled onto her side, blinking away her tears, and rubbed her eyes with the heels of both hands. When she opened her eyes she saw that woodworm was attacking the bottom of the chest of drawers. 'Everything is falling to pieces,' she said, getting to her feet. Then she put on her cardigan and made her way downstairs.

The children were left to watch television. The adults set off down the hill, on the mile-long walk to the tank. It was nine months since Mattie had hurtled down this way on her bike, on a mission to tell her father that smoke from his stubble-burning was obscuring visibility. Now the horizon was scarely any clearer. None of them knew what they were expecting to find. Were they walking towards the scene of a crime, or a mere mystery? Were they going to find a dead body, or a missing belt? Three members of the party were not even sure what sort of destination the 'tank' was. All of them wondered if they were acting on the whim of a six-year-old boy.

They walked in silence, with the exception of the vicar, who pursued an aimless hum. What was in their minds? Jean was thinking nostalgically of beetles. Geoff was wishing he had worn jeans instead of a cassock. He had not reckoned on a country walk.

Hayes was looking at the land around him and feeling that everything he knew and loved was threatened. He held Mr Payne accountable for this – not because he suspected any link between the tenant and Jack's disappearance; it was unlikely that the men had ever exchanged more than a few words. Hayes' fear was not directly related to the current crisis, but a more nebulous response to the changes he knew were coming. Farming was entering a new age, becoming an enterprise for scientists employed by large agrochemical companies. The farmers of his father's generation had provided everything – seeds, feed and fertilisers – for themselves. Now they were mere servants of technologists and the technocrats in Brussels. A future of bureacracy, of rules, regulations and form-filling loomed on the road ahead, and Hayes wondered if he would prove equal to it. Mr Payne's undesired presence beside him seemed to symbolise the menace of the inspectors and his powerlessness to escape them.

Isabel was possessed by a giddy unreality. She heard the noise her shoes made on the road, but could not sense the contact her feet made with the ground; it was as though she were floating above it. She registered, too, the vicar's irritating hum, but could find no way to connect these outward stimuli with her mind's activity. A succession of images came to her, of Jack singing 'The Internationale' to the Siberian swans, of the time they had met at the jumble sale, of Jack lying next to her at the cottage. The pictures were vivid, but they came to her only at intervals, because the rest of the time she was wondering what to cook for dinner, or when to do the ironing. All at once, memories of her childhood crowded in on her, together with snatches of songs she had heard on the radio at different points in her life, and disjointed remarks from people she had once known. The effect was to produce such a commingling of mental images that she felt unable to focus on what was happening to her at this very moment. To think that she had fallen in love with a man, that he had disappeared and might now be dead – and had he died because of her? – these were fantastical notions on which she could build no substantial thought. Instead, her mind filled up with extraneous information: things she needed to buy, socks that required darning, items that were waiting to be glued. She asked herself: 'What has happened to me? What will become of me?' And the only answers that came were to do with leftovers and shopping lists.

There was, besides, the possibility that Tom was wrong: that idea had crossed all their minds, but particularly troubled Mr Payne. Why were they acting on the impulsive suggestion of an over-imaginative six-year-old boy? He did not much like children anyway, and Tom seemed to him a fine example of an attention-seeking brat. He had invented a wild story, followed it up with a tantrum and, hey presto, got them all out of the house so that he could watch television with his sisters. The boy was not stupid! Hayes probably thought that this episode let him off the hook, but Mr Payne would not be deterred. There was no word too strong to denounce Hayes' violent methods. This was rape, desecration, environmental vandalism . . .

'I will not get ill again,' Isabel thought to herself, 'and this is the method: to keep placing one foot in front of the other, to carry on, to keep walking.' She felt faint though, and noted the world beginning to spin around her – the hills and trees and then, scattered beyond view, the compass points of her adult life: the church, the post office, the school, Miss Prince's house. Her mouth was dry and her heart banged a dull downbeat. The world revolved around her, but she saw Hayes, steady at its centre. She ran forward a few steps to give him her hand and he held onto it tightly. He looked at her and, without saying anything, smiled. It gave her heart.

They were approaching the tractor shed and the tank. From his sheltered spot at the back of the shed, Mikey saw the procession pass and felt relief. He was exhausted by his secret and, after three days, would do anything to give it up.

Mikey's first reaction, when Jack's head hit the floor, had been one of swelling satisfaction: that would teach the bastard! He had stood, with his hands on his hips, thinking of clever things to say when Jack came round (usually there was no time to think of a decisive put-down). From where he was standing, he had seen only the back of Jack's head lying on the concrete floor. But when Jack did not move, Mikey approached him cautiously, walking slowly around him. Then he saw Jack's open eyes and the spreading pool of dark-red blood under his head, and he was very scared. He retreated to the back of the shed and stayed there for a long time among the tyres, shivering and crying, chewing his thumbnail to the quick. After a while, the fear gave way to anger: it was only a punch, for Christ's sake! If the man had not been so clumsy, he would not have tripped as he fell and everything would be all right now. Mikey had tried remonstrating with Jack to get up, pacing around him in circles until he had even shouted at him to get up. He had shouted that he was sorry, for Christ's sake. His mother said that he never apologised – well, if it would make a difference, he was willing to make an exception now: the thing with the lynchpins had been a stupid joke. *Sorry* – all right?

After Jack had hit the ground, the day turned dream-like; the hours slowed. Several times Mikey had left the shed and set off down the road, meaning to tell Hayes, or the first person he met, that there had been an accident, that Jack was really badly hurt. He had thought of running up to the farmhouse; it was not too late – no one would know that he had waited more than an hour before raising the alarm. They would be able to telephone for an ambulance, and by the time any help arrived it would seem as though Jack had died in the interim. This struck him as a plausible course of action, but he could not commit himself to it. Each time he set off down the road he turned back after a few yards and went into the shed again, shaking and crying, retreating to the tyres. He sat there and cried, biting his knuckles hard, because he wanted the distraction of pain. Then he took a swig of cider from the flask and it made him feel better. He began to calm down. He thought he might go home and have a rest, or go to the pub. He needed to go back anyway, to feed Blue, left at home today because he had been limping with a sore paw. He persuaded himself that in the morning Jack would be better and everything would be all right. He began to say these words aloud to himself as a mantra: 'Everything will be all right.' He may have sat like that, murmuring these words to himself, for an hour or more. Finally dusk fell and, with it, a cool realisation that Jack was certainly dead: he had killed him.

By then Mikey knew that he could not go home, or to the pub, without doing something about the body. The idea of seeking help or going to fetch someone else was no longer practicable: he had waited too long. Now he was on his own. It made him shake again to think that he would have to touch a corpse. Outside in the long grass beside the shed he vomited, then drank more cider. The sting of the alcohol revived him, but it made him dizzy, too, and he squatted down in the grass, leaning against the shed's corrugated-iron exterior. The noise of his pulse throbbed in his ears. He looked across the hills and seemed to see, in the half-light, some distant figures. He knew, without feeling any sense of alarm, that these were not real people, but perhaps the ghosts of labourers who had worked on the land a century ago, come to show him that he was not alone. It was a comforting visitation and he sat watching them for a time, until he had achieved a measure of composure and knew what he was going to do next.

Returning to the shed, Mikey approached the body, this time with more confidence. He grasped Jack by his booted ankles and began to drag him out of the shed and towards the tank. When he saw the quantity of blood that was dragged along under Jack's body, he heard himself whimper like an animal and the sound gave him a fright. But he remembered the calming effect of his mantra, and the gentle figures on the horizon, and began to speak softly to himself again: 'It will be all right. You're nearly there.' It was only about twenty yards to the tank, then there was a short metal ladder of five steps up to the edge of the water. It would be too hard to pull Jack up that by his boots. He had to grip Jack under his arms, which meant that the dead man's head lolled back against his thighs, bloodying his boiler suit. Mikey felt himself about to cry again, but by now he had learned to control his fear. With a giant heave, he pulled the body up the steps and over the ledge, and let it slide into the water. As Jack's body sank into the sediment, his arms drifted away from his sides and his chin tilted upwards, and for a moment he looked as though he was floating pleasurably on his back, somewhere hot.

Mikey's heart was pounding and he was sweating, but it would not be safe to rest yet. He returned immediately to the shed, took the length of hose – the same coil that had caused Jack to trip – and attached it to an outside tap. Working now by the light of his torch, he sluiced the blood away, watching it run in rivulets down to an outside drain. He cast around for something to cover the body. At the back of the shed was a pile of hessian sacks that had once contained potatoes for animal feed. For years they had lain there in a mouldering pile, stiffening with mildew. He prised six of the sacks from the pile – evicting a colony of harvest spiders that scattered on the ground like beads from a broken necklace – then carried these stiffened shrouds back to the tank. Mikey could not see his feet as he edged carefully along beside the water, because the load in his arms blocked his view, so he tried to feel the lip of the brick border through the soles of his boots. Dropping the sacks into the water, he feared that they might float, but their years of vegetative waiting had made them heavy, and soon enough they sank and cloaked the body. Then he went to the silage clamp, took off one of the tyres and pulled back a section of polythene sheeting. The noxious gases rising from the fermenting hay were almost over-powering and for a minute he had to stand back and take deep breaths of fresh air. He took a wire broom from the shed and used it to spread some of the foul-smelling run-off from the silage over the area where the blood had been, so that any remaining stains would become confused with the effluent. When he had finished his work Mikey returned to the shed, took off his boiler suit and hid it in an empty fertiliser bag. Hayes often asked him to make bonfires of rubbish – never suspecting what useful therapy this was for a latent pyromaniac. He would easily find a reason for another bonfire soon, and then he could burn the evidence and put the events of this afternoon behind him.

After this work Mikey felt very tired, but he could not yet go home. He stood for a time in the shed without moving. The evening's silence revolved around him and he felt more alone than ever before in his life. The thought came to him that he had always been alone, and would always be lonely. His mother was on the Costa del Sol and his father off the face of the planet. There was no one to care for him, and that thought made his chest ache. While sluicing down the blood he had remembered Jack talking about his travel plans, and how his eyes lit up when he mentioned visiting France and Spain. That was soon after they had first met, when they still talked to each other in a friendly way. Jack's passport and other documents would be up at the cottage. If Mikey could dispose of them now, he could make it look as though the Australian had decided to go away earlier than planned. The logic of this course of action gave him an infusion of energy and somehow made him feel more hopeful; he would persuade himself, too, that Jack had moved on to sunnier climes. He sat down to finish the cider, draining the flask in a few gulps – then he set off for the cottage.

The darkness went in his favour that night. When he came to the top of the hill he saw only one window at the farmhouse lit by flickering light. This was all to the good. He turned right, down the path that led to the cottage. While walking, he had been worried that he might find the front door locked, in which case he would have to think of some other way to get into the cottage. He had not thought to look for keys in Jack's pockets, before dumping him in the tank. Stupid fucker! If the door was locked, he would have to jemmy up a window round the back – and that complicated things. When he found the cottage door open he wanted to shout for joy. Inside the house Mikey worked quickly. Jack's passport and some money were in a drawer upstairs. A wallet was in his jacket, on the back of a chair in the kitchen. He took some chocolate that was on the table and set off again. That was when he had run into Isabel and cooked up the story about going to the pub with Jack.

He had not gone to the pub, of course, but back to the semi on the green, which felt very empty now that his mother was in Spain. Outside the door, putting his key in the lock, he heard Blue's excited scuffles on the other side and was grateful to think that at least he was going to see his dog. But as Blue greeted his master, furiously wagging his tail and hindquarters, he caught the scent of blood on his jeans and began sniffing at his leg with such avidity that Mikey could hardly push his muzzle away. The dog's blood-lust filled him with revulsion. Mikey took Blue by the collar into the dining room and left him shut up there. In the kitchen he fumbled in the dark to empty a can of dog food into a bowl, then took this and some water to the dining room, without letting his dog escape.

He could not bring himself to eat anything. Instead he lay in the dark on the sofa until he noticed that the power was back on in the houses on the other side of the green. Then he put on the television and watched it until close-down was announced and the national anthem played. Upstairs, without undressing, he lay on the bed. He did not go to sleep, but was pursued by nightmares all the same: Jack's open eyes stared up at him through the murky water in the tank. He had been so angry with Jack, hating him, and now he felt dreadfully sorry for him. It did not seem right that he should have the comfort of a bed while Jack was lying at the bottom of cold and dirty water.

At first light Mikey got up again, put on a clean boiler suit over his clothes and returned to the farm. He was light-headed and nauseous as he walked along the bottom road – the combined effect of too much alcohol and not enough food or sleep. He shook as he climbed the metal steps up to the tank, remembering the previous evening's ordeal. This time he did no more than glance into the water, reassuring himself that the body was obscured by sludge and the bright-green algae that covered most of the water's surface. It was not as if anyone ever looked in the tank, anyway. He waited in the tractor shed until it was time to start work. The routine of farm labour had always seemed so boring to him, but now it was a luxury that he would do anything to retain. Hayes had a meeting early in the morning, so it was not until later that he came looking for Mikey, told him that Jack was missing and asked if he knew anything about his whereabouts. Mikey found himself so perfectly able to feign surprise and concern that he almost convinced himself he was innocent of the knowlege, let alone the crime. Give this time, he thought, and life could be normal again. At dusk, though, all his fears returned and he felt that he had very little energy to fend them off.

At home he foraged in the cupboard for food and ate randomly out of tins and packets. He ate not because he desired food but because he realised that some minimal fuel was necessary. He could not be bothered to warm anything up, although he would have liked a cup of tea, if there had been any milk. He spent the night hunkered down on the sofa, shivering and delirious. He began to entertain the idea that Jack might be alive, alongside an absolute certainty that he was dead. This same confusion pervaded a dream in which Jack climbed out, sopping, from the tank and congratulated Mikey on his joke and they embraced. When he woke up the next day, Mikey was hugging the cushions and the close-down signal from the television sounded like a police siren. He might have lain there for hours, but Mikey heard Blue whimpering in the dining room and wanted the company of his dog so much it brought tears to his eyes. He could not release Blue without having a bath and washing off the incriminating odour of Jack's death. Upstairs, for the first time since the accident, he took off his clothes, shaking all the time because he was so frightened that some of Jack's blood might have seeped through the material onto his skin. He imagined that his mother was there. 'Come on, off with them dirty things,' she had always said, when he was a child preparing to step into this same bath. He spoke aloud to himself: 'Off with them dirty things.' He stuffed the clothes into the laundry basket and immersed himself in the water. He soaped and scoured all of his body, but particularly his legs. When he was cleaned and dressed, he let Blue out and gave him a hug, taking heart from his dog's thumping tail on the carpet.

They had been together ever since. On Saturday Mikey had stayed at home and kept the curtains closed, praying that the proximity of the fête would not bring any visitors to his door. By Sunday afternoon he knew that he must return to the tractor shed. He had no clear idea about how long he expected to wait there; all he knew was that he had a duty to keep Jack company. It was wrong to die and be buried without any ceremony, with no mourners. He had a superstition, perhaps acquired from his mother, that it might mean Jack's soul could not go to heaven. In so far as he was able, he would try to make a ceremony for Jack. He took his mother's Bible from her bedside, a candle, matches and some food for himself. He returned to the shed with a calm feeling of purpose. At the back of it, beside the tyres, he produced the candle and lit it. He took out his mother's Bible and held it in his hands. Then he kneeled and prayed for Jack's soul.

Mikey could not have known that Tom had come to the tank to play with the newts on Saturday, and yet it did not surprise him to see Hayes approaching, with his wife and the others, on Sunday afternoon. His first thought was that his prayers had been answered: here were mourners for Jack – and even a priest. Mikey felt the relief of a lookout guard who has spent a night on duty alone and desperately wants to sleep. He did not wonder how Jack's resting place had been discovered. It did not matter, anyway. He knew that Jack would be in good hands now. Mikey had worked at Hill Farm for five years and he trusted Hayes more than anyone else he knew. He thought that Hayes would take care of the situation: make things right. Mikey was not at all scared. For the first time in three days he felt released from fear.

There were holes here and there in the corrugated iron, and Mikey found one that gave him a good view of the tank. He wanted to watch Hayes and the others when they first looked into the tank and saw Jack lying there. As a teenager, Mikey had lingered at the scene of several fires he had started, waiting to see the expression on people's faces. This was different, though: he was not looking for kicks, but for confirmation of his crime. He needed to see a reaction register on the people's faces before he could be sure that the events of the last few days existed outside his mind. He watched as the curious-looking party approached the steps up to the tank and formed a single line, like school children. Hayes prepared to climb the ladder first and then, seeming to think better of it, stepped backwards, causing everyone behind him also to take urgent steps back or risk falling over. Mikey almost laughed to see it – but what was Hayes up to? He watched through the spy-hole as Hayes wandered around near the tank, inspecting the ground; the others also seemed to be casting about in the long grass beside the farm road. Were they looking for traces of blood?

Hayes picked up a long stick, or perhaps a branch, from the verge. That was a good idea: he could poke the stick into the water, then Jack would be able to grab onto it and be pulled out. Now Hayes returned to the metal ladder and climbed up it, with the others following. The priest had to pick up his skirts to avoid tripping over them. Mikey watched them inch along the edge of the water and knew how hard that was, because he had done it himself. He saw Hayes study the water, then plunge his long stick into the tank; he must have been trying to draw all the algae to one side, to make an area of clear water through which to look down on Jack. The others watched intently, following the progress of the stick. Then Hayes stopped, looking into the water as though he saw something immeasurably sad there. He was the only one to remain completely still. The women raised hands to their faces, the priest crossed himself and the other fellow looked away. For a few seconds the figures stood together like this, a silent tableau. When the cry came, it tore across the valley, and Mikey turned away from his spy-hole.

He had seen enough. He began to pack up the things he had brought with him. They would come looking for him soon enough, but he did not want to wait for them in the shed. He would like a walk, and a drink. The pub would be opening soon, and Hazel was probably already behind the counter polishing the brass pumps. He could sit at the bar and have a pint. He would like to sit and talk to her, uninterrupted, to buy her a drink and a packet of crisps. Perhaps he would be bold enough to ask for some peanuts.

He started walking across the fields.

ACKNOWLEDGEMENTS

I wish to thank Ralph and Pat Needham for their warm hospitality and for the invaluable advice they have given me on different aspects of farming and breeding cattle. Any inaccuracies remaining in this book are mine alone. Gillian Stern read and re-read the manuscript with dedication and generosity; I feel very lucky to know her. Thanks also to my agent Patrick Walsh and my editor Becky Hardie for all their encouragement and good ideas. I owe a special debt to my father, whose love and knowledge of the countryside underpin this book in so many ways.